KELLY RIMMER

Undone

HEADLINE
ETERNAL

The right of Kelly Rimmer to be identified as the Author of
the Work has been asserted by her in accordance with the
Copyright, Designs and Patents Act 1988.

Published by arrangement with HQN Books,
An imprint of Harlequin, a division of HarperCollins.

First published in Great Britain in 2020
by HEADLINE ETERNAL
An imprint of HEADLINE PUBLISHING GROUP

1

Cataloguing in Publication Data is available from the British Library

ISBN 978 1 4722 5761 1

Offset in 12.6/15.67 pt Times New Roman by Jouve (UK), Milton Keynes

Printed and bound in Great Britain by Clays Ltd, Elcograf S.p.A.

Headline's policy is to use papers that are natural, renewable and recyclable
products and made from wood grown in well-managed forests and other
controlled sources. The logging and manufacturing processes are expected
to conform to the environmental regulations of the country of origin.

HEADLINE PUBLISHING GROUP
An Hachette UK Company
Carmelite House
50 Victoria Embankment
London EC4Y 0DZ

www.headlineeternal.com
www.headline.co.uk
www.hachette.co.uk

The character of Jess was inspired by
badass women everywhere. If you see something
of yourself in her, then this book is for you.

Undone

CHAPTER ONE

Jess

GRANDMA CHLOE, IF *you can hear me from wherever you are, you better be proud of me for sticking this out.*

My grandmother died four years ago, but I will always live my life by the principles she taught me. She used to say that when your friends or family need you, you move heaven and earth to be there for them. That's one reason I'm putting myself through the sheer torture of attending a wedding tomorrow—one of my least favorite things to do, by the way, especially in this case, because I'm not just a guest, I'm a bridesmaid. Oh, and did I mention this is the second time I've been a bridesmaid for this couple? I'm basically a saint for doing this.

Or maybe I'm doing this because the bride is basically a saint.

Yeah, that's more like it, and that brings me to the other reason I'm putting myself through this clusterfuck of a weekend: the bride is my best friend, Isabel.

Isabel has big blue eyes and natural curls in a

startling shade of ash blond. She's recently turned thirty-five, but she looks much younger even on rare occasions like this one, when she's wearing a full face of makeup. I think her anti-aging secret is her wholesome lifestyle, which is obviously an extreme measure and not one I'd ever be willing to try myself. I'm thirty-five too, but when I'm not wearing makeup, I look like an aged, freckled version of Pippi Longstocking, if Pippi partied way too much in her twenties.

It's fair to say that Isabel and I are the unlikeliest of friends. She's sweet, I'm sharp. She's kind and gentle and softhearted, I'm... Well, I'm just not. We've had a lot of great times together, but we also have very different approaches to life, and every now and again I wonder why she puts up with me at all. What I don't wonder about is why I've kept her around. Izzy is the lite version of humanity—all of the goodness, none of the calories. She's easy to love, and for the most part, quite uncomplicated when it comes to her friends—a rare trait, and one I value highly.

I'd be lost without her. Completely, hopelessly lost.

Right now, maybe for the first time ever, I wish that Isabel wasn't an exceptional human being. In fact, I'm wishing that last year, when she abruptly decided to divorce my business partner Paul, I'd have done what I usually do when people around me do something stupid—told her exactly what I was thinking. If I'd been harsh enough, she'd probably have cut me out of her life. Yes, I'd have been lost and miserable and sad and I'd have missed her forever, but then again, even feel-

ing miserable and lost and sad would have been pref-
erable to what I'm feeling right now.

Anxious. I'm anxious, which isn't like me at all. I
have no idea what to do with such an uncomfortable
feeling simmering away inside me, and that's why I've
decided to drown it in champagne.

Izzy and Paul sorted their shit out—only this happened just a little too late to stop the divorce, and now
they want to get remarried. So here we all are, at their
brownstone in Chelsea for the rehearsal dinner before
their second wedding takes place tomorrow. There are
fairy lights and candles and big vases of fragrant white
roses on the long table that centers their dining room.
There's soft, orchestral music playing on the speakers.
Isabel and Paul are both radiant. It's all so joyous and
romantic that it makes me a little ill.

Don't get me wrong: I'm utterly delighted that they
sorted their shit out and they're both happy again. It's
just that all of his haste and love and joy and renewal
means that instead of ordering my first wine for the
night in a bar somewhere and scanning the room for a
companion, I'm sitting here chugging champagne like
it's water and watching the door as if it's about to burst
open to reveal some kind of Jess Cohen kryptonite.

Which it kind of is.

Because Paul's brother Jake is due to arrive any second now, fresh off a flight from the West Coast, where
he now lives. And…okay. I'm not exactly thrilled about
being a part of this wedding party tomorrow, but it's
maybe just a tiny bit possible that my imminent en-

counter with Jake has more to do with my anxiety than the festivities themselves.

"What's up with you?" The voice belongs to Marcus, my other business partner, who's sitting to my right. He speaks quietly—keeping his voice low, no doubt so as not to upset the other members of the wedding party. Paul and Isabel are opposite me, and Abby, Marcus's fiancée, is in the restroom. She's very pregnant with twins. As far as I can tell, being very pregnant with twins means you spend half your time looking exhausted and terrified, and the other half peeing.

"What's up with you?" I snap at him unthinkingly, and he slowly raises an eyebrow.

"Ho-ly shit," he whistles.

"What?"

"Jessica Cohen—are you upset about something?" The incredulity in his tone suggests that the very idea of this is impossible. I'm kind of pleased that I've managed to fool him into thinking I really am some kind of superwoman, and also immediately depressed that one of my best friends has no idea I have any emotional depth at all.

"Mind your own damn business, Marcus."

His expression grows serious, and he leans even closer to whisper, "Is everything okay?"

"Everything's fine."

"Things are clearly not fine," Marcus says, frowning. He glances down at my hands, and I realize I'm tapping the table. I stop, but as soon as I do, my knee starts to bounce.

"Seriously, Marcus, leave it," I whisper back to him, but the words come out as a half growl, half hiss, and he winces.

"Okay, okay," he says, raising his hands in surrender. Just then, the doorbell rings and my heart is suddenly beating so hard and so fast I feel a little faint. I have butterflies in my tummy, and in my back. That's *not* normal. Maybe I need medical attention.

Isabel squeals and stands.

"That'll be Jake!"

And off she goes to answer the door, while I try to figure out just how upset Isabel and Paul would be if I tell them I can't stay for their rehearsal dinner. But what would be big enough an excuse to justify such a dick move? I can't say it's a date. That would make me a bitch. What else is there? Why didn't I come up with an excuse earlier?

Aaaand… Now it's too late.

My stomach drops. I stop tapping my knee, but now my hands start to shake, so I fold them together and hide them on my lap.

Jake Winton strides into the room wearing jeans and a plain gray T-shirt that stretches over the bulky muscles of his arms and his chest. Goddammit, I *hate* how good he looks. Unlike his brother, Jake is very broad and very tall—far too large for my tastes, really. I like a man I can look eye to eye in my heels, and Jake is six foot six. I'm good, but even I couldn't manage thirteen-inch heels.

Jake is just a veritable giant in every way. Yes, including that one. Men spend a lot of time worrying about size, but frankly, I'd take a skilled guy with a sensibly sized appendage over a horse like Jake any day. I want a man who can get in there, get the job done, then walk away—leaving me able to walk away too…as opposed to limping away. Maybe it's just me, but I like to enjoy a guy's company and not need an epidural if I want to go to spin class the next day.

Not that I was complaining all that much when Jake and I were together. Probably because he *was* a skilled guy. In fact, I do remember relishing that sometimes-morning-after tenderness because it reminded me of the hours I'd spent with him. I was so lust-addled at the time that I actually thought that was a good thing.

But sex is better without complications like that—delicious memories, emotions, huge dicks. So yes, in hindsight, his is definitely too big. And he's definitely too tall and broad. And too compassionate. And too… *argh*… These days he's just too West Coast. He looks so relaxed, and I can't miss the light tan on his skin and the way that his muddy-blond hair has brightened up several tones. Then again, Jake always loved surfing and hiking. Even when he lived here in Manhattan, he was forever planning trips away to commune with nature or some shit. When his job gets too much, he heads to the outdoors to decompress.

Yes, Jake Winton was and is all wrong for me, in pretty much every way.

I look away, and I plan to continue looking away—but my eyes are drawn back to him and I find myself staring again immediately. I've just missed him so much, and it's been two and a half years since I saw him—apparently that separation has left me weak and hungry. I note the smattering of gray at his temples and just for a moment I wonder if I put it there. Then I do the calculation and realize he'd be thirty-nine now, so I guess a hint of silver makes sense. Also, I'm really not into salt-and-pepper guys, so that's excellent.

Except that it suits him. He is a doctor, after all…a specialist at that, and there's something about the hint of gray that makes him look even more distinguished. And the horn-rimmed glasses? They're new too. He used to make fun of my reading glasses in that flirty, melt-my-panties way of his. He always said they made me look like a sexy librarian.

Seriously, who has sexy librarian fantasies?

Me.

Right now.

I'm fantasizing about a very broad, very tall, very sexy male librarian who's actually a doctor with a huge dick and horn-rimmed frames on his brand-new glasses.

"…glad to be here. Marcus, congratulations on the engagement and the twins and—oh! Hey there, Abby! Wow, you look amazing. When are you due?" Jake's going around the table greeting everyone and by the time I check back into the conversation, he's already up to me. His gaze lands on me, and after a split second of panic I force my brightest smile. "And Jessica," he says, then he returns my smile with a very tight smile of his own.

There's barely disguised antagonism in his gaze, and it seems I've made a critical error here. I knew I was at real risk of throwing myself at him like some kind of lust-sick idiot tonight, but I figured *he'd* be on his best behavior. I mean, come on: Jake's the nicest guy I've ever met. It really didn't occur to me that he'd *ever* look at me like…this.

It seems that in all of my wasted hours over the last few weeks, worrying about seeing Jake again, I have neglected to consider one very important thing: I'm the villain here. It was my idea to hide our relationship from our friends. My idea to end things. My idea to "give one another some space" after we broke up.

It was *his* idea to pack up and move to California to get away from me, and I probably should have given a little more thought to the level of hurt that might have been behind that decision. I just told myself the job offer at Stanford must have been too good to be true, and that he was probably ready for a change after living his whole life in New York. It was easier to believe my own lies than it was to think about what might actually have been going on for him.

"Hello," he says now.

"Hi, Jake," I say. My gaze lands on the almost-empty bottle of champagne in the middle of the table.

"We need some more bubbles!" My voice is a little too light and a little too high. I glance toward the kitchen, where Marcus's brother-in-law and a pair of apprentice chefs are preparing our meal as part of his wedding gift to Paul and Izzy. "I'll just—"

"Sit down, Jess," Isabel says, laughing. She waves at me, playfully dismissive as she rises. "I'll get it. You guys can all catch up before we talk through the plan for tomorrow."

"I need to walk a bit," Abby says, and she stands with some difficulty. Didn't she just get back from the bathroom? I move to rise, but Marcus is right beside her and before I'm even on my feet, his arm is around her waist and he's leading her away from the table.

"Let me come, Abs," he says softly. "Want to go outside for some fresh air? How's the heartburn?"

"All good." She flashes a smile that's just a little too bright. "Fresh air sounds great."

That leaves me, Jake and Paul. I mentally beg Paul to stay but because the universe hates me, he stands immediately.

"Sorry," he says, then he gives us a cheeky grin. "I've been waiting all night for Isabel to get distracted. I've organized a surprise for the honeymoon and I just need to check some details."

They're going to New Zealand for their honeymoon. I'm pretty sure the "surprise" is tickets to a rugby game—Isabel is sports-mad. In any case, Paul leaves the room, and... Now I'm alone with his brother.

I down the last of my champagne in one gulp, then

glance hesitantly at Jake. He's staring at me, his gaze hard, and I try to force myself to be polite and to make an attempt at small talk.

"How have you been? It's been too long," I say. It's possibly the stupidest thing I could *ever* have said to Jake Winton. Jesus. I don't know even why I said it. It's just what people say, isn't it? My voice is all wobbly. Where's my supposedly endless confidence when I need it? Where are those "balls of steel" lovers and business rivals have accused me of having? Oh God. I want the earth to open up and swallow me whole.

Jake sits. He leans back in his chair and surveys me for a moment, then he sighs impatiently.

"We have to play games when the others are around because that's how *you* wanted it to be. But when we're alone, let's not pretend this isn't uncomfortable."

Even as I nod in agreement, I feel my heart sink. There's no mistaking the disdain in his tone. I usually don't give a flying fuck what other people think about me, and I'm still not sure what makes Jake so different... But he is different. And I *hate* the idea that he might hate me.

I'm saved by the return of Izzy with the champagne, and she immediately launches herself into rapid-fire chitchat about the meal. Everyone else returns soon enough too, and at first, I figure the tension between Jake and me will dilute, at least a little, as we settle into the company of our friends.

But I'm wrong about that too. Jake is polite enough to ignore me in conversation, but tense enough to narrow his gaze every time our eyes meet.

CHAPTER TWO

Jake

HERE'S THE THING: I'm a nice guy. I'm a healer by trade—an oncologist, actually, which is a pretty unsexy profession and not one you choose unless you genuinely care about people. I do care about people. I donate money to charity. I help little old ladies cross the street. I rescued a dog last year. Her name is Clara and she's the ugliest fucking thing you've ever seen— as far as I can tell, a cross between a pug, a Brussels griffon, and that ball of hair and gunk that clogs up the bathroom sink after a while. I found myself at the shelter just before closing time on what happened to be the very last day before Clara was due to be "put to sleep." She looked up at me with her one remaining eye and for some reason I just couldn't bear the thought of the shelter staff putting such a young dog down.

Well, Clara may be young, but she's not exactly healthy or even cute. In addition to that missing eye, she has a terrifying overbite, she's an odd shape, her fur is patchy, and the shelter staff told me they suspected she was abused by a previous owner because she has severe anxiety. I pay more for her monthly medication than I did to adopt her, and I let her sleep not just in my bed—but on my pillow. Sometimes I wake up and she's actually lying on my face. No matter what I do, her endlessly mangy ears always wind up smelling awful—awful enough that my guests often exclaim some variation on, "Holy shit! What is that smell? Is that a dog?!"

Right at this very moment, I'm paying a dog behaviorist to act as dog-sitter, which is costing me a stupid amount of money. The woman actually has to sleep at my house because Clara can't go to a kennel and has a very bad habit of shredding everything in sight if she's left alone overnight.

And despite all of that, I love my dog, because that's the kind of guy I am.

A nice guy. A tolerant guy.

And yet, I'm sitting here staring at Jessica Cohen, and I'm struggling to find *any* goodwill toward her whatsoever.

I've had a lot of time to think in the two and a half years since our breakup, and I've come to a few hard realizations about our relationship. I desperately want to confront Jess, and I plan to do just that—*after* the reception. I'm due to fly out for a hiking trip on Sunday night, and I'm pretty sure Paul and Izzy aren't going to fuck this marriage business up again, so there's a very good chance tomorrow night will be the last time I'll see Jess in our lifetimes.

I'll say what I need to say, and then I'll finally be able to let her go.

Izzy hands me a bottle of champagne and I pop the cork. I pour some for Marcus and myself and then Izzy and Paul. Abby returns to the table, so I offer her some too, although I know she won't drink it. She points to her water with a sigh, then I flick a glance at Jess. She already has a flute in her hand, but just as I look at her, she avoids my gaze, lifts her glass and drains it.

I should offer her a refill.

I mean, I *should*. But I can see she desperately wants a refill, so I don't. Jess has always had a way of drawing out aspects to my personality I didn't even know were there. It turns out, she can even inspire me to petty childishness.

"How are things for you?" Paul asks me, when I've finished sharing the champagne. "How's Clara?"

I feel Jess's eyes on me, and just for a minute, I let myself enjoy the possibility that she might think Clara is a girlfriend rather than a particularly high-maintenance pet. It was Jess's decision to end our relationship so I'm sure she's not jealous, but I really do like the idea that she might be. It's ridiculous, and maybe I'm not such a nice guy after all, because I'm deliberately ambiguous as I say, "Clara is great." Then I smile broadly. "Sure makes life better having someone to come home to each night. But I don't need to tell you lovebirds that—how long have you been back home, Izzy?"

"A few months," Isabel says, then she just beams at

me. I glance at Paul, and he's wearing the same stupid grin. I chuckle.

"I can't wait to officially welcome you back to the family tomorrow."

She sighs happily.

"Everything is just perfect, isn't it? I'm so glad you could be here. I know the timing wasn't great…"

I wave her apology away.

"Even the timing was perfect. It was easy to push my trip back a few days—much easier than moving patient appointments if I hadn't been planning a break already."

"Where are you off to, Jake?" Marcus asks across the table, where he sits right beside Jess.

"I'm hiking the John Muir Trail—doing an ultra-light trip, so taking minimum supplies and walking it as fast as I can. I was originally thinking Paul might join me… I thought he'd want to be distracted when his first post-divorce wedding anniversary rolled around." I glance at my brother, then wink at him. "Turns out he had a better idea."

Paul laughs softly.

"I forgot all about that."

"Well, I decided to do it alone anyway. I'm flying back Monday morning and I'll start the trail on Wednesday. I expect to finish in about eleven or twelve days, depending on how I'm feeling as I go."

"How far is this trail?" Abby asks with visible horror. I laugh at her expression.

"About two hundred and twenty miles. I'll try to

average twenty-two miles a day so I can have a few rest days along the way."

"You do realize you're completely insane, right?" Abby shakes her head at me and I grin at her.

"Maybe when the twins arrive, you guys can plan a hike with me. Marcus and I can carry the babies in backpacks."

"That does sound like fun," Marcus murmurs playfully.

"You know very well that it sounds like my worst nightmare." Abby scowls at him, and I laugh again.

"There's nothing like it, Abby. Fresh air. Silence. Disconnecting from all of the noise of modern life is the best way to nurture your soul."

"Clara doesn't mind you leaving her, then?" Paul asks, and he's teasing, of course, but this time I have no doubt at all that anyone who hadn't made my terrifying pet's acquaintance would hear this and assume he was referring to a partner. I flick a glance at Jess. I'm both delighted and instantly irritated to see that she's visibly jealous. In fact, she's close to incandescent green.

"Clara is incredibly loyal," I say slowly. "It's one of her best qualities."

"She'll greet you at the door when you get back, and she'll be humping your leg—" Paul says, and I cut him off hastily.

"Classic Clara. So what's the deal for tomorrow?" I ask Izzy.

"The food is just about ready," she tells me. "I'll run you through our plans when we're done eating."

WE SPEND THE next hour gorging ourselves on the incredible four courses the caterers have prepared for us, and just as we finish with dessert, Paul hands me another bottle of champagne. While he and Izzy rise, I quickly top up another round into everyone's glasses. I studiously ignore Jess, then set the bottle on the table between us, so, unlike *everyone* else, she has to fill her own glass.

Yeah. I might not like Jess anymore, but I definitely do not like the guy I've become tonight.

"First, I'd like to thank you all for coming here tonight, especially on such short notice," Paul says. "I never dreamt that I would get a chance to do this again, and it means the world that you'd all be here again to witness it."

"Don't worry," Isabel assures us all. "Tomorrow is going to be very low-key."

She gives us the basics in about thirty seconds: Marcus and I are to meet Paul here at his home. Abby, Isabel and Jess will meet at a suite at a hotel for hair and makeup and whatever else it is that women do on wedding days. Truth be told, I tune out of the details after that because I'm pretty sure it's all I need to know. Instead, I busy myself staring at the roses in the center of the table, just so my eyes are pointed in Jess's vague vicinity, but my staring contest with the roses doesn't last long because my gaze drifts automatically toward her. She catches me and we both scowl, then look away, just as Paul and Isabel take their seats again.

As best man, it's only appropriate that I make a toast, so I reach for my glass.

As soon as I'm on my feet, Jess snatches her own glass up and stands too. We stare at each other just as we've been doing all night, only this time, the moment isn't fleeting. It's still painfully uncomfortable—but neither one of us looks away.

I'm all too aware of the confused gazes around us.

"I was going to make a toast," I say carefully. I am Paul's brother, after all, and the best man, and traditionally a toast would be my responsibility. Besides, I stood up first. The polite thing for Jess to do is to sit down, or maybe even to apologize and then sit down.

Jess is anything but polite.

"I was going to make a toast too," she says pointedly, and she remains stubbornly standing. Her gaze is pure challenge. *I dare you to make a scene.*

I try to wait her out, but we end up standing there in an awkward game of chicken. The moment stretches and stretches until I realize that no matter how long I wait there, Jess is not going to be the first to sit down. Given the opportunity, she'd stand and glare at me until the dinner finished, until the wedding happened without us, until we both starved to death and our bones decomposed. And as the earth crashes into the sun in seven or eight billion years, the last thing my ghost would see would be Jess's ghost, still glaring at me as we dissolved into a ball of fiery doom.

If I don't sit, we're either going to stay here literally forever, or one of our friends is going to have to intervene to break the stalemate. This leaves me very little choice but to say, "Well, ladies first, then," and soon I'm the one taking my seat while Jess makes a very poetic, very touching speech about how wonderful it is to be in their wedding party for the second time, and how glad she is to see them back together.

The whole time I'm staring at my champagne flute, watching the bubbles rise, trying not to admire how eloquent she is, and trying to talk myself out of acting like a spoiled brat. It's been well over two years since we split, and we were together for only four fucking months. The woman should have no hold over me whatsoever, and the fact that she does is kind of humiliating.

Jess finishes her toast, and everyone raises their glasses, then she says sweetly, "Jake, did you still want to add something?"

I glance up at her, and she flutters her eyelashes. I rise, lift my glass, and tilt it toward my brother and his lovely bride-to-be-again as I say, "Paul, Izzy, I'm just so happy for you both. Not much to add to Jessica's wonderful speech, other than to say… Welcome back to the family, Izzy. I couldn't be happier for you both. To Paul and Izzy."

As I sit, I glance at Jess, and find her smirking. Yeah, she definitely won the "battle of the speeches." There's open triumph in her eyes. As the others start to chat again, she leans forward and whispers, "*That* was for pretending you didn't see I needed champagne."

"If that slurred, rambling word-vomit was any indication, more champagne is the last thing you need tonight," I whisper back. Jess looks like she's about to leap across the table and rip my face off, so I turn to Isabel and try to slip into her conversation. She's laughing with Paul about how "lucky" it was that they ran into one another at the vacation home six months ago. I catch the undertone but don't understand it, so I ask in surprise, "Was that not luck? Did you go out there to catch him on purpose?"

"Oh, no," she laughs, and then she flicks a meaningful glance to Jess. "It's a funny story, and you won't believe it—but it turns out it was all Jess's doing."

All roads lead back to Jess Cohen. Of course they fucking do. The woman has a finger in every pie.

"How so?" I ask, but my tone is resigned. I glance at Jess briefly and find she's smirking at me again.

And then Izzy tells me all about how Jess engineered for her and Paul to arrive at their vacation home for the same weekend away, and how they were both too stubborn to leave, and by the time Monday came around, they were in love again.

"Jess had a hand in bringing us together too," Abby sighs happily, from across the table. "I was pretty determined that I wasn't in love with Marcus until Jess tried to set him up with one of the programmers from work. Nothing is more effective for curing denial than hard-core jealousy."

"Brave of you to intervene in your friends' lives like that," I murmur to Jess, and she lifts one perfectly arched eyebrow at me.

"Brave?" she repeats.

"Either situation could've worked out very differently."

"I knew it was worth the risk in both cases," Jess says, then she leans back in her chair and begins to study her immaculately polished fingernails. Something about her lack of concern for my observation irks me even more, and I lean forward just a little.

"But either scenario could easily have turned to disaster," I say. "Did you ever think about that before you went about playing God with your friends' lives?"

"Playing God?" Jess repeats. Her tone rises just as her eyebrows disappear into her hairline, so this is exactly the rise I was looking for.

I shrug and say casually, "Some people might consider what you did in both cases to be...manipulative."

I'm pretty sure no one was listening to us a minute ago, but in a heartbeat, all of the chatter in the room has stopped. Four shocked sets of eyes are now on me and Jess—and Jess is glaring at me with such intense rage that if I was just a little smarter, I'd be looking for something to hide behind.

Sudden, brutal regret grips me. I can't believe I let this escalate—but just as I'm trying to figure out how to undo the scene I've just made, there's a sudden shift in Jess's expression.

Holy shit. And now her big blue eyes shine with the unmistakable gleam of tears.

Jess turns sharply and reaches down for her handbag below her chair. She withdraws her phone and begins to press the screen frantically as if she's texting. She's blinking rapidly, but a smidge of moisture leaks out anyway, and she swipes at it—accidentally smudging her heavy eye makeup.

No one says anything. Perhaps the rest of our friends are in shock too.

"Izzy, I am so sorry," Jess says, raising her gaze. "I forgot I had a date."

The silence has been fraught, but in an instant, it becomes incredibly awkward.

"A date?" Isabel says hesitantly.

"A date," Jess says, as if this is the most normal thing in the world. She picks up her phone again and begins to madly press the screen. "But we're done here, aren't we?"

I suppose we are done. The plans have been discussed, the food has been eaten, toasts have been made. It might even be fine for Jess to leave now, if it weren't so painfully obvious that she's not leaving because we're "done."

The problem with revenge is that it's never as satisfying as you think it's going to be. I wanted to get a reaction out of Jess, to dig the knife in and to twist it a little, because she hurt me, and I wanted her to feel bad. I got exactly what I wanted, but it feels disgusting. I just don't know how to fix this without embarrassing Jess even more… And an embarrassed Jess is likely to be a dangerously unpredictable creature.

There's a flurry of activity happening around the table. Abby and Isabel are trying to convince Jess to

cancel this serious, last-minute, surprise date that Jess
is now arguing she absolutely must go on. Paul and
Marcus also appear to be convincing Jess that she
should cancel her date, without actually telling her
that she should cancel her date.

Probably because they're trying to avoid poking
the bear. Paul and Marcus are definitely both much
smarter than I am.

I'm silent, watching all of this unfold, also trying
to figure out exactly what I said that got such a reaction out of her. Was it the manipulation comment? The
"playing God" comment? The whole night of awkward tension had built up and up. Did something just
get to her?

Maybe she's sick?

Maybe she didn't know I was coming tonight?

Maybe she's been secretly pining after me for two
years?

Well, that last one seems unlikely. It was her decision to end our relationship, not mine. I was all in—I
had the fucking engagement ring in my underwear
drawer, just waiting for the right moment.

I'm still sitting in useless silence right up until Jess
leaves. And just as I suspected, the minute the front
door closes, all eyes are on me.

"What just happened?" Abby doesn't say the words,
she growls them. I clear my throat.

"I didn't mean to upset her—" I say helplessly. I
open my hands, because I read somewhere that if you
expose your palms to an angry person, you're show-

ing vulnerability and they'll go easy on you. The gesture does nothing to soothe the angry pregnant lady, who rounds on me like she's going to body-slam me.

Isabel approaches from the other side and says sharply, "You upset Jess Cohen. I didn't know anyone *could* upset Jess Cohen. What did you do?"

"She didn't manipulate us," Abby says sharply. "She tried to help us, can't you see that?"

"I know," I say defensively. "I really didn't mean to hurt her. She's clearly oversensitive tonight—"

"Oversensitive!" Abby gasps.

"Jake, do you *want* them to kill you?" Marcus mutters, wincing. I stand, and I throw my hands into the air.

"She did manipulate you guys. I'm glad it worked out for the best but what she did was pretty ballsy, and it all could have ended in disaster. I'm super glad you all ended up together, but what right does she have to interfere in other people's lives like that?"

"If you knew her like we know her," Isabel says, voice shaking with feeling, "you'd understand that her intentions are beautiful. She has a tough exterior, but beneath it, she's one of the most caring, loving people I've ever met. And you upset her tonight, Jake Winton, so you need to fix it before you ruin our day tomorrow. I don't know how you're going to do it, but *you are going to fix it.*"

And there, shimmering in the eyes of my sister-in-law, are the second set of tears I have put in a woman's eyes tonight. I thought I could sit Jess down and have it out *after* the festivities tomorrow, but apparently, I lack the self-control to keep things civil until then. I sigh heavily, run my hands through my hair.

"You all know that Jess and I have always grated each other." That's the understatement of the century. We spent more than a decade clashing, four months fucking and then the past two years pretending the other didn't exist. Apparently, Jess and I don't just run hot and cold, we can exist in the same space only as steam or ice. "I'll go see her now, clear the air and say sorry."

"Thanks," Paul says before he sighs. "Jess can be difficult, but so can I. And you get me better than just about anyone, so I know you can handle her." He gives me a crooked smile. I feel like a heel.

"I really am sorry about this, Paul."

"I get it. If I had a dollar for every time I said something awkward, we'd be living in a castle of pure gold."

I slip my wallet into my pocket, scoop my phone off the table and open the Uber app.

"Don't you want to know her address?" Abby says sharply.

"Uh…"

"She bought a condo. Two years ago."

Jess and I broke up just before she moved into that place, so she didn't invite me to the housewarming, but we were definitely together when she was house hunting. I helped Jess pick that apartment, and she actually lived with me while the contractors were re-modeling it for her. Abby just has no idea about any of that, and now I have to pretend I need Jess's address, when I know it by heart because I actually figured I'd wind up living there with her one day.

That's the problem with lies. You tell one, and the next thing you know you're drowning in them. I never wanted to hide our relationship from these people in the first place.

But Jess was adamant that no one know we were ever together, and only in the last few months have I figured out why.

CHAPTER THREE

Jess

FOR A WHILE when I first came to New York, I had a poster on the wall of my bedroom at my grandma Chloe's apartment. It said: "Tears are weakness leaving the body."

I'm older now and I'm wiser. These days, I know that motivational posters are, literally without exception, bullshit. I also know that tears have nothing to do with weakness, nothing to do with strength even—they have everything to do with losing control.

And under ordinary circumstances, I *never* lose control.

I thought the worst-case scenario for tonight would be that Jake would ignore me. Never in a million years did I consider the possibility that he'd be living with another woman. Paul never mentioned it, but then again, why would he? Paul has no way of knowing I have a vested interest in Jake's life. That little tidbit knocked me off-kilter, then Jake's hostility finished the job. I'm home now, but I'm still feeling jealous and bruised and embarrassed. There was no date—of course there wasn't, I'm not a complete asshole. Instead, I've pulled on my PMS pajamas, and I'm curled up in my wing chair with a bottle of Riesling and a tub of low-carb ice cream. Life is all about balance, you see.

I hear the sound of a key in the lock and then my door swings open, and my friend Mitchell Cole silently steps inside. He's wearing a confused frown and his typical date uniform of designer jeans and a button-down. Mitch is tall and classically handsome, and clean-shaven with his hair slicked back like it is tonight, he looks like he's just taking a break from his starring role in a romantic comedy. He silently closes the door and drops his keys and wallet onto my hall table, then, as he walks toward me, lifts his hand and wags his finger from my toes to my hair. "And what exactly am I seeing right now?"

"This is what sulking looks like. Deal with it." I dig into the ice cream, then I survey his own attire again and sigh. "Didn't realize you had a date tonight. Sorry."

"Don't worry, it wasn't going well. She doesn't drink."

"So?"

"She's not one of those 'oh I just don't like to drink myself' teetotalers. She's one of those 'no one is allowed to drink because it's poison and the body is a temple' types. I could feel her judgy eyes boring holes in me all night. She was gorgeous, but disapproval is a very effective boner-killer."

Mitchell Cole would be the most famous person I know if he wasn't safely hidden away behind a pseudonym. He's a bestselling author, my best guy friend, my perma-wingman, holder of all of my secrets and the only person who's seen me cry since I was a kid. Well, he *was*, until tonight. He sits heavily opposite me now, spreads his legs and rests his elbows on his knees.

"What happened? Did the rehearsal dinner go badly?"

"It went perfectly," I mutter. "Right up until I cried."

Mitch frowns at me.

"Cried?"

"You heard me. Jake made me cry."

"I don't understand."

"He said mean things and I burst into tears."

Mitch blinks.

"I'm not following you. Cried? Like....tears? In public? Since when do you cry in front of people? And since when does Jake say mean things?"

I sigh and slump again.

"He called me manipulative."

"You are manipulative."

"Fuck off."

"And that right there is the reaction I would have expected from you."

"Maybe *cry* is a strong word. I just got teary, but I know they all saw."

Mitch rises and walks to help himself to my liquor cabinet. He pours himself a drink, then turns back to face me, leaning against the cabinet as he sips at what

I know is my twenty-year-old single malt Macallan. The man has expensive tastes. When I first met Mitch, he was working as a barista and that bottle of whiskey would have cost more than a week's salary for him. It's a *very* good thing he's richer than God these days. It's also very annoying that he never lets me forget it.

"Jake was the one that got away," he says gently, and I open my mouth to protest, but he continues pointedly. "Yes, I know he got away because you sent him away, but you can't actually tell me that wasn't hard as shit because I had front-row seats for the aftermath." I close my mouth and look away. "Jess, you've managed to pretend Jake disappeared into thin air for two years, but the reality is, he didn't, and confronting him again was always going to be difficult."

"I just…" I reach down and scoop up my phone, which has been resting on the coffee table between us. I turn the screen on and flick it around to read the notifications on my lock screen. It's been pinging non-stop since I ran out. There are several messages from Abby and Isabel, one from Marcus, even one from Paul. Paul, who wouldn't notice another human's suffering if it was happening on his lap, is worried about me. On the eve of his wedding day. "Everyone is panicking, and I want to punch my self in the fucking face."

"So, tell them you had a bad night." Mitch shrugs as he takes a seat back on my sofa. "I know you don't have bad days, but everyone else does. Sometimes those bad days are badly timed. Or you could just tell them all that you and Jake dated, and things ended badly, and then they'll completely understand."

"You know I can't do that."

"You wanted to keep things with Jake quiet in case it ended badly, right? You didn't want it to upset your relationship with Paul?"

"Yeah."

"Well, it did end badly. And it did not upset your relationship with Paul. I kind of understood why you insisted on secrecy at the time, but I don't have a clue why you're still hiding it from them now."

"It's not even about secrecy at the moment. It's simply me not wanting to steal their thunder on their wedding day." He gives me a skeptical glance, and I sigh impatiently. "Come on, Mitchell. Surely you get that."

"This secrecy strategy just resulted in you sobbing like a baby at their rehearsal dinner, so maybe it's time to reconsider it."

"I didn't sob like a baby," I snap. Mitchell grins and kicks his feet up onto my coffee table. I glare at him, and he rolls his eyes at me.

"You sent me a 911 text, Jess. It must have been bad. The last time you did that was the night you broke up with him, and we both know you did sob like a baby that night."

I groan and press the cold surface of the ice cream carton against my heated cheeks.

"Did you know he's living with someone?"

Mitch gives me a quizzical glance.

"No. He's not."

"He *is*," I mutter. "He was talking about her tonight. Just before he accused me of playing God with Abby's and Isabel's relationships. It hurt."

"I've tried very hard to stay safely in no-man's land between you since you guys split, but I saw him two months ago, and he wasn't even seeing anyone then." This doesn't reassure me one bit because I know that Jake is the kind of guy who might move fast if he met the right woman. Or even if he met the wrong one, like me. "Also, Jess, you *did* play God with their relationships." I glare at Mitch and he gives an exaggerated sigh. "This friendship works because we're honest with one another. If you're going to change the rules and expect me to fear you like everyone else, I'm going to have to rethink this whole arrangement." I snatch a cushion off the couch and throw it at his head. He dodges it easily and laughs. "I've known you for a long time. You have your faults, and you do tend to meddle like a grandchild-obsessed senior citizen hell-bent on matchmaking her kids, but your intentions are always good."

"For a novelist, you sure do love an awkward metaphor."

There's a sudden, dramatic knock at the door. I look to Mitch and find him downing the whiskey.

"Don't leave," I blurt, and he sets the glass on my coffee table and says very gently, "That's either Abby, Isabel or Jake. Right?"

I squeeze my eyes shut and I nod.

"If it's Abby or Isabel, you don't need me here. And if it's Jake, you don't want me here."

"I do want you here."

"Jess, you're a lot of things, but you're nothing like a coward," Mitch says, so gently that I could almost cry again. Almost. "It's time to face the music, especially if things between you two are still so tense you're about to ruin this wedding. I know you don't want that."

Stupid Mitchell and his stupid insight.

There's another knock, then Jake calls out, "Jess. Open up, I know you're in there."

I groan in frustration and rise.

"Wait here," I snap at Mitch, who raises one eyebrow at me coolly.

"Why?"

I wave my hand down toward my PMS pajamas. I have quite a few regrets from tonight, but the pajamas are now at the *very* top of that list. If I'd been thinking clearly, I'd have considered the possibility that Jake would come here.

"I'm not answering the door like this."

Mitch sighs and stands.

"I'll let him in while you change—"

"No," I say, and Mitch hesitates.

"Jess…"

"I'll talk to him in the hall. I'm not letting him in. If I let him in, I'll…"

I'll what…? I'll throw myself at him. I'll beg his forgiveness. I'll apologize profusely. I'll make an idiot of myself. At least in the hallway, I'll be in a neutral public space, and then maybe I'll feel in control. As I'm struggling for words, Mitchell's expression softens.

"Okay, Jess. Go ahead."

I HAVE ABSOLUTELY no choice but to try to bluff my way through this, because if I'm going to maintain a shred of dignity, I'll have to stick to my original lie and insist that I did have a date. I can't stand Jake thinking that while he goes home each night to this—no doubt—flawless, glamorous Clara woman, I'm schlepping around here in my Winnie-the-Pooh onesie.

I throw the ice cream in the bin as I sprint toward my bedroom. I'm gone for just a few minutes, but when I saunter to the living room, Mitchell nearly chokes.

"This is a bad, bad idea," he says flatly. "Don't you *dare* seduce that man. Nothing has changed. You still don't want what he wants—"

"I'm not seducing him," I snap as I adjust the neckline on my *very* short tube dress, then scrub my teeth to make sure the bright red lipstick I hastily applied hasn't spread. The makeup is far from perfect, but my boobs are pretty much hanging out over the top of this thing. Jake probably won't even notice I still have a face. "I told them I had a date... Well, this is how I would look if that was true."

"And how are you going to explain my presence?"

There's another, more determined thump on my door. I shrug as if I have no idea how to answer that question, even as I walk to Mitchell's side. I reach up as if I'm going to kiss his cheek goodbye. At the very last minute, I plant a kiss right near his mouth. Just as I'd hoped, the bright red lipstick lands heavily and when he reaches up to wipe it off, it smears onto his lips.

Perfect.

Mitch leans back and stares at me warily.

"Jess…"

I shrug innocently, then reach up and tussle his hair. He finally realizes the scene I'm trying to set here, and he all but leaps away from me.

"You've got to be fucking kidding me."

"I'm just trying to get through a difficult situation, Mitchell," I say lightly. Mitch is genuinely pissed, and for a second, I think I've gone too far, especially when he scoops his keys and wallet up from the hall table and turns furiously toward the door. Jake steps back in alarm as Mitchell throws the door open with some force.

"Hey, Jake," Mitch says. "Still on for breakfast Sunday? Good. By the way, she is manipulative, she totally loves to play God and you did upset her so…good fucking *luck*." He turns back to scowl at me, but at the very last second, his expression softens. "I'll see you at the wedding, you friggin' weirdo."

Mitch and I have a longstanding "plus one" reciprocal arrangement, one that means either one of us can easily bow out to go home with a groomsman or bridesmaid if the opportunity arises. Actually, the opportunity did arise at Paul's last wedding, and that's exactly what got me into this mess.

I already feel bad about what I just did to Mitch.

He's a great friend and he doesn't deserve to be treated like a prop in my stupid game with Jake. Tonight is officially a disaster, and it isn't even over yet. Jake is standing in the hall looking completely bewildered, and so I force myself to raise my chin and take two more steps, until I'm blocking the doorway. I walk quickly, because I don't want him to come inside, but not too quickly, because I want to seem slightly annoyed and not panicked.

Do I feel like a sex goddess right now?

No. No, I absolutely do not. I feel like an idiot—exposed, embarrassed and somewhat bewildered by how easily tonight has spun completely out of my control.

But if there's one thing I'm sure of in this life, it's that you fake it till you make it, and that's why I pin a sultry smile on my face and lean into the door frame and I stare Jake Winton right in the eyes. I'm rewarded for my quick-fire outfit change when those eyes nearly fall out of his stupidly handsome head. I feign confusion and calm.

"Jake, what a pleasant surprise."

"Jess," he says, then he clears his throat. I can see him struggling to keep his gaze on my face and I suddenly regret this plan. I didn't want to admit I lied about a date, but I haven't thought this through at all. Does he think I'm trying to seduce him? Knowing he has a live-in girlfriend? Jesus. I'm off-kilter tonight, frazzled and reactive. I hate it. I'm both disappointed and relieved when the lust-addled expression on Jake's face clears and he raises his gaze to my eyes. He's pissed at me too now, but maybe that's for the best. "Cut the bullshit. We need to talk."

"There's nothing to talk about," I start to say. "And as you can see, you interrupted something—"

"You and Mitch? Please," Jake snaps. "Did you forget you told me that you two hooked up once?"

Actually, I did forget I told him that. I try to forget everything about the time Mitchell and I hooked up. Also, "hooked up" is a bit of an exaggeration, given we had so little chemistry, I actually gagged when he put his tongue in my mouth. Not a polite-cough gag either. I was very nearly sick, and that's saying something, because my lack of a gag reflex is legendary.

"Clara is a dog," Jake suddenly says.

My jaw drops.

"Did you *seriously* just call your girlfriend a dog?"

"Jessica. Clara is a dog. She's—" He groans and reaches for his phone. "She's a dog. An actual dog. That's her species, not an insult. Now can you put some clothes on and stop acting like a crazy jealous person so I can apologize for being an asshole back there?"

"What kind of a name is *Clara* for a dog?" I scowl.

"The kind of name a rescue shelter gives a pet, actually," he snaps as he spins the screen of his phone around so I can see it.

So, two things here:

First, Clara-the-dog has clearly had a tough life— it looks a little like she's recently emerged from some kind of blender. Even so, she's fluffy and tiny, and in the photo, Jake is holding her high in his huge, strong arms and they are the most adorably mismatched pair I've ever seen. I'm so relieved I could cry all over again, and now I kind of want to punch myself in the face for that too. I absolutely hate jealousy—it's an emotion that never leads to anything good. Besides, I have no right to be jealous when it comes to Jake Winton.

Two: Jake just accused me of being jealous and crazy. The nerve. That kind of does make me crazy. I cross my arms under my boobs—pushing them higher instead of blocking his view from them—and I raise an eyebrow.

"Did you just call me crazy?"

"I didn't call you crazy, but your behavior most definitely qualifies," Jake says, and his gaze briefly drops down over my body before he closes his eyes and grinds out, "For fuck's sake, Jess. Let me inside, put a robe on and let's talk."

I want to slam the door shut and go hide under my duvet. I want to pretend he's not here and I don't have to face him. I want to pretend I don't wish things could have been different. I want to pretend I don't relive those months with him when I'm lonely or sad, or that the hours we spent in bed together haven't secured VIP status in my spank bank listings. I want to pretend that throwing Jake Winton away isn't one of the only regrets I *ever* let myself think about.

But Jake opens his eyes and he's now staring at me, an apology in his gaze, and I feel myself weakening.

I sigh and step out of the doorway, then without waiting to see if he comes inside, I head for my bedroom.

"Make yourself at home," I mutter. "I'll just change." Again.

CHAPTER FOUR

Jake

WHILE JESS IS in her bedroom, I look around her apartment. She still has a particularly unique sense of style.
Most of the walls are white, but there's a feature wall
behind her TV that's a vibrant, fire-engine red. It's so
bright it almost hurts my eyes. Over the glass dining
table, she's hung a huge crystal chandelier, and all of
her appliances are a glossy red to match the feature
wall.

She has most of the same furniture I remember, but
she has a new, brightly colored wing chair and a white
leather sofa. Between them, a bright red rug sits over
whitewashed floorboards.

The white sofa is incredibly low—it looks like it's
been designed for preschoolers. Given it's in Jess's
apartment, I assume it's insanely expensive and designed for style over comfort. I feel like I'm falling to
the ground as I try to sit, and then once I'm down, my
knees are almost as high as my head is.

This is fucking ridiculous. But I have a feeling the

wing chair is Jess's throne, and if I take it, she'll feel attacked. So I settle into the stupid miniature sofa and try to do some rapid-fire strategizing. I have two options here. I can prance around the issue and try to gently ease my way into a conversation with her, treating her like she's fragile, which she'll hate, and which will probably make her angry.

Or I can do what she'd do if she had initiated this chat: address it head-on. Like a bull charging at a red flag. Or, in this case, like a bull charging at a red flag in a china shop that's balancing precariously on some kind of cliff, because our entire history is littered with fragile things.

"I'm sorry I upset you," I say as soon as Jess reenters the room. She's pulled a floral satin nightgown on over that skimpy minidress, and she's put on an air of determined calm. She curls up on the wing chair, then tilts her head and raises her eyebrows at me.

Jess looks like a vision, like a queen surveying her kingdom. She looks serene and magnificent and perfect, right up until she opens her mouth and spits out, "You did *not* 'upset' me."

Oh my God. This woman.

"Sorry I made you cry, then."

She stiffens, then her carefully neutral expression shifts into a glare as if I've insulted her.

"I didn't *cry.*"

"It doesn't even matter," I groan, already exasperated. "Whatever happened back there, I'm here to tell you I'm sorry."

"You already said that. In the hallway. So, are we done?"

I'm pretty laid-back and it takes a lot to piss me off. Jess has always had a way of hitting that threshold miles faster than anyone else.

"Christ, Jessica. What do you want from me?"

"Nothing. I don't want *anything* from you. That's the whole point."

She is the most infuriating woman I've ever met. I groan and tilt my head back to stare at the ceiling as I expel a frustrated breath.

"We need to clear the air," I say. "We can't make tomorrow about us."

I drag my gaze back to her, and after a particularly fraught moment where we just glare at one another in silence, Jess sighs heavily and shakes her head. I know she's let down her guard the minute her gaze softens.

"I'm sorry too. I don't even know what happened tonight."

"There's a lot of tension between us these days, it seems."

"There was always tension between us. This wasn't the usual tension." She clears her throat, then raises her chin stubbornly. "I really didn't think there'd be any hard feelings between us."

I'm trying not to gape at her, but I'm failing miserably.

"Are… But… I mean… You're *kidding*, right?"

Her gaze narrows.

"We are fundamentally incompatible. We agreed we were fundamentally incompatible and so we ended it."

I was madly in love for the first time in my life. When Jess's inheritance from her grandmother came due, she went hunting for an apartment and insisted I come with her. I really thought that was some kind of hint that she was thinking about us making it official and moving in together eventually. A few days later, I walked past a jeweler and my gaze snagged on an emerald ring in the window...a flawless, perfectly round stone, set alongside two diamonds in a rose gold setting. It screamed Jess to me, and I already knew I wanted to spend the rest of my life with her, so I walked in and bought it then and there.

Then I went to the West Coast for a week for work, and when I came home, she said she wanted to talk. Her expression was cold and hard, and she spoke so formally, I felt like I was at a job interview that was going horribly wrong.

I'm sorry, Jake. This has just gotten out of hand. We want different things from life.

We talked for a while, but it was pretty obvious that we weren't going to find common ground. Jess had no way of knowing I was about to propose, but she was right to assume that I did want a commitment from her and, I suppose, at least honest enough to be up-front about the fact that she did not want that.

I've never been angry that she broke up with me. She wants what she wants, and I respect her for knowing her own mind. No, I was and am angry at the way that she discarded me as if I was nothing to her, and if I'm really honest, I'm pretty pissed off that she insisted we hide our relationship. When we first started seeing one another, she said she was just trying to keep her business and personal lives separate. Maybe I wasn't entirely convinced, given she's close friends and business partners with both Paul and Marcus, but I did respect that romantic relationships can be more complicated than friendships.

Mostly I went along with it because I had no idea how things between us were going to play out. Besides, I thought that once we fell into a rhythm together, we'd just come clean to our friends.

That's not how it played out at all.

I don't know what the expression on my face is, but I'm guessing it's pretty dark, because Jess looks flustered for the second time tonight. Maybe for the second time in all of the years I've known her.

"We fell in love so hard it rocked my entire world, Jessica," I grind out. "It wasn't a simple case of us just not seeing one another anymore for me. And you won't convince me it was that simple for you either."

"We weren't 'in love,'" she gasps, focusing on entirely the wrong part of my announcement. I blink at her.

"What were we, then?"

"Lust, Jake. It was lust," she says pointedly, but then she avoids my gaze as she tightens the tie on her robe.

"Lust?" I repeat, gaping at her.

"I assume that even Saint Fucking Jake is familiar

with the concept?" Jess says, a little bitterly. I frown, then tilt my head at her.

"That's the story you tell yourself even after all of this time, isn't it? You convinced yourself what we had was just physical, so you didn't have to feel guilty about how cruel you were."

"I don't want to do this," she blurts. "I don't want to have a postmortem. I don't want to dig up the past. Can't we just go back to the way it was for the next few days?"

"The way it was?" I repeat incredulously.

"When we were friends, Jake. We had a lot of good years when we were just friends."

"Jessica. You and I were *never* just friends."

She raises her chin stubbornly.

"You're angry because of the breakup. Even after all of this time. I really thought you respected my decision. Frankly, your attitude reeks of 'entitled male' right now."

Oh, she did not go there.

"You treated me like shit," I say flatly.

"I did not!"

"You used me like a dirty little secret. You had no regard whatsoever for my feelings at any point during our relationship or after it, when you just cut me out of your life as if I was nothing to you. You didn't even invite me to your housewarming party, for fuck's sake. Do you know how hard that was to explain to everyone else?"

"I thought it would be better—"

"You thought it would be easier," I correct her. She's staring at me, lips pursed and nostrils flared, and my fragile hold on my frustration slips. When I speak again, my voice is low and harsh.

"Maybe your Tinder dates don't care if you use them like a piece of meat, but I should have been more than a hookup—we'd known each other for more than a decade! I deserved better. For fuck's sake, the whole reason I looked like an asshole again tonight is that you insisted we keep our relationship from our closest friends. Am I bitter? You bet your ass I am, but not because you ended things. No, I'm angry with myself because I let you use and discard me. And the worst thing is, I'd watched you do it to other guys for years, but I was still stupid enough to think I was different." I shift to lean forward and look right into her eyes. "I figured out why you didn't want anyone to know about us, by the way. You knew all along where we were headed. You knew you'd end things with me, and you knew how I felt about you so you knew it wouldn't be pretty. That's why you didn't want anyone to know we were even dating, so you could use me and discard me without facing their disappointment in you."

The words burst out of my mouth, and I'm not sure which one of us is more shocked by them. She's staring at me with her mouth open and her eyes wide. I groan and run my hand through my hair, then unfold myself from her stupid fucking fun-sized sofa and stand.

"This is stupid."

"Jake," she says, and I'm already turning for the

door, but the softness in her voice gives me pause. I glance back at her, and she bites her lip, then says very quietly, "You're wrong. It was never my intention to hurt you."

"Well," I say flatly, "you did anyway."

She follows me, but I pause in the hallway and turn back to her. All of a sudden, her beauty hits me hard in the gut—it's like I'm seeing her again for the very first time. The big blue eyes framed by those eyelashes that I know are really light beneath the mascara. The skin of her face, so pale it's almost translucent, dotted with freckles beneath her makeup. Sometimes she dyes her hair an artificially bright fire-engine red. Sometimes she colors it almost burgundy. Sometimes, like now, it's her natural shade—a red that's rich with copper tones and gold.

I have tried to move on these last two years. I've dated a little, including a few months with Vanessa, a woman I met on a hike. I ended that because as much as I want to settle down and find a partner, I couldn't give Vanessa my heart, and I knew she both wanted and deserved it.

After all, wasn't that the same problem as me and Jess, just in reverse?

Staring down at Jess in this hallway, I'm painfully aware that the reason I couldn't give Vanessa my heart is that Jess still holds it. I'm furious with her, I don't particularly like her—but I want her, and I can see the echoes of desire in her eyes even as she stares up at me less than *sixty fucking seconds* after an argument.

She moistens her lips and I'm reminded that beneath that flimsy gown, she's wearing a dress so tiny that she could leave it on while we made love. I'd lift her up onto her kitchen countertop, push the dress up to her thighs, slide the panties to the side and—

"Jake," she whispers throatily.

"Yes?" I whisper back. The air around us is thick and we're both breathing heavily, the space between us shrinking by the second.

"You should go," Jess whispers, and the spell breaks.

Because she's right. I need to go, before she shatters me all over again.

I nod curtly and walk away as fast as my legs will carry me.

CHAPTER FIVE

Jess

I'VE BEEN IN New York for seventeen years, and for the first few years, I felt like a grain of rice on a beach. That analogy sounds like something Mitch would say and I'd definitely give him shit about it if he did, but I came here straight from small-town Georgia. The size of the city was terrifying—not to mention the fact that I didn't feel like I fit here. Not at first.

In fact, the city began to feel like home only after a few years, once I'd built a family beyond my grandmother. First came Paul and Marcus, and Abby too, because she and Marcus were a package deal long before they were a couple. Then Jake popped up in my life because he and Paul were always hanging out and Paul and I were living and working together as we tried to get our company off the ground.

And not long after that, I met Mitchell.

We met in a ticket line, of all places. Abby's mom was in town for a last-minute visit and she desperately wanted to see a particular smash-hit musical. It was sold out months in advance, but luckily for Abby's mom, my grandma Chloe was the kind of woman who had a contact in every industry. Chloe made a call for me, and I was waiting in the ticket line to see the friend of her friend who was going to hook me up with tickets.

But as I waited, I chatted with the guy in front of me. He was waiting to enter the ticket lottery—a long shot, but his mom was also in town and she was *desperate* to see it, so he figured he'd give it a try.

Obviously, I offered to get him tickets too. I mean—why wouldn't I? Mitch was cute and flirty, and once we realized that even Grandma Chloe's friend of a friend could manage tickets only for the following night, we decided to leave Abby and the moms to fend for themselves so we could go out for dinner and drinks alone.

It was a fantastic dinner. Mitch and I drank too much and laughed hysterically the whole time, and I got the real sense that I was in the presence of someone exactly like me. He invited me back to his crappy apartment, and I said yes without even a second thought. That's where the wheels fell off. Because it turned out that Mitchell was exactly like me, and not even I am narcissistic enough to want to fuck myself. We gave it a real shot—but after just a few minutes of an exceedingly awkward attempt at kissing, I sprinted for the door.

I'd never have seen Mitchell Cole again, except that the very next night we had theater tickets together, and when his dear, sweet mother heard how we got the tickets, she insisted on sitting next to me. During the intermission, she let slip why she wanted to see that particular show.

"What do you think of the female lead?" she asked me.

"She's amazing," I said.

"See, Mitchell? Even *Jess* thinks she's amazing," his mother said pointedly, then she turned to me and explained, "They used to date. He broke her heart. I may never forgive him."

Mitch looked so mortified that I started to feel a little sorry for him. And by the end of the night, when Mrs. Cole insisted Abby and Mrs. Herbert and I join them for a late dinner, I felt very sorry for him. Mrs. Cole is a lovely lady. She's also a dreadful nag, and if I had to hear one more time about the adorable grand-children Mitchell had robbed her of, I was going to scream. That's why, somewhere between the appetizers and the main, I switched places with Abby and leaned into Mitch.

"Will she shut up about this if we pretend we're dating?"

He gave me a confused look.

"Probably."

"Good," I said, and I linked our hands and slammed them on the table so everyone could see. Our sad little ploy worked and after Mrs. Cole was placated, the rest of the evening was a blast. That's when I realized Mitch and I really did have a lot of chemistry—just not the sexual kind. By the time we parted for the night, I'd scrawled my number onto a napkin.

"I think you and I are basically the same soul walking around in two different bodies," I told him, and at the flash of panic in his eyes, I burst out laughing. "*See?* That's exactly how I'd react if a guy said that to me. Let's be each other's wing-person. And let's promise one another that we will never, ever again try to have sex."

He shook my hand and took the napkin and we've been best friends ever since.

Last night's stupid game was probably the shittiest thing I've ever done to him, and I was so distracted by the seemingly never-ending drama with Jake that I forgot to clear the air before I went to bed. That's why, as soon as I opened my eyes this morning, I was sick with guilt. It took me a while to draft an appropriate text.

Jess: I am so sorry. It's no excuse, but I was particularly frazzled and I panicked. And I'm sorry I didn't call you to say sorry last night. Jake and I had another argument and I was distracted. Basically I'm a selfish bitch and you deserve a better best friend.

Mitch: Did you even stop to think about MY friendship with Jake? And how complicated that would be if you and I were actually—shudder—fucking?

Jess: No, I didn't think. But I really am sorry.

Mitch: You're not a selfish bitch, but you definitely are an insensitive cow.

Jess: So you've told me. Am I forgiven?

Mitch: Let me think about it.

Mitch: Okay, thought about it, and I have a demand. I'll forgive you if you promise not to drag me to that shitty hipster cocktail bar for the rest of the year.

Jess: Sorry, not worth it. I guess I'll just have to find a new guy best friend.

Mitch: Please. If that was even a remote possibility you'd have done it years ago.

Jess: See you at the reception?

Mitch: I'll be there with bells on.

Mitch: P.S. You're forgiven. Yes, you absolutely are an insensitive cow, but you're MY insensitive cow.

I exhale a breath and drop my phone onto the bed beside me, because my alarm isn't even due to go off for another hour, but I've been lying here feeling awful about Mitchell for a while now. And now that all is right with the world again, I have to think about the other shocking events of the previous evening.

Jake.

I know that despite the busy day ahead, I'll be thinking about the near miss with him in the doorway all day long. Even on Monday when I'm back at work and Jake is God-only-knows-where gathering berries or bathing in puddles or whatever the fuck he does when he's "hiking," I'll still be both relieved and miserable about the fact that I didn't get to kiss him again.

I could have. I could have stood up on my tippy-toes in that way he used to tease me about. I could have put my hands on his shoulders and pulled him down toward me. I could have pressed my lips to his and reminded myself that despite his size and how very different we are in pretty much every way, we also fit together in ways that always blew my mind.

If I ever managed to fool myself into thinking I hadn't hurt Jake Winton, last night he proved otherwise. I can be a bit insensitive sometimes, I'm well aware of that, but despite what Mitchell probably thought last night, I'm not a sociopath. As much as I'd have loved to kiss Jake again, doing so would have been unforgivably cruel.

I get up and dress, then while I sip my first coffee of the day, I answer emails. I'm the CEO of the software company Paul, Marcus and I founded after college. Brainway Technologies makes only one product, a somewhat fancy internet browser. It's taken twelve years to build the company to the point it's at now—with offices on both sides of the country and the world at our feet. I love what I do, enough that I work round the clock most days. Today's actually a rare exception, because once I close this laptop, I'll be completely offline until tomorrow.

Just as I'm about to log out and order a car, the inter-office chat client sounds a notification.

Marcus: Morning, Jess. Are you okay?

Jess: Are you seriously logged in and working the morning of Paul's wedding?

Marcus: Are you kidding me right now? Hypocrite, much?

Jess: Go play groomsman.

Marcus: I never understood you and Jake. You've always had such a weird dynamic.

He's not wrong about that. Jake and I seem to have two modes: push or pull. We fight or we fuck. But Marcus doesn't know that, he only knows about the fighting part, and especially with a mild-mannered guy like Jake, that probably does seem strange. I guess me and Jake have never made much sense to anyone, ourselves included.

Jess: I had a bad day, and sometimes, bad days are badly timed.

I do give Mitch a lot of shit about his awkward metaphors, but the man really does have a way with words.

Marcus: We were all really worried about you.

Jess: I'm definitely signing out now.

Marcus: And worried about Jake too, to be honest. He seemed determined to put you on the spot and I don't really get why he was being a jerk like that. He's really not a jerk, is he? Still, if you need me to kick his ass, you just let me know.

Jess: We both know Jake could pick you up and snap you like a twig.

Marcus: Jake is essentially the human version of one of those oversize teddy bears. By the way, should I ask him about it today, since you're not quite ready to explain what that was all about?

Jess: Mind your own damn business.

Marcus: Yeah because that's how this group of friends works.

Jess: See you at the pier later.

Jess: And please just leave it. What happened last night wasn't even Jake's fault. We talked and we've cleared the air, everyone should just let it go.

I shut the laptop before he can reply and then I order a car.

CHAPTER SIX

Jess

ABBY IS WAITING on the sidewalk outside her building looking ready to pounce, as if she'll quickly hop into the back of the car if the driver just slows down enough. But when the car stops to let her in, she waddles toward the door with visible discomfort. I leap out to help her inside.

"I'm fine," she says, but she's out of breath and clearly miserable.

"Oh, honey," I sigh, squeezing her upper arm as she slides inside. The driver behind us is leaning heavily on his horn so once she's safely seated, I flip him the bird, mouth some obscenities in his general direction, then I join her in the car. Abby shifts until she's something like comfortable, catches her breath, then glares at me.

"Fess up, Jess. What the hell was that last night?"

"I had a bad night. It was badly timed," I say, wondering if I need to start paying Mitch royalties for the phrase.

"I'm going to ask you a question and before you

answer it, I just want you to know I will never, ever forgive you if you lie to me."

"Jesus, Abby."

"Did something happen between you and Jake?"

"Just a squabble—"

"I always knew you didn't get along, but watching you two carry on last night, it occurred to me that maybe it was actually the world's longest mating dance."

"Ah—"

"Oh my *God*. You *didn't*."

"What?" I say, defensively. She gives me a pained look.

"Did you seriously fuck Paul's brother the night before his wedding? That's bad even for you, Jess."

I'm a little relieved I can deny her accusation without lying, but mostly I'm just desperately wounded by the horror in her eyes.

"I did not," I say. I know I successfully keep the defensiveness out of my tone, although I'm not entirely sure I can hide how much she just hurt me. Abby is pregnant and cranky, but she's generally a wonderful person who would never intend to cause me pain. For a moment I think the moment has passed, but it actually gets worse, because Abby is visibly relieved to hear I kept my slutty mitts off Saint Jake.

"Thank God for that," Abby breathes, then she laughs weakly as she pretends to wipe sweat off her brow. I frown at her.

"We had a chat, cleared the air and then he left. Happy?"

"Phew."

"Are you okay? You look…" I scan her expression, then pause. "You look really cranky, actually."

"I am," Abby groans. "I snapped at Marcus because I slept through my alarm this morning, so he figured I was tired and he let me sleep. I snapped at one of my contractors yesterday because she edited a video too quickly and I was worried she hadn't done it properly. I even snapped at Izzy yesterday after you left because she asked me if I knew what was going on with you and Jake."

"Par for the course I think, babe," I say, motioning toward her enormous belly.

"I've had such an easy pregnancy so far," she sighs. "This week, it just seemed to hit me in a way I wasn't prepared for. I mean—look at my feet."

We both glance down, and I gasp at the size of her ankles. Her feet are in flip-flops, but the bands are tight beneath her toes.

"Do you still fit into your shoes for today?" I ask her hesitantly.

"Yeah, I tried them on last night when we got home. They still fit, but only just." She sighs heavily, then rubs her belly. "So yeah… It turns out a twin pregnancy isn't exactly a walk in the park after all, and I'm tired and headachy and cranky and swollen but… okay. Excited. I can't believe they'll be here so soon."

"How far along are you? I've lost count again."

"Thirty-one weeks yesterday," Abby sighs happily.

"I'm so excited for you," I say, and I mean it. Abby and Marcus are totally in love, and they'll make exceptional parents.

"I am too. But I'm also so excited to get today over and done with so I can put these cankles up." Abby gives me a pained look, and we laugh.

"If you need a rest, you let me know. I'll find a way to make it happen."

Abby leans her head on my shoulder as she says, "I know you will."

ISABEL IS BESIDE HERSELF. I was there when she met Paul. I was there when they fell in love, and there at their first wedding. Hell, I was even there for the breakdown of her marriage, but I've never seen her like this.

"It's finally the day! I just can't wait," she says, throwing open the door to the hotel suite and beaming.

"Dear God, how much coffee have you had?" I ask her, aghast.

"I've been up since four. I couldn't sleep! I've had a lot of coffee, I guess. Six cups. No, seven. Maybe I need another?"

She's speaking so fast I can barely keep up with her. Abby reaches out and grabs Isabel's forearm to stop her bouncing.

"No coffee," she says firmly. "You need champagne, not coffee. Jess?"

"On it," I laugh, and I push my way into the suite and make a beeline for the kitchenette. It's all ele-

gant furnishings and glamour and flooded with natural light through the floor-to-ceiling windows. My
assistant, Gina, arranged some supplies for us yesterday, so I know there are all sorts of goodies waiting
to get us through the day. I pour some sparkling apple
juice into a flute, then pour two sparkling wines for
me and Isabel, and return to the living area to distribute the glasses.

"We need to make a toast," Abby says, then she
gives me a cheeky glance. "Should I call Jake so you
two can arm-wrestle again to see who goes first? That
was super fun last night."

"What was that about?" Izzy asks with a frown.

"I've already interrogated her about it. She promised
it was just a bad day and nothing untoward is going on
with Jake," Abby answers for me.

Isabel frowns at Abby, then glances at me and turns
back to Abby. I have an awful feeling Isabel is about to
defend me somehow, and I also have an awful feeling
it would take very little to leave Abby in tears today,
so I hastily raise my glass.

"To Isabel, our dearest friend. May today be everything you've dreamed of."

Isabel's expression softens and she raises her glass
too.

"And to you two. Both of you. Thanks for being
there for me while Paul and I figured all of this out.
I'm not sure how I'd have survived the last eighteen
months without you."

We all clink our glasses, and just as I raise my glass to my lips, Abby bursts into tears.

Called it.

"Happy tears," she assures us. "I'm so happy for you, Izzy. *So* happy."

WE EAT BRUNCH, then assemble for a team of stylists to work their magic. While Yvette refreshes my mani/pedi, Shondra does Abby's makeup and Isla styles Isabel's hair—and then we all rotate. It's an almost perfect day, with no more accidentally insulting comments from Abby. I'm with two of my best friends in the world. There's almost as much laughter in the air as there is chatter, and believe me, we three can chat.

"Thanks for letting us pick our own dresses," Abby says to Isabel, when we gather in the bedroom to dress. Izzy gives her a gentle look.

"The ceremony is going to be really casual and I wanted you to be comfortable. Even if you wanted to wear sweatpants, we'd have made it work."

"Sweatpants were an option?" Abby jokes, then snaps her fingers. "Dammit. Wish I knew earlier."

I've chosen a simple dress in light green silk, with a fitted lace bodice and an asymmetrical skirt that falls above my knees at the front, but almost to my ankles at the back. Abby's gone for a soft blue baby-doll dress that flatters her pregnant shape in the most beautiful, feminine way. To her mother's horror, Isabel refused to wear a traditional bridal gown this time around—instead, she selected a blush halter-neck cocktail gown, paired with a sky-high pair of sandals and some blindingly sparkly bling.

"I just adore this dress on you," I murmur as I help Izzy zip the back.

"Mom is still pretty pissed." She smiles ruefully. "But this is my day, not hers."

I remember at Izzy's first wedding, the way her mom railroaded her into a much more formal day than Izzy and Paul ever wanted. This time around, Izzy grew a backbone—and that's exactly why her mom isn't even here, helping her dress this morning. *No family drama*, Izzy told me a few weeks ago, which is why neither Paul's dad nor Izzy's parents and brothers were at the rehearsal dinner. Jake got a free pass because he's in the bridal party, but all other family members will meet us later at the event space at Chelsea Piers.

Abby shuffles out from the bathroom in her dress, face flushed and eyes downcast.

"Abby, you look amazing," Isabel says gently. Abby gives a self-conscious smile and does half a curtsy. I frown at her sharp intake of breath as she bows, even as she quickly straightens. I open my mouth to ask her what's wrong, but she gives me a pointed look, then shifts her gaze to Isabel. I nod, reading her silent message loud and clear, and focus on helping Izzy get her jewelry on.

But as soon as Isabel excuses herself to use the bathroom, I turn to Abby with a frown.

"Is it your back?"

"It's my shoes, Jess," she whispers urgently. "They don't fit."

"But you said they fit last night."

"They did. But they're way too small now. I don't know how it happened."

She drops the shoes onto the floor beside her feet and I feel my stomach drop. Her ankles were huge this morning—now, they are enormously swollen and the skin beneath them is pitted and flushed. I don't know how she's even walking.

"Abby," I whisper. "That's…"

"I just need to put my feet up," she interrupts me. "As soon as we get through the ceremony, I'll sit down at the reception and prop them on a chair. I promise. Don't make a fuss, but you have to help me find something I can wear on my feet."

I look at her helplessly. She's close to tears, her gaze pleading with me, and I sigh and reach for my phone.

"What are you doing?" she asks me in alarm.

"I'll text Mitch and get him to swing by the—"

"What's going on?" Izzy asks, returning to the room. Her gaze drops to Abby's feet and she gasps. "Abby! Oh my God, are you okay?"

"I'm fine," Abby says, but her lip wobbles just a little now. "I'm so sorry, Izzy. My shoes don't fit."

"Can you wear your flip-flops?" Izzy asks, without hesitation.

"Of course, but—"

"So wear them. Who cares?"

"Izzy, they'll look ridiculous," Abby says, her voice uneven.

"Don't wear any shoes, then."

Izzy and I exchange a glance, and then at the exact same time, we grin.

"Barefoot bridal party. Like a beach wedding!" I say, bending to unbuckle my own shoes.

"Oh my God. Why didn't we think of this earlier?" Isabel asks as she bends to slide off her own shoes. As soon as she kicks them away, she exhales in bliss. "Ah. That's better already."

"You two are insane. We can't all be barefoot at your wedding!" Abby protests, laughing tearfully.

"Actually, I can do whatever I want at my wedding," Isabel says pointedly.

"She makes an excellent point," I agree.

"Plus, this will really piss my mom off. So, it's a win-win."

We all laugh, but then Abby's smile fades.

"Are you sure? I'm sure we could find someone to pick me up some…I don't know…clown shoes or something," she mutters. Isabel laughs and shakes her head.

"We're definitely doing this. Come on, then! Are you two ready?"

I help Abby up from the bed, and we both stare at Isabel, who has already bounded out of the bedroom.

"God, she's exhausting like this," Abby laughs softly.

"Abby," I say, very quietly, and I catch her elbow before she moves to follow Izzy. When she turns back to me, I keep my expression soft. "I want you to promise me you'll call your OB about this swelling tomorrow."

"I will."

"Okay, then. Let's go get this Energizer Bunny married off before her batteries run low."

CHAPTER SEVEN

Jake

PAUL, MARCUS AND I stopped in early at a bar on the pier for a drink. Partly to kill time, but also, as Marcus suggested, because maybe a beer might help my brother relax.

"Unless you could prescribe him something…like a light general anesthetic or something?" Marcus suggested under his breath as we watched Paul pace up and down the length of his apartment. He was already fully dressed when Marcus and I arrived, and for the entire hour we sat at his place "to keep him company," Paul paced.

"I actually like my medical license, so no, probably not a great idea to anesthetize my own brother on his wedding day."

Marcus is at the bar ordering, and Paul and I have taken seats looking out over the water, enjoying the view. It's a beautiful afternoon. The sun is hitting the water just right, so the light is fresh and golden, but not blinding. I breathe it all in, then glance at Paul, who is now sitting with his hands over his stomach as if he's seasick.

"You're positively green," I say. He gives me a pained looked.

"I just have this feeling she's not coming."

"She's going to show up," I laugh softly. "Do you really think she'd let things go this far if she was going to back out at the last minute? You did this last time too, I recall."

"Yeah, I did," he sighs heavily. "Distract me. Tell me what happened with Jess last night."

I wince and scan the crowd for Marcus, hoping he's about to return with beers so I can avoid the question. I find him at the bar, waiting behind a crowd of what looks suspiciously like a bachelorette party. He's going to be a while, dammit.

Sometimes, I still can't believe I ever let Jess convince me to lie to Paul. And then I can't believe I didn't come right out and tell him the truth about our breakup when it happened. The only reason I didn't was that I felt like I should give Jess a heads-up, and I was too hurt, and then later, too angry to get in touch with her.

Now, I'm kind of torn. I probably could just tell him what really happened—except that it's his wedding day, and I don't want to complicate anything for him right now.

And so, yet again, I find myself lying to Paul.

"I was overtired. She was obviously having a moment too. We talked and cleared the air. Everything is fine now."

"Hmm," Paul says thoughtfully. He gets this intense expression on his face when he's thinking about something really hard. After growing up with this guy, I know it well. And I'm not particularly thrilled to see it.

"What does *hmm* mean?"

"*Hmm* means I can't believe she reacted like that. It's almost like she overreacted. Which I don't need to tell you, is not like Jess at all."

"Everyone has bad days, right?"

"I suppose they do. Yes, that would explain it. Jess has been working very hard this week, preparing for me to go away, starting to get ready for when Marcus's twins come. So that explains Jess's odd behavior but… What about yours?"

"Me?" I blink at him.

"You seemed determined to embarrass her last night, unless I'm reading the situation incorrectly," Paul says carefully. He glances at me, hesitating just a little. "Am I reading the situation incorrectly?"

I sigh.

"We have a complicated dynamic. She pisses me off like no one else. She always has."

"Have you ever asked yourself why?"

Only every day for the last fourteen or fifteen years.

"It's…complicated."

"So you keep telling me," Paul chuckles. "Care to elaborate?"

"Remember when I lived here and we used to hang out all of the time? The six of us?"

"Of course."

"Remember how Jess and I could never agree on anything? I mean, if I wanted pizza for dinner, she'd go out of her way to insist on Thai food. And if I wanted to see a film, she'd insist on going to a club instead."

"Yep."

"And remember that time when we got into an argument about coffee? She was actually trying to convince me she didn't like coffee. As if I hadn't met her."

"Oh, I remember."

"So last night was just the continuation of a messed-up friendship that's been hovering around confrontation for what...? Fifteen years now?" I say, trying to reassure him.

"Fourteen years, eleven months, six days, and I'm going to go right ahead and guess about twenty-two hours," Paul says. He's not joking, by the way. To say Paul has a mind for dates would be an extreme understatement.

"See? We have a very long history of driving each other bonkers," I mutter.

"Jake, we both know I'm not great at interpersonal relationships," Paul sighs. "But even *I* can see through your bullshit. You were both on edge all night and you know it was bad for me to notice it. I have to assume there's more to your recent history with Jess than I know about. Am I right?"

I blink at him. I was worried about what the others thought last night, but it didn't even occur to me that Paul might guess the truth about my relationship with Jess.

"Uh…"

"You don't have to tell me if you don't want to." My once-clueless brother shrugs, but then pins me with a look. "But can I give you some advice?"

"Um. Okay?"

"Sometimes what feels like hate is actually disappointment."

"Beer," Marcus announces, sliding three mugs onto the table in front of us. Paul gives me a sage nod, and I open my mouth, then close it again and reach greedily for the beer.

"Beer," I repeat weakly.

I don't know when my little brother became so wise, but it seems that these days, he's extending his IT-and-not-much-else genius status into whole new areas.

CHAPTER EIGHT

Jess

GOD, I HATE WEDDINGS. I hate them with the same intensity I usually reserve for people who walk too slowly on the sidewalk and those who chew food with their mouths open. I've been known to accept an invitation to a wedding but to skip the ceremony, turning up at the reception for food and booze and to party—because *those* things, I know how to handle. Unfortunately, that's not an option when it comes to a wedding like this, given I'm in the bridal party. So, when the music begins, I hug Isabel, then pause to adjust the hair around her shoulders.

"You ready?" I ask her gently.

"I'm so excited," Isabel whispers through a grin. "I can't wait another second to marry him again."

"Then let's do this," Abby laughs softly, and she steps out from behind the curtain to walk down the aisle. When I see that she's more than halfway down, I step out to follow her.

There are ninety-six people here, including a bunch

of my employees. Paul's new development manager, Audrey, stands out among the crowd with her pastel-purple hair and a pink-and-white-polka-dot vintage dress. Frankly, I'm more than a little relieved she didn't wear a cartoon T-shirt, given that's exactly what she wears to the office every day. She's on the aisle side of the back row beside a whole group of programmers, two of whom are typing on their phones. I pause at their aisle and death-glare them like a teacher on playground duty, and they slide their phones into their pockets.

Programmers, am I right?

Mitch is a few rows in front, and he gives me a very unconvincing leer as he scans his gaze over my dress. I roll my eyes at him, and he laughs.

But then I can't avoid looking toward the front of the room. Paul and Marcus wait beneath an archway adorned with white roses. I know that Jake is standing between them, but I can't bring myself to look at him, so instead, I offer Paul what I hope is an encouraging smile. He actually looks like he's going to puke. I make a mental note to stand as far away from him as possible.

As I continue down the aisle, I hear movement from behind, and I turn just in time to see Isabel burst out from behind the curtain. She's grinning, and she mutters an awkward "excuse me" as she sprints toward me. I laugh softly and step to the side to make room for her. She darts gracefully around Abby as if she's playing soccer, and then she hitches her dress up and throws herself at Paul. He catches her, and her bare feet cross at the ankles behind his waist. As they start to kiss, the lights shine against the moisture on his cheeks.

"I love you," I hear him choke.

"I love you too," Isabel croaks back.

My eyes are suspiciously moist, but when I scan the crowd, I see that pretty much everyone is blinking away tears. If I have to publicly display my shocking ability to shed tears for the second time in twenty-four hours, at least I've got company.

"Well, that was quite an entrance," the celebrant chuckles.

"Sorry!" Isabel says as she slides down off Paul and straightens her dress, then rests her hand flat against his chest and gives him one last kiss. I hear her voice over the celebrant's microphone as she whispers, "You just looked so nervous, like I wasn't going to come out. And…" She turns back toward me and Abby and gives us a rueful smile as a blush creeps up her cheeks. "I know I didn't do it right. Sorry, everyone. I just couldn't wait to marry him again. I just can't wait."

Now, the assembled crowd is all chuckling softly. I laugh too, and then unthinkingly, I glance at Jake. He's laughing, and he's looking right at me. We share a smile that's almost easy, and I skip ahead to catch Abby's arm. We walk the rest of the way to the front of the room with our elbows linked.

But as we near the archway, I glance down at Abby's hand, and I feel a little sick when I realize that her hands are almost as swollen as her feet. A tiny bit of my joy recedes.

Maybe I'll ask Jake about that later. He's no OB-GYN, but he is a physician, so he might know whether this is normal pregnancy swelling…or something I really need to worry about.

I HATE ALL WEDDINGS, but there's *one* kind of wedding ceremony I hate much more even than the others: the kind when I cannot fucking stop crying. Honestly, it's like someone burst a dam in my brain this weekend because my tears just will not let up. I cry when Paul and Isabel exchange vows. I cry when the celebrant reads a poem about love. I cry when Paul surprises Isabel with a new wedding ring.

"Because this represents a new union between us," he tells her unevenly. "We're not in the old pattern anymore."

And then I cry when she exclaims, "But I didn't get you a new ring."

And then I cry again when Jake quietly passes Isabel the ring Paul bought for himself.

When it's finally, *finally* over, Isabel and Paul link arms and leave the room, Abby and Marcus link arms and follow them, and I can't avoid Jake's gaze any longer. He extends his arm to me, and I take it grudgingly. I forgot how tiny I feel standing right up against him. I forgot the way his scent seems to hook me in and pull me closer to him. I forgot how strong these stupid tree-trunk arms of his are.

I give his muscles a quick squeeze just to remind myself of that last one.

"Did you seriously just feel me up?" he asks me, irritation lacing his voice. I keep the ultrabright smile on my face as I nod to greet Mitch, then Audrey and her motley band of misfits, then I shrug.

"Like you *haven't* checked out my rack in this awesome dress."

Jake doesn't reply, but when I glance up at him, there's a red flush seeping under his skin and his jaw is set hard. So, we're not quite ready for jokes yet. Fair enough.

Paul and Jake's father, Martin, and his new girlfriend, Elspeth, are waiting in the foyer, along with Isabel's massive family. She has at least four hundred brothers at last count, although when I comment on this, Jake snaps at me that I'm exaggerating. Okay, so it's not quite four hundred, but there's definitely at least five of them and when Isabel stands with her family, she almost disappears into the brawn.

There are seemingly endless hugs for the happy couple and Marcus and Abby are talking quietly to themselves, leaving Jake and me to stand in awkward silence as we wait. The photographer eventually calls us all to order, and then we spend another painful half hour posing for photos all together. Finally, everyone except Isabel and Paul are released to go to the reception.

I'm startled by the rapid transformation of the room where the ceremony took place. In the last hour, the staff set up round tables and centerpieces, and waiters are mingling among the guests with finger foods and trays of drinks. I snatch a glass of champagne from a passing waiter, down it, then immediately reach for another.

"Want to slow down there? We ruined the rehearsal dinner. I don't think Paul and Isabel are going to be quite so forgiving if we ruin the reception too," Jake murmurs, nodding toward the waiter as he also takes a champagne flute.

"I'm pretty sure you didn't use to be this paternalistic, Jake, but you should keep it up," I say pointedly. "Being an arrogant asshole really suits you."

"I was just trying to…" He begins, then he groans and sighs. "Did we always bicker like this?"

"Not when we were fucking." I shrug. "We could do that instead. Meet me in the restroom in five?"

He scowls at me, then shakes his head and walks off. I sigh and nurse the champagne while I scan the room for Mitchell. I find him seated at one of the round tables, chatting with Audrey. He must feel my eyes on him, because he looks up and meets my gaze.

Don't even think about it, I mouth. He grins and winks at me, then goes back to chatting. I briefly consider warning him that she's got a wicked temper and a third-degree black belt in judo, but then I decide it'll be more fun for him to find out for himself.

Next, I see Abby sitting at the bridal table, her feet up on a chair as she promised me, and she's talking quietly with Marcus. He's holding her hand and smiling at her. My gaze drops to their entwined hands, and that reminds me that I was going to ask Jake for his thoughts on her swelling, but now I've gone and pissed him off.

I sigh and wander over to take my seat beside Abby, determined to get a feel for her well-being before I go another round in the ring with Jake.

"Beautiful ceremony," Marcus remarks.

"Sure was," I say, downing the rest of my champagne before I glance between them. "Is that the kind of relaxed feel you two will go for? Or are we talking about ice sculptures and pomp and circumstance?"

"Somewhere in the middle," Abby says with a shrug.

"And by that she means, we'll have ice sculptures, but they'll be small ones," Marcus qualifies. Abby thumps him gently. She seems in good spirits, so I relax a little.

"And when is the big day?" I ask. "Have you decided yet?"

"I'm thinking I want the twins to walk me down the aisle," Abby announces. Marcus scowls at her and I can tell he's genuinely pissed. I may have just inadvertently opened up a can of worms.

"We are not waiting that long," he says.

"Um, we will wait that long if that's what I want," Abby snaps. "It's my special day, remember?"

"Oh God," I groan. "Don't you two start squabbling too. *Jesus.*"

I take my empty champagne flute and leave them be.

After all, this is a wedding. There has to be a single guy here somewhere.

Other than Mitch and Jake, of course.

CHAPTER NINE

Jess

THREE HOURS LATER, I'm nicely buzzed, but just on the right side of "humiliate my friends and colleagues by making an ass of myself" drunk. Mitchell seems to have given up on Audrey, and so he and I have been dancing and laughing and doing what we're actually particularly good at together—having a terrific time and forgetting all about our exes.

I've even managed to do a passable job of ignoring Jake all night, other than a few times when I caught myself looking for him. He's been circulating the crowd, no doubt impressing every person he speaks to with his unique blend of humility, compassion and all-round amazingness. He also had an unfortunately long chat with Audrey. I couldn't very well forbid him from flirting with her like I did Mitch, so instead I shot her my fiercest death glare and she immediately excused herself and went to the restroom. When she returned, I shot her a pleased, approving smile and ever since she's been hiding in the middle of the pro-grammer pack.

Now, I'm starting to get thirsty—proper thirsty, for water preferably, or at least something nonalcoholic. Most of the formalities are over, other than the triple chocolate and caramel wedding cake, but the night is still young—it's only just passed ten. I excuse myself, leaving Mitchell to dance alone—something the man is not afraid to do—and pad back to the bridal table. As I walk, I take a moment to appreciate just how unsore my feet are. Normally, I love expensive shoes—towering heels, razor-sharp stilettos, sparkly sandals are all totally my jam… But this barefoot thing does have its advantages.

As soon as I think about this, I realize I haven't seen Abby for a while. I scan the room, my heart rate starting to accelerate. Marcus is easy enough to spot—having an animated conversation with Jake at the bridal table—but Abby's chair is empty.

I walk briskly around the room, finally feeling a brief flash of relief when I see her sitting in a darkened corner by the kitchen. I make a beeline for her, scooping up two glasses of water from a waiter's tray on the way. As I near her, I'm pleased to see she has her feet up on a chair, but the relief is short-lived because once I'm close enough to see her face, I know that something is terribly wrong.

In the last few hours, Abby's face and neck have swollen up. Now, her entire body seems bloated, and she's sitting in an odd position, her shoulders up and stiff, but her head slumped forward.

"Abby," I say urgently as I pull up a chair beside

her. She lifts her head and gives me a smile that's visibly forced, even as she takes the water and sips at it cautiously.

"Hey there. Having fun?"

"Cut the shit. What's going on?"

"Just a little headache," she says, her smile slipping a tiny bit. Oh God, why did I drink that last glass of wine? I'm a ball of feelings right now, none of them good, and the wall between those feelings and the rest of the world feels dangerously fragile. Maybe it's not even a wall. Maybe it's a membrane, and maybe it's straining under pressure.

"Why are you sitting like that?" I ask her.

"Heartburn," she says uneasily, motioning vaguely toward the top of her abdomen. "Normal pregnancy problems, Jess. It's fine."

I scan down her body.

Severe swelling.

Headache.

Heartburn.

Upper abdominal pain.

A memory rises like a bubble and pops at the front of my thoughts. I'm sitting in my room at Grandma Chloe's apartment on the Upper East Side. It's late at night and I'm scared to make too much noise because I don't want to wake her up. She gets so upset when I'm upset, and that's why I'm silently weeping as I read through page after page of internet forum postings.

Right now, my vision is tunneling on Abby. I'm suddenly, frighteningly sober.

"Babe. Listen to me," I whisper urgently as I lean even closer to her. "You need to call your OB. You need to do it right now."

"I will tomorrow," she promises me. A waiter pushes open the kitchen door, and her face is suddenly properly illuminated. My stomach drops all over again.

"I don't think it can wait," I say. My voice sounds faraway and tinny. I hope I'm projecting an air of urgency, but I also need her to think I'm calm because the last thing I want to do is panic her. Inside though, I am a swirling torrent of anxiety and uncertainty. Abby gives me a weak smile and promises me, "I don't want to make a fuss tonight. I'm sure it's fine."

Eric will get angry if I make a fuss. I can't make a fuss. I'm sure it's going to be fine. It has to be fine.

There's some serious shit in my past, but I will not be the kind of woman who lets it float to the surface in a moment of crisis. I press the memories down—hard—and squeeze Abby's swollen hand.

"Abby. Please," I whisper. "I think we need to get you to an emergency room."

She stares back at me, but her gaze is unfocused.

"They deserve this night to go perfectly. We haven't even cut the cake yet, Jess. I'll pop some Tylenol and if I'm still feeling unwell later, I'll call my OB. Okay?" She hesitates, then admits uncertainly, "It's just... I know she's out of town this weekend, but I can call... maybe there's an on-call number..."

Abby is scared to cause a scene. Abby is scared to put people out.

I feel that membrane inside me burst as surely as if it was a physical thing, and just like that I know I'm going to lose my shit. The best I can hope for now is to hold myself together until I can get Abby some help.

I rise, then smile and nod as if she's convinced me. "Sure. You rest up. I'll go fetch you some Tylenol."

There are almost one hundred people in the reception hall, some dancing on the dance floor at the center of the room, the rest mingling around the tables chatting. I scan the room, and when my gaze lands on Jake, now standing with a group of the programmers near the kitchen, everything else fades away. The next thing I know, I'm slipping my arm into the crook of his elbow and flashing my staff a brilliant smile.

"Sorry, gentlefolk. Could I please borrow Dr. Winton here for a moment?" I say brightly. I sound totally at ease and confident. I don't know if I'm proud or ashamed of the way I can project this shiny veneer even while I'm dissolving into a puddle of utter terror.

Jake opens his mouth to protest, but I'm already leading him away from the group. He's much stronger—he could easily resist if he wanted to—and I feel the tension in his muscles. He's considering it. *Please, Jake. Please come with me.* But soon enough, he's come as far as the exit to the foyer. I push the door open, and my gaze lands on a disabled restroom. I'm going to break, and I need privacy to do it, and the urgency to lock myself away before I lose my grip on my composure is driving my footsteps faster and faster. I'm almost running now, but Jake's stride is so long he keeps up easily. When he realizes where we're headed, he tenses again and stops walking altogether.

"Are you fucking serious right now? I'm not hooking up with you tonight," he hisses, voice low and flat. "And I'm sure as shit not hooking up with you in a restroom."

I shake my head mutely. I'm going to break, and the best I can hope for is to do it behind closed doors.

I pull on his arm, *hard*, push the door open with my bare foot, then release his arm and run inside. Jake does follow me, albeit with visible reluctance. When the door closes behind him, he turns and then, with a heavy sigh, flicks the lock closed.

By the time he turns back to me, that membrane between my feelings and my facade has entirely dissolved. I've wrapped my arms around my waist, trying to warm myself up, because I feel *so* cold…*so* scared. Words cycle on a loop through my brain and I can't focus on anything else but the fear and the panic.

Abby's in trouble. She's in trouble and she doesn't know it. She doesn't want to make a fuss, but she doesn't know. She doesn't know that if she doesn't get help—

Jake knocks the seat down on the toilet and those big, strong hands land on my shoulders, then he guides me to sit. I am putty in his hands…weak, trembling putty. I'm hardly one to suffer low self-esteem, but right in this moment, I am everything I hate.

"Jess? What is it?" Jake's voice is so gentle. I blink and focus my gaze.

"I think Abby has preeclampsia. Maybe even HELLP syndrome."

I croak the words out, and see the shock and concern register in Jake's face. Those eyes—my God, those beautiful green-blue eyes are so kind. I'm frantically blinking away tears at the unquestioning empathy and compassion Jake offers me.

He's the best man I ever knew, and I hurt him so much.

"Tell me what's going on," Jake says. I guess this is what Dr. Winton sounds like in action. His voice is firm and soft, all at the same time. His eyes have locked with mine and I know I have every ounce of his focus and attention.

"Her shoes fit last night. But her feet are so swollen they didn't fit this morning. That's why we didn't wear—" It suddenly occurs to me that I'm barefoot in a public restroom and I shudder. *Focus, Jessica.* "That's why we didn't wear shoes for the ceremony. She's swollen all over now and it's getting worse so quickly. And she's got a headache—she's trying to be brave, but I can see she's in pain. And the heartburn, Jake." I'm pleading with him with my gaze. *Help her. Please. Help her.* "It came on so suddenly a few days ago and she's in so much pain her posture is all funny because she can't sit normally. She doesn't want to make a f-fuss but she needs help and she just doesn't know. She doesn't know it can all slip away."

I'm speaking so fast that he probably can't even understand me. Jake's hands on my shoulders tighten.

He's crouching before me now, so tall that when he kneels, our eyes are almost level.

"Jess, I need you to take a deep breath," he says gently. "You're starting to hyperventilate."

"But Abby—"

"We can't help Abby if you pass out in a toilet. Breathe with me, sweetheart. That's it."

I've been terrified of this ever since Abby told me she wanted to have a baby—not that she'd get sick, but that I'd project my own shit onto her and see complications where there were none. I've had friends become pregnant before and it's always been fine, but I knew it would be harder with a close friend like Abby.

I'm staring at Jake, breathing in time with him, conscious of the heat on my cheeks. I'm so ashamed of my weakness right now, I can barely stand it. I could have gone to Mitchell. But he knows about my past and he might have focused on me instead of Abby. That would have cost time, and I just don't know how much time Abby and her babies have.

My instincts drew me to Jake. Whatever is going on here, real or imagined, he will scoop all of this up in those massive bear claws of his and if it needs to be sorted out, he'll know how to sort it.

Even as these thoughts filter through my addled mind, I feel myself start to calm.

"Do you think she's in trouble?" I whisper.

"It doesn't sound good," he admits, then he puffs out a breath of air. I can see the wheels turning in his mind, and I'm suddenly convinced that he has this under control. The last of my panic recedes, and I straighten my posture, rising out of the slump I'd fallen into. Jake must see the calm returning too, because he stands from his squat and gives me a searching look.

"Are you okay now?"

"I'm fine," I say, a little stiffly. Fucking hell. I can see confusion in his eyes and I know that once we get Abby sorted out, he's going to ask me some questions I can't answer. "How do we get her to a hospital without panicking her?"

"You're going to go out and quietly let Isabel and Paul know that she's leaving. I'm going to go get Marcus, and I'll take them straight to an emergency room."

I throw my arms around his neck and press my face into his shoulder.

"Thank you," I whisper. "Thank you."

His arms wind around my waist, then contract.

"It's going to be okay," he murmurs. "I'll look after her. You just go and take care of Izzy and Paul."

I glance in the mirror as I leave the restroom. My mask is back in place, and I look fine—in fact, I look fantastic. I pause just for an extra second to admire the fact that my hair is still perfectly in place. My lipstick could do with a touch-up, so I'll grab my clutch and come back to tidy it up, but beyond that, I look just as polished and poised as I did when we left the hotel this morning.

If I keep projecting this sense of calm and purpose, no one will ever know.

That's been a principle I've relied on since I came to New York seventeen years ago, and it's still working for me even now.

CHAPTER TEN

Jake

I'VE SEEN A lot of shocking things over the years of my medical career, but this is something else. Not Abby— I haven't even seen her yet.

I'm talking about Jess. The fierce, unflappable Jessica Cohen, who just dissolved into an absolute fucking puddle at the thought of her friend being unwell. The proud, sometimes cold Jess, hyperventilating at the thought of Abby's pregnancy being in danger.

And probably even more mystifying—how the hell does Jess know about an obscure, rare pregnancy complication like HELLP syndrome? I did a six-month OB-GYN rotation as part of my residency and I saw a single case of it.

"Hey, Jake," Marcus greets me as I approach him. He's chatting with a waiter, nursing a glass of what I know is water, because earlier he told me that our beer at the bar was all he'd drink today, just in case Abby needed him. He must see something in my gaze, because he leaves the waiter and steps close. "What's up? You look…"

"Abby needs to go to an emergency room, Marcus," I say quietly. I'm used to delivering bad news, so I know from experience that the direct approach is best. Marcus's eyes widen, and he's suddenly scanning the room.

"But I just saw her ten minutes ago—"

"Jess tells me she's quite swollen and suffering from a severe headache. She doesn't want to let Izzy and Paul down, but since she's pregnant, those symptoms are concerning. We need to get her checked out, and we need to do it right now."

Marcus is already walking away from me, so I quickly drop my hand onto his shoulder. He turns back, looking almost as panicked as Jess did five minutes ago.

God, I miss these guys. I miss our close-knit friendship circle. I've made new friends in California, but these people were *my* people, in a way I don't think I'll ever really replace.

"You can't panic her, okay?" I say gently. "We need to keep her calm."

Marcus nods curtly, and then I follow him around the dance floor. Abby is just where Jess said she'd be—sitting in a dark corner by the kitchen.

Jess was right—Abby's face is starting to swell. She's got her eyes closed and she's now propped one elbow on the back of another chair so she can rest her head on her shoulder without slumping forward. I glance at her feet, and feel a chill run up my spine.

If her blood pressure isn't sky high right now, I'll eat my hat. During that residency all of those years ago, if a patient came to me with symptoms like these I'd have been sprinting for my attending. Hell, even if a nonpregnant patient presented like this now, my adrenaline would be pumping.

"Hey there, my love," Marcus murmurs, crouching beside her. Abby opens her eyes and smiles.

"Having fun?" she asks.

"I have been," he says, then he smiles right back at her. "Abs, we're going to go to the hospital now, okay?"

"What? No!" Abby protests. "I'm fine—"

"You aren't fine," Marcus says softly. "I know you're trying to be brave and you don't want to steal Izzy's limelight, but I can see it in your face. You're in pain, and we need to get you checked out."

"It's probably nothing. All of these things are just part of pregnancy," Abby says, but her voice is thick, and finally, there's real fear in her gaze. She glances at me, and a tear slides onto her cheek. "Tell him, Jake. Tell him this is all normal."

I walk to her other side and slide my hand under her elbow, gently easing her to her swollen feet.

"If it was just a bit of swelling in your feet after you'd been standing all day, or heartburn that you'd had for a while, or even a mild headache, I'd agree with you," I say quietly. "But, Abby, you're swollen all over, and I know you've got tenderness in your right upper abdomen. Am I right?"

"Some," she admits reluctantly. I can tell just from her grimace as she straightens that by *some*, she means *a lot*.

"We just need to get you checked out. We'll go to the emergency room and they'll run a few tests, and if this is nothing, you'll be home and in bed, resting easy by midnight. How does that sound?"

"But Paul and Izzy—"

"Jess has gone to let them know what's happening. They'll understand. I know they'd want you to get checked out much more than they'd want you here for the cake."

"But I was really looking forward to that cake," Abby says weakly. Marcus chuckles softly as he promises her, "I'll text Jess and get her to save you some."

We make it out of the reception area and into the foyer without much fuss. There, Marcus helps Abby into a chair, and I call for a car on my phone. I'd call an ambulance, except that my old hospital is only a mile away, so it won't be any faster and I don't want to panic her.

"The car is three minutes away," I assure them.

"I'm sorry," Abby whispers, in tears again. "I'm ruining their night. I feel so bad about it."

"Isabel is glad to be rid of you," Jess announces suddenly, walking proudly across the room to crouch beside her friend. "No one wants a bridesmaid outshining them on their big day. You're lucky she didn't send you home earlier."

"Yeah, I'm sure I look fantastic right now," Abby whispers, grabbing Jess's hand. "I'm scared, Jess."

"You're going to be absolutely fine," Jess says firmly.

"Will you come with me?"

She hides it pretty well, but I see a flash of fear in Jess's face that I just don't understand. She blinks it away, then raises her chin.

"Are you sure you want me there? You'll have Marcus…"

"I was going to come too," I add. "But I can stay—"

"No. You come too," Abby interrupts me.

"So Paul and Izzy's entire bridal party is leaving their reception?" Marcus says hesitantly.

Jess and Abby are staring at each other now. Abby's hands are linked with Jess's in a vise grip.

"I'm scared, Jess," Abby says again, and her face crumples and she starts to sob. "I've been telling myself all day that this is nothing to be worried about but now that you're all rushing me off to the emergency room, it's suddenly real. Please come with me."

Jess throws her arms around Abby and I hear her whisper, "Of course I'll come. We're all here for you, and you and the babies are going to be fine."

"The Uber is here," I say slowly. I glance among the four of us. "I'm not even sure we'll fit. It's a Prius."

"We'll make it work," Jess says. There's not even a hint of a wobble in her voice now—she's back to her calm, intimidating herself, and that makes it impossible to argue with her. Before I know it, we're all walking toward the front door, Jess and Marcus on either side of Abby.

Marcus helps Abby into the car, then folds himself up to take the middle, so Jess can take the other side. I automatically move to the front passenger's seat—there's no way I'll fit in the back. Just as I move to slide into the car, the front door to the event space opens and Mitch appears. He runs out toward us, a frantic expression on his face. I'm confused by how distressed he seems—I know he and Abby aren't close—but then I realize his gaze is on Jess. She steps away from the car and pushes him back a few feet away from us, so I can't hear what they're saying. Are they arguing? He's visibly frustrated and he grips her forearms, then pulls her close and plants a kiss on her cheek before Jess runs back to the car. Mitch gives me a slightly stiff wave, and I frown as I wave back.

"Let's go," Jess breathes. The driver signals to leave the curb, and she leans forward to nod toward me as she murmurs, "If you get us there fast, I'll make sure he tips you so well you can take the rest of the night off. Got it?"

The driver grins and tears into the traffic, just as my phone vibrates. I slide it from my pocket and see a text from Mitchell.

Don't ask me why but keep an eye on Jess tonight. She's not great with hospitals at the best of times and this situation is nothing like the best of times. She's only going because Abby asked her to.

I glance toward the back seat. They really are crammed in like sardines back there. Abby is crying silently, her head on Marcus's shoulder. Jess is staring at her lap.

She looks calm, but suddenly I know she's not. And Abby's situation is frightening, but I still don't understand how Jess even knew to be so concerned.

Unless...

I've known Jess since the year she graduated college—virtually a lifetime ago.

But it strikes me that for all of the years we've been "frenemies" and friends and lovers, there are still a lot of things about the infamous Jessica Cohen that just never added up.

CHAPTER ELEVEN

Jess

I SAY I HATE WEDDINGS, and it's true that I don't love them, but the hate I feel for hospitals is on a whole other level. I wish there was another English word for it. We've got *loathing* and we've got *dislike*, but those words just aren't strong enough. And what's worse than hate?

Worse than hate is what I feel for hospitals. I hate the harsh lighting and the misery and the fear and the medical equipment everywhere and the beeping machinery and the way the staff has to be just a little bit cold with their patients to even survive. I hate the constant reminders that life is so fragile. I hate all of those things, but the thing I hate the most is the smell of antiseptic. It has some god-awful, mystical ability to remind me of days I've spent my life trying to forget and stirs up such a tension in me that I'd always make Jake shower before I even kissed him when we met up after work.

He seemed completely perturbed by this at one

point, so I managed to convince him I'm a germaphobe. Maybe I really am a germaphobe. I'm now barefoot in a hospital after being barefoot in a restroom and when all of this is over, I'm going to soak my feet in bleach.

Abby and Marcus are filling out paperwork. I'm confused by why she hasn't been rushed off to be examined, but apparently getting her insurance details is a higher priority than treating her. I'm impatient enough that I can't sit still, and so I've slipped my phone out of my pocket and I'm scrolling through the website for the hospital. I find the board of directors and zoom in on the CEO and the list of members.

I know a lot of people in this city, especially in the corporate world. Grandma Chloe taught me a lot of things—but the best skill I learned from her was to always maintain a large, diverse network. I hoped I had some connection to someone senior here so I could speed this all up, but for once, I've got nothing.

Beside me, Jake has also been on his phone. He rises suddenly and walks to the counter. I see him flash the clerk a smile, and then he bends to speak to her through the window. A nurse appears a few seconds later, talks to Jake, and then the door to the triage area opens.

"Come on through, Abby. We'll sort the insurance out soon enough," she says quietly. Marcus and Abby rise, and the nurse waves to Jake, then to me. "You two, as well. Let's go."

Jake waits for me at the door, and as we follow Abby

slowly along the long hallway, I ask him quietly, "How did you do that?"

"One of the nursing unit managers on this ward used to work with me at the oncology unit. She's not on shift, but she made a call for us."

"Why hasn't Abby been taken straight to the maternity ward?"

"That isn't how this works, especially not this late at night. She has to be examined down here, but I imagine once they triage her, they'll either call a consult or just take her right through." He glances at me. "It'll speed up now, Jess. She's going to be okay."

We're shown to a room somewhere in the bowels of the hospital, deep behind the reception area. Marcus and Jake help Abby up onto the bed. She's cold now, and so they cover her with a sheet. The nurse pulls the curtain closed as she leaves but assures us a doctor is on his way. For the first time, I start to feel agitated. Abby is still quietly crying, and although she says she's cold, her face is flushed raspberry. There's a blood pressure cuff right there. Jake could just check it himself…

"I don't have admission rights at this hospital anymore," he says, correctly interrupting my questioning stare. "But if someone doesn't come soon—"

The curtain slides open and a startlingly young man appears. He's wearing a lab coat, but he has a certain air about him that I recognize immediately. It's the slicked-back hair, the too-white teeth, the haughty expression and what might just be a fake tan. He looks like he's about to go to a frat party. He looks like the kind of kid I knew at college, the one who'd barely study all semester, then have a tantrum because he didn't get the marks he wanted.

It's fair to say I feel something like insta-hate for this Doogie Howser wannabe.

"So, it's absolute bedlam in here tonight and Milly just called my personal cell and told me I need to ignore my other patients for five minutes to check you out, Abigail," he greets us. He says it like a joke, but I can see he's deeply unimpressed with Jake's queue-jumping skills. "Apparently you and your entourage here are VIPs. I'm Dr. Nolan. Can you tell me a bit about what's happening here?"

"It started with heartburn a few days ago," Abby says, her voice wobbly. She's only just beginning to explain herself, but Nolan seems to have heard enough. I hear the sigh he tries to stifle as he scans the shape of Abby's body without even lifting the sheet. When he raises his gaze to her face, there's a curl to his lip.

"And how much did you eat tonight?" he asks. Marcus, Jake and I all stiffen. Abby only blinks. "All I'm saying is, you're heavily pregnant. With twins, or so I've been told. It's crowded in there, and you're obviously overweight—there's a lot of fat around your internal organs. If you overeat, you're going to suffer for it."

Marcus and Jake both open their mouths as if they're about to tear into this kid, and fair enough. But if they tell this guy to fuck off, we'll have to wait for someone else to tend to Abby and we just need to get this process started. I leap in before the guys can blast this idiot, because there's a smarter way to proceed here.

"Dr. Nolan," I say as politely as I can, given that I want to tear this ignorant idiot a new asshole every bit as much as Jake and Marcus do. I let what remains of my rural Georgia accent roll on out as I ask him, "Tell me, do you know who the CEO of this hospital is?"

"Of course I do," he says flatly.

"Now look, I doubt as a resident you're spending much time with the CEO, so let me give you a bit of a tip…" I'm wearing my most cordial smile and speaking very slowly. I learned this trick from Grandma Chloe too. She used to say that there's no better way to make someone underestimate you than to lean into a stereotype.

Stereotypes are two-dimensional, Jessica. There's no depth to them, no complexity. And as soon as someone feels like they know all there is to know about you, they think they can control you.

I want Nolan to think I'm some redneck hick, out of my depth in the big city. I want him to underestimate me. In about two seconds flat, his body language relaxes and he becomes visibly impatient as he waits for me to make my point. His guard is down because he thinks I'm *no one*, so when he opens his mouth to dismiss me, I pounce.

"Cindy and I go to a corporate leaders' brunch together every month, and I've known her a long time."

My polite smile slips, and I feel my expression transform. This is my fierce face—and if this moron cries, it won't be the first time I've brought a man to tears with a few well-placed comments and a glare. "If there's one thing Cindy hates, it's text messages from her friends at eleven on a Saturday night, asking for her to intervene because she has a resident in the emergency room who's too ignorant and fat-phobic to treat a patient with the dignity, respect and urgency she deserves. So what you're going to do is to take whatever observations you need to take, then you're going to call us a consult from obstetrics and get the fuck away from my friend. Do you hear me?"

Nolan steps toward the bed and reaches for the blood pressure cuff, even as he mutters, "A nurse should be doing this."

"Well, sweetheart, the nurses are smart enough to know that Abby here is a VIP who deserves immediate attention from the guy with the medical degree. So do your fucking job."

Abby's eyes are closed now, and there are silent tears rolling down her cheeks. I don't really know Cindy Lang, but I'll be speaking to her next week anyway. This bastard needs to pay for making Abby feel small in one of the most terrifying moments of her life, and I'll personally make sure he does. Jake shifts subtly, and for a minute I think he's moving closer to me to tell me to back off—but then I realize he's shifting to see the monitor.

We all know the second her blood pressure reading

appears on the digital monitor because Nolan nearly trips over his own feet as he fumbles for the phone on the wall of the cubicle.

"Page an obstetrics consult. And get the rapid response team in here stat."

"What's happening?" Abby asks frantically. She's trying to sit up, wincing with the pain as she does. Marcus looks from Abby to me and Jake, the color draining from his face.

"Jake?" he whispers.

"She'll be in good hands in a minute," Jake says, shooting a filthy glare at the resident, but then he turns to me and takes my hand in his. "We have to get out of here, Jess."

"But—"

"Don't go!" Abby sobs.

"Sweetheart, your blood pressure is far too high," Jake says very gently. "There's a team of doctors and nurses who are coming in here to help you right now— they'll be here any second. Marcus can probably stay, but Jess and I really need to clear out to make room for them to work, okay? Your job right now is to lie there and to take nice, deep breaths."

"Are my babies okay?"

I'm not moving fast enough, so Jake slides an arm around my waist and physically pulls me out of the cubicle. I hear Marcus trying to console Abby as a team of hospital employees comes running down the corridor to flood the cubicle.

I was scared before, but seeing this response, I'm

terrified because it's exceedingly clear that Abby is not okay at all. Nolan backs out of the cubicle too, glances at me and then takes off down the hallway as if he's scared for his own life. Huh. Maybe he's smarter than I thought.

Jake and I stand in stunned silence in the corridor, staring back at Abby. She's crying now, but a doctor speaks to her and Marcus in urgent, calming tones. Someone is drawing blood, and someone else is preparing an injection. The curtain slides closed and then I can't see her anymore. I give a frantic, panicked squeak.

"We can't stay here," Jake says quietly.

"We can't leave her!"

"We have to, Jess. Come on." He's still holding my hand, and he tugs gently, leading me away from Abby's room. My feet are numb, so I let him drag me away.

"Where are we even going?" I whisper.

"Let's go back out to reception—"

"Dr. Winton?" The nurse who led us in from reception jogs to catch up with us, then gives us a sympathetic look. "She's in good hands now. I'll take you to get settled in the quiet area up at maternity."

The quiet area. I know what this means. This means she's going to set us up in a space where if bad news comes, we have privacy to deal with it. There's a heavy, warm weight on my shoulders, and I'm only vaguely aware that this delicious comfort is Jake's arm around me.

I look up at him. My gaze is blurry. My mouth is so dry.

"I don't think I can do this," I choke. I can hear my pulse in my ears and my knees feel so weak. Jake's expression softens.

"Do you want to go home?"

"I can't leave them. What if they need me?"

"Abby's here where the staff can help her, and not back at the wedding reception suffering in silence. And you did that." He draws in a deep breath, then bends to bring his face closer to mine as he whispers, "You've done enough, sweetheart. If you need to go home, I'll call Mitch. We both know he'll come and get you."

I could go with Mitch. Then I could melt down in the privacy and comfort of his apartment or mine, and that sounds divine right now.

But if I do, I'll have to spend the rest of the night waiting...worrying. And besides, if the worst happens, Marcus and Abby are going to need my support.

I make a decision then: I'll have a minor meltdown now, and then I'll pull myself together before anyone actually needs me.

"I'm staying," I say.

"You're sure?"

"I'm sure."

I'm barely even aware of the walk to the maternity ward. I'm barely cognizant of the nurse letting us into the quiet room, of the lollipop lady who brings us sweet tea and cookies that I can't bring myself to touch. It's only when Jake and I are alone again that I take a deep breath and fill my lungs with the scent of hospital antiseptic, and I finally let out a sob.

"Hey," he murmurs, pulling me close. I'm limp in his arms as he lifts me like I weigh nothing at all and settles me on his lap so he can wrap his arms all the way around me. Jake the man-mountain. God, he gives the best hugs. It's like he's completely wrapped my body in his. Like he could shield me from the whole world.

The problem is that it's not the outer world causing my distress right now. It's my inner world. He can't save me from it, but I can draw comfort from his embrace, and I do. I feel his breath in my hair, and he rocks me very gently as he whispers soothing words to me with love and care that I know he actually feels for me, even if I don't deserve it.

"It's okay, Jess. Let it out. It's okay."

CHAPTER TWELVE

Jake

I HAVE NO fucking idea what's happening right now. I mean that quite literally—because I'm blind to what's happening with our friends downstairs in Emergency, but I'm also blind to what's happening right here in my arms.

Jess is a mess. She's sobbing in a way that I would never have imagined she would ever sob. Her whole body shakes with waves of grief and fear, and I hold her close and I whisper reassurance to her, but something is going on here that I just can't figure out. Jess is tough, but right now, she's hopelessly out of control.

"Sweetheart," I whisper. "You have to help me out here. I want to help you, but I don't understand what's going on for you right now."

"I can't," she chokes.

"How did you know that Abby needed help?"

"Please don't ask me that now," she weeps, and my arms contract around her.

The door opens suddenly, and Jess's sobs abruptly

stop. She presses her face into my chest, apparently unwilling to let this intruder see her tears.

"Sorry to interrupt," the kindly nurse says. She gives me an awful, sickly look. "I just thought you'd want to know that they're taking her through now. Her husband is walking her to surgery, then he'll be up here shortly."

"Surgery?" Jess repeats, still facing away from the nurse.

"For a C-section?" I ask, looking at the nurse, who winces and nods. "General?"

"Yes. It needs to be done now."

When she closes the door, I sit Jess up and look right into her bloodshot eyes.

"Marcus is going to come here in a minute or two and he's going to be a wreck. They're taking her through for an emergency C-section right now, and they don't have time to give her a spinal block so she's going to have to have a general anesthetic. He won't be able to stay with her."

"I have to get my shit together." Jess correctly hears the point of my explanation and pushes me away. She stands, straightens her dress and raises her chin. A hic-cupping sob erupts from her throat, and she clenches her fists. "I need a bathroom."

I wait in the quiet room while she disappears into the hallway. Just a few minutes later, she's back. Her eyes are red and swollen, but she's fixed her makeup and hair, and she's completely composed. It's almost eerie—like a shutter has come down over her emotional turmoil. She sits calmly on the sofa opposite me, and then helps herself to the now-cold tea, holding the mug with her forefinger and thumb as if it's the finest china and she's dining with royalty. Right now, Jess is a picture of dignity and composure.

The door opens again and Marcus appears. I can tell he barely sees me. His eyes search for Jess, and then he walks to stand in front of her. She sets the mug down and stands too, just as Marcus throws his arms around her and bursts into tears.

"You saved her life," he says. His voice breaks. "You saved their lives. They said another hour or two and—"

"Don't," Jess says fiercely, her voice muffled against his chest. "Don't you even say it. She's here now, and she's going to be okay. They're all going to be okay."

"Luca and Austin went out of town this morning," Marcus chokes, referring to his brother and his husband. "And I've called my parents, but they won't be here for hours."

"I'll stay with you," I say immediately. Marcus gives me a bleary but relieved look.

"I'm not going anywhere either, Marcus," Jess says, and her voice is strong and clear. She leans away from Marcus's chest and stares up at him. "We're here for you. As long as you need us."

I do not understand this woman. Jess is clearly in a great deal of pain herself for reasons she can't even share with me, but Marcus needs her, and she's dug deep enough to find the strength to push all of that aside to become his support. He's sobbing now, and she pulls him down to sit with her on the sofa.

Our eyes meet over Marcus's head, and she swallows, and then through dry lips, she mouths a silent thank-you.

CHAPTER THIRTEEN

Jess

MARCUS NEEDS ME. *Marcus needs me. Marcus needs me.*

It'd be easy for me to run away tonight. I've done it before—I could do it again. People don't know that grief really can be outsmarted. People don't understand that if you move fast enough, the pain doesn't destroy you. It still catches you. It still hurts. But it can't drown you if you're busy enough with distractions. It can't ruin you if you're focused on building something new.

Right now, I want more than anything to run, to busy myself with distraction…but I don't. I can't, because, like Grandma Chloe used to say, when your friends and family need you, you move heaven and earth to be there for them.

Jake would stay, but it's me Marcus is sitting with. Jake is on the other side of the room, on alert, like our emotional security guard. He's primed and ready to support if all hell breaks loose, but for now, he's just waiting.

We're all waiting. And the minutes feel like hours.

But I stay, even though every breath of that antiseptic-filled air makes me feel more vulnerable. And I stay, even though I want more than anything to leave and to run. And I stay, because maybe I'm a coward when it comes to my own pain, but I would never, ever leave my friends to deal with theirs alone.

IT'S JUST AFTER 1:00 a.m. now. We spoke a little at first but time has stretched, and we've been sitting in silence for over an hour. I don't know how long twin C-sections normally take, but I can tell from the growing anxiety on Jake's face that this is just too long. I'm so tense I feel like I'm positively vibrating with anxiety. Marcus has been sitting with his elbows on his thighs, staring at the floor.

"What if she doesn't make it?" he blurts suddenly. "Or what if the twins don't make it?"

He's probably been wondering about this for a long time, but the words can't be held back now. They burst out of him, raw and desperate.

"That isn't going to happen," I say flatly.

I'm not at all an optimistic person by nature, but I know when a person needs words of encouragement. I can't do much for him other than to be here, but I can point him toward the best-case scenario, not the worst.

I'm all too aware that if the worst is going to happen, forcing him to stay positive in these minutes of not knowing about it yet is actually a small mercy. Besides, he needs to conserve his strength, because either way, he's going to need it.

Marcus looks up at me, then goes right back to staring at the floor.

"I don't know how I can love someone I've never met," he whispers. "But I love them. So does Abby. She's my whole world. Why didn't I know how sick she was?"

"She didn't even know how sick she was," Jake points out gently.

"But—"

The door opens quietly, and we all jump in fright. It's a doctor in scrubs, and Marcus flies to his feet.

"They all made it," the doctor says without preamble. I see Marcus slump with relief, but it's a brief reprieve. "I'm not going to mince words with you, sir. Another hour and it would have been a different story. Abigail's liver and kidneys were starting to fail, and both of the twins were in severe distress."

"Where are they?" Marcus blurts.

"Abigail is being taken through to the ICU. She's going to need some support to stabilize her tonight. But I'll take you through to meet your children now—they're in the NICU. One is strong, the other has needed a bit more help, but is stable now." The doctor hesitates. "Did you know their sex?"

"No…"

"Sometimes in these situations, the dad wants to keep the sex a secret until the mom wakes up. So the mom is still one of the first to know."

Marcus turns back to us, tears in his eyes again.

"She thinks girls, I think boys. I don't know if she'll

ever forgive me if you guys know she was wrong before she does." A sudden grin transforms his features,
and his voice breaks as he says, "Jess. I'm a dad." I
throw my arms around him, and as he returns the embrace, he bends to whisper in my ear, "I will never forget that you did this for us."

"Go see your kids," I say, feeling my throat tighten.
The second he releases me, he's already lifting the
phone to his ear and I know he'll be calling his and
Abby's parents, who are in the car together on the way
down from Syracuse.

"Mom? They're here. They're all okay," he croaks,
voice heavy with emotion as he walks out the door
after the doctor. I turn to Jake the minute the door
closes behind them.

He's been my safe place tonight. Even after all of
this time, Jake Winton still feels like home in a way
that terrifies me, but there's no way I can deny that tonight, that magic has saved me. I don't know if I could
have been here for Marcus without Jake's support.

"I'm going to cry again now," I warn him stiffly.
"And this time, it's going to take a while."

Jake opens his strong arms and motions for me to
join him on the other sofa.

"Have at it, then. I'm ready."

I DON'T CRY much after all, maybe because my tears
have run out. Instead, I sit close to Jake, just holding
on to his hand with a vise grip. After a while, I close
my eyes. I'm not sleeping, but I am thinking.

"Do you want to talk about it?" he asks me eventually. It's well past 3:00 a.m. now. The only thing keeping me awake is adrenaline and the three cups of coffee I've had since Marcus joined us in the quiet room. As soon as his and Abby's parents arrive, we'll leave, but I didn't need to ask Jake to know he'll be happy to stay here with me until they do.

"I don't know if I can," I admit.

"You don't have to tell me. But if you want to, I'll listen."

I think about this for a while. I think about how I might explain—what words I might use. The words are so hard to say—that's why I've said them only once in the last seventeen years. How would Jake react?

He already knows, you idiot.

I open my eyes as it occurs to me that after my reactions to Abby's situation tonight, he's probably already made some assumptions. I sit up away from him and survey his face and I know I'm right. He's giving me space to talk about it, but he's already figured it out. Something about this realization makes it easier to say.

"I had a son. I was young, still a teen. He was still-born."

My voice wobbles, but it doesn't break and I don't cry. The last time I told someone about Tristan, I was blind drunk and weeping all over Mitchell. That was seven years ago. I don't leave my apartment on Tristan's birthday now. No one can say I don't learn from my mistakes.

"Was it eclampsia?" Jake asks me.

"No. My blood pressure was perfect and they never figured out what went wrong. They said it was just some freak thing…supposedly nothing I could have done to prevent it. That didn't stop me from torturing myself for years researching causes of neonatal death. I'm a walking encyclopedia of useless information about pregnancy complications that I didn't actually have because my pregnancy was perfect. Uneventful. And then he was gone anyway."

"I'm so sorry, Jessica," he whispers. Jake is the empathy master. He looks so fucking sad for me. If anything was going to make me cry again tonight, it would be the look of sheer pain on his face. I have to look away, because he's mirroring my private inner world so closely, and that's forcing me to face it.

We knew he was dead before I went into labor. They told me a vaginal birth would be better and then they induced me. I didn't want pain relief, but they offered it to me constantly. I wanted to feel everything—I wanted to punish myself for letting him down. Twelve hours of pain and pressure went by and then he was born and there was nothing—just silence, and a silence that felt oh so wrong. Even though I knew he was gone, I was still waiting for the cry once he left my body.

Tristan's perfect little face springs to mind—flawless, other than the fact that he was so bewilderingly still. I remember those ruddy eyelashes and the auburn curls that were stuck to his skull, and the deep-red lips that never had the chance to smile. I remember how it felt to hold him against my chest, his body still warm because he'd just left mine. After a while, he became cold and I was irrationally active, rubbing his skin, wrapping him in more and more blankets, just trying to warm him back up. When the nurses came to take him, I remember thinking I'd never survive the agony of it.

"What was his name?"

"I called him Tristan," I whisper. *Tristan*. The baby I never wanted in the first place, the baby I came to love more than anything in the world, the baby I lost anyway and now the baby I still miss every day.

"Was it hard for you? Watching Abby's pregnancy?" Jake asks me. I shake my head, shaking away the memories and the question.

"No. It was…nerve-racking. Tonight was hard. I couldn't tell if I was panicking because of my…" I clear my throat. "You know. My baggage or whatever. I had no way to know if she was really sick, and I was worried all along I'd see problems with her pregnancy that weren't really there. But I wanted this for her. I've been waiting years for someone to make me an aunt."

"Mitchell knows?"

I turn to frown at him.

"How do *you* know that Mitchell knows?"

"He didn't tell me," Jake assures me. "But he did text me to ask me to keep an eye on you tonight."

"The bastard," I say, but I don't mean it at all.

"Why don't you talk about Tristan, Jess?" Jake asks

me softly as his gaze searches mine. I give him a sad smile.

"Because I don't want people to look at me the way you're looking at me right now."

"And how is that?"

"Like I make sense. Like you understand my trauma, and now you understand why I am the way I am."

"You're seeing what you expect to see," Jake says, raising his eyebrows. "I'm not looking at you that way at all. Do you want to know what I'm thinking?"

"I have a feeling you're going to tell me whether I want to hear it or not," I mutter.

"You were willing to come here tonight to be there for them when it must have been impossibly raw for you." He brings our hands to his lips and kisses my knuckles. It's not a sexual gesture, but one that speaks of a depth of affection I don't know how to process. "I always admired you, even when I thought I hated you. Right now, Jessica Cohen, I'm in absolute awe of you."

I close my eyes and let him bring our entwined hands to his cheek. I let my guard down for just another second or two as I focus on the warmth of his skin against mine.

"Jake?" I whisper, eyes still closed.

"Yes, sweetheart?"

"I couldn't have done this without you. Thank you."

He pulls me close and wraps his arms around me. Just for a minute or two, I think.

I can't have him forever, and I can't ever afford to

get used to leaning on him. I'll just enjoy his comfort for another minute or two, and then I'll make myself be brave again.

CHAPTER FOURTEEN

Jake

THE ROSS AND HERBERT parents descend on the quiet room in an avalanche of tears and gas station flowers just after 4:00 am. A nurse goes to find Marcus, and after he returns to hug each of them, he points to me and Jess and then the door.

"You two. Go home and sleep."

Marcus is composed now, beaming with pride and relief, although visibly exhausted, and no wonder. He tells us that he's seen Abby, and although she's drugged to her gills, she woke up long enough to see a photo of the twins on his phone. He's disappointed that she's a long way from well enough to go to the NICU to see the babies, but he's also proud as punch to have spent some time with them himself.

"And I got a photo of each." He grins.

"Can we know what sex they are now?" Marcus's mother asks as she greedily takes the phone from his hands. A sob bursts from her lips as she sees the photo. "Oh God, Marcus, please tell us. You said you would as soon as Abby knew."

Marcus blinks away sudden tears of joy and then he tells us all, "Girls. Abby was right. I have two magnificent daughters."

There's a cheer all round, and I glance at Jess. She's beaming, genuinely overjoyed for her friends.

She shouldn't be alone tonight. And even as we say goodbye to the assembled family members and promise Marcus we'll both return after some sleep to check in on them, all I can really think about is Jess. About her courage. About her pain. About how alone she's been with her loss, and how vulnerable she is after the intensity of the night we just shared.

We walk in silence to the entrance to the hospital and she slips her phone from her clutch. I know she's about to call a car, and I reach out and touch her hand gently to stop her.

Emotional upheavals in hospital rooms are basically my day job. Even so, I don't want to be alone tonight, but I could do it. I'm used to the emotional toil, but I'm also used to going home alone after a long day or night at the hospital.

I simply cannot stand the thought of her going home and crying alone over all of this.

"Come to my room with me," I say. She looks up slowly and searches my gaze. I see relief in her eyes, and I'm glad I asked the question.

"Just for tonight?" she asks, her voice soft.

"Just for tonight."

CHAPTER FIFTEEN

Jake

IT'S NOT LONG before I'm unlocking the door to my hotel room and Jess and I are stepping inside. I flick on the lights and glance at the alarm clock by the bed. God, it's almost 5:00 a.m. now. I'm in that weird state where I can't wait to lie down, but I'm so wound up I know I won't sleep right away.

There's only one bed in this suite, and the sofa is far too small for me to sleep on. Jess might fit on it, but it would be cruel to suggest it. We've shared a bed without sex before, and tonight we'll just have to do the same. It'll be an innocent comfort to be near one another after the evening we just shared.

That is, I assume it'll be innocent. Until I turn around and Jess has already stripped her dress off and thrown it over the back of the sofa. She's wearing a skimpy balconnette bra and a matching black lace thong, and she's walking toward me like she's about to eat me alive.

"Jess!" I groan. Okay, that's a lie. I want to groan,

but instead, I kind of moan it like a prayer or a plea, and then I cover my eyes with my palm because my eyeballs refuse to stop staring at her. I've relived the nights I spent with Jess in my daydreams over and over the last few years, and it's no comfort that my memories didn't do her justice. She's a strong woman—not just emotionally, but physically. She's toned and muscular, her compact frame honed for power and strength. Jess is beautiful—but that's not her best feature. No, her very best feature is her complete confidence. I'm sure there are flaws there somewhere, hidden among the pale curves and freckle-dotted limbs. Hell, now that I know she had a child, there's probably even a stretch mark or two.

But Jess is at home in her skin in a way that I've never seen in any of my other lovers. It's more than enticing. It's a delicious trait, and one that I came to revere in her. Even now, she's stripped right down to virtually nothing but she's standing proud, hand on her hip, challenge in her gaze.

She knows she's beautiful, she knows what she wants, she knows how to ask for it.

"This wasn't what I wanted when I invited you back here," I tell her gently.

"Oh," I hear her say.

"I just… I thought it would be better if we were at least together. Just to sleep."

I peek out between my fingertips and find she's paused thoughtfully a few feet away. She shrugs and turns toward the bed, then slowly peels back the covers, bending over in a way that's completely unnecessary… But it forces my gaze to focus on her ass, and I know that's exactly why she did it.

Jess slides against the sheets as if it's the most sensual sensation on earth, then she rolls onto her side and props herself up on one elbow. She must know how incredible her breasts look in this pose; Jess never does anything by accident. I'm sure I'm all but drooling as she raises an eyebrow and murmurs throatily, "Are you sure you don't want to…take a trip down memory lane?"

How does she make the words *take a trip down memory lane* seem positively obscene?

"It wouldn't be a good idea." I groan—this time successfully—and all but sprint across the room to my suitcase. I take out a clean T-shirt and throw it over my shoulder, hoping it lands in her general vicinity. I wait until I hear movement, and then turn back to look at her hesitantly.

Jess is standing by the bed now and the T-shirt swims on her, coming to rest around her knees. She's crossed her arms over her chest and she's scowling.

"You're kidding, right?" she says, lifting the hem of the shirt and letting it drop. "I can't wear this to bed. I'll get lost in here."

"Well, you can't wear nothing to bed either," I say. My voice is choked. Jess sighs heavily.

"But we are sharing the bed, then?"

I glance again at the tiny sofa and I'm starting to regret my decision to bring her back here. Then I turn my gaze to Jess and see that although she's pulled a mask over the pain in those bleary eyes, shadows remain. In fact, this moment is somehow the most vulnerable we've shared tonight.

"Let's just go to sleep. No talking, no...anything else. We'll keep our hands to ourselves and if you don't want to talk, you don't have to."

Jess rolls her eyes and walks toward the restroom. As I pull on a pair of boxer shorts, I hear the sounds of her using the toilet, then brushing her teeth. She comes to the door, my toothbrush in her foaming mouth, and I raise an eyebrow at her.

"Sorry," she mumbles, although I doubt she means it, especially because she seems to have come back out here to make *sure* I knew what she was doing. "I figure this is okay. Given...well, you know. I've had much more intimate things of yours in my mouth in the past."

I sigh and nod, then wait my turn to use the restroom. Unlike Jess, I close the door. When I come back out, she's lying on her side on the bed—and it's funny how I still think about beds in terms of my side and hers. But Jess always likes to take the side of the bed farthest from the door, and now she's facing away from me, her legs curled up toward her waist. I flick off the light and climb in beside her.

"Good night," she says.

"Good night, Jess," I murmur.

Ten minutes later, I'm *this* close to sleep when she whispers, "Jake? Are you awake?"

I pry open my eyelids and turn my head toward her.

She's shifted now, so that she's stretched out on her back. In the dim light of the hotel room, I can see that her eyes are wide open and she's staring at the ceiling while she waits to see if I react.

"Yeah." It's half a lie—sleep was so deliciously close. But if she actually wants to talk now, I'm here for that.

"I can't shut my brain off."

I roll toward her, and she swallows, then rolls toward me too. We're staring at one another in the semi-darkness. Jess looks so weary.

"It was an intense night," I say softly.

She ponders this for a moment, then quirks an eyebrow at me.

"You always were more sensitive than me."

"You hide it well," I murmur. "But I know you're more sensitive than you let on. Insensitive people don't give a shit. You give a shit." I expect her to make a smart-ass comment, but instead, she sighs. "Why is Tristan a secret?"

Jess gnaws her lip as she ponders her response, then she admits, "When I first came here, I was an eighteen-year-old mother without a baby. I was a mess, but that mess wasn't me. I didn't want people in my new life to define me by my loss. I learned to compartmentalize. Maybe I got a little too good at that over the years since, but in the beginning, I just couldn't forge the life I wanted if everyone was defining me as the girl who got knocked up and then lost her kid."

"You don't think people would have understood?"

"Quite the opposite. If people know your secrets, they think they understand you. I didn't want people to look at me and assume that I was this woman because of that tragedy."

I'm so tired I can't quite untangle that.

"What does that even mean?"

She sighs impatiently.

"I'm not everyone's cup of tea, Jake. I'm ambitious to my core and I'm loud and I'm blunt and I'm…" She searches for words, then gives me a searching look. "I like dating and sex and men and partying and going out to bars and doing naughty things. But I have always loved those things. I'm not this way because of any flaw or any wound from my past—it's just who I am."

"I know all of that. Knowing about Tristan now doesn't change how I see you."

"Ah, but that's because you've known me forever. Imagine if we'd only just met. Imagine if Paul introduced me as his new business partner all of those years ago, and as soon as I left the room, he told you I'd just given birth to a son who was stillborn."

"First, Paul didn't introduce you as his business partner. He forgot to introduce you at all and you had to introduce yourself. Second, he would never have thought to tell me you'd lost a baby. He'd have let me put my foot in it with some careless comment."

She smiles faintly.

"You just proved my point—your brain has already gone right to the ways you might have hurt me because of my trauma. If you knew I'd lost a child, you'd have been on edge with me. Careful with me, like I was fragile. I mean, think back to when we met. What did you think of me?"

"You were astounding. A force of nature," I murmur. The urge to reach up and tuck that flaming hair behind her ear is almost overwhelming.

I think back across the years to the night I met her. Paul, at the ripe old age of not-quite-nineteen, had just graduated summa cum laude and was the proud owner of a brand-new information science degree. Every academic who encountered Paul over his studies had been convinced that he was destined for a career at the college, including our own father, who's a pure mathematics professor. "He hasn't met an intellectual problem he didn't like, and he hasn't met a person he does like. Of course he'll be an academic," Dad said to me, just a few months earlier.

You can imagine our surprise when, instead of doing an honors year and then signing up for his master's like a sensible genius, Paul asked Dad for a not-insignificant loan and announced his "two best friends" were going into business with him, to develop, of all things, an internet browser. Dad and I had both met Marcus and found him impossible to dislike. Marcus clearly saw potential in Paul and seemed to tolerate my brother's…shall we say…quirks.

But Marcus was also young and impossibly green, and Dad and I were nervous. We hadn't yet met Jess but she seemed to be the driving force behind this project, and she was now in control of a lot of Dad's money. She, Paul and Marcus had set themselves up in a crappy apartment in a very ordinary neighborhood in Brooklyn—the "incubator," Paul was calling it. He'd told us that they'd each put in the same amount of money, but if that was true, why hadn't that kind of combined coin secured the little start-up an office...or at least, an "incubator" apartment somewhere slightly less...homicide-adjacent.

That's why, on a steamy summer night like this one, I arranged to catch up with Paul. He met me at the subway station, and as we walked to his new home, we chatted.

"I can't wait for you to meet Jess. You're going to love her."

My brother was the most literal person I'd ever met. Ordinarily, when Paul said something, I knew I had to take it at face value. That's why I was so confused by his statement.

Did he think I'd love her, because he had a crush on her himself? Or did he think I'd *love* her, because he'd concluded that this Jessica Cohen girl and I were somehow soul mates? Or did he think I'd love her, because for once in his life, he'd managed to use a phrase loosely, instead of literally?

"Why?" I asked him. He thought about this for a moment, then shrugged.

"She's smart in many different ways, just like you are. I'm sure you'll mutually appreciate each other's charms. I've been quite certain that you two would really hit it off ever since she came into business with me."

I wasn't sure how to feel about that. As we approached their apartment, I could hear a woman speaking.

"...oh for fuck's sake, you can do better than that, Himanshu!" The owner of this particularly feminine voice was Southern, and her tone was positively brimming with what some might call "sass," and what other, less charitable folk might call "snark."

Paul slipped his key into the rusty lock of the front door, and the hinges screamed as he pushed it open, to reveal Marcus sitting at one of the many laptops that littered the vinyl dining room table. He was sporting a wiry beard and heavy gray bags under his eyes. He glanced up at us, smiled warmly, then went right back to tapping on the keyboard.

Paul walked right up to the table to stare down at Marcus's screen, pointed at a line near the top, and rattled off a few corrections. I scanned the room for the source of the voice, and that's when I saw Jessica Cohen for the very first time.

She was sitting on a Swiss ball in the darkest corner of a dark room, a cell phone at one ear. It took my eyes a moment to adjust to the dim lighting, but when they did, I drew in a sharp breath.

"I'll call you back," she said, then dropped the cell onto the carpet beside her feet and stood to run her gaze from my feet to my eyes. I actually felt myself blushing from the undisguised hunger in her gaze— suddenly wondering if she was thinking about mounting me right here in front of an audience or sautéing me to literally eat me.

Actually, now that I think about it, the hungry look she gave me tonight was pretty much the same one she gave me the first time we met.

"Well, well, well, Pauly," she whistled, voice low, his name drawn out slowly. "This delicious hunk of man can't possibly be your famous brother."

"It is," Paul said, without glancing up from the monitor.

"Hello there, Jake. I'm Jess, and I'm enchanted to meet you," Jess said as she made a beeline for me. I resisted the urge to cover my eyes with my hand, instead resorting to looking away as I said, "Uh…isn't it a little early to be wearing your…" I glanced back, skimmed my gaze up her body, then swallowed and croaked, "…pajamas?"

If her clothes were indeed pajamas, they were teeny, tiny, skimpy pajamas, the shorts *so* short that I knew I'd see the curve of her ass if she turned around, the tank so small that one halfhearted jump and her breasts might have bounced right out of there.

"It's hot as balls, Jake," she said, laughing as she approached. "The rent is dirt cheap, but apparently that kind of dollar doesn't buy you a working AC or even a functional super. And I bet you didn't even notice that Marcus is shirtless, did you?"

My gaze skipped back to Marcus, who was indeed shirtless, and I belatedly noticed the rivulets of sweat that ran down between his shoulder blades.

"Oh," I said, glancing back to stare over her head so I didn't have to look down at her eyes, which were dangerously close to her breasts. "Sorry."

"I hear you're a doctor."

"Yeah. I've just started an oncology fellowship."

"Are all oncology fellows deeply sexist, or are you just a relic from humbler times?"

I dropped my gaze to hers.

"I'm not sexist," I said, but I was fumbling to regain some sense of control, so I tried to turn on the charm. "Just slightly less attuned to the half-naked male form than I am to beautiful, half-naked females in my immediate vicinity."

A loud laugh burst from her lips.

"Oh, we're going to get on just fine, Dr. Jake. Come in and have a lukewarm beer and some coupon pizza."

It's telling that I remember this moment so vividly after all of this time. Maybe I was in love with her right away, even if it did take me more than a decade to come to grips with it. All I knew was that I suddenly wanted to spend an inordinate amount of time at my baby brother's god-awful apartment-slash-office, and I'd soon been sucked into a friendship group that I came to love.

My career had been my entire world for years, and the change was subtle at first, but soon became undeniable. I'd work a twenty-hour stint at the hospital, then instead of crashing at my apartment nearby, I'd be dragging myself onto the train to go "visit Paul." I told myself that the only reason I spent any time with

Jess at all was that I was worried about my brother. Maybe there was a degree of truth to that—it was several years before Brainway started making money. But even when I didn't trust her, I was also drawn to Jess like a moth to a flame. And maybe it was a while before I realized she really knew what she was doing with that business and, by extension, Dad's money.

It was even longer before I figured out that our near-endless bickering was never going to ease up, but for all of that time and for all of those years, and even while I was learning more about her, I was entranced.

"Well, obviously I was and am amazing," Jess says lightly now, and my attention returns to the present. "So when you met me, I'm sure you were fascinated. But if you knew then what you know now, how would you have viewed me? Would you have assumed I'm driven because I have something to prove? Would you assume that I was dating like it's a competitive sport because I was trying to heal some kind of psychological wound?"

She rolls onto her back again, not waiting for my response. I reach out and take her hand in mine. She winds our fingers together and squeezes.

"Maybe I would have," I admit. "But I do think you underestimate your own confidence. It's hard to question why someone is the way they are when they are so…" I hesitate, and she looks at me "…intimidating."

"I never intimidated you."

I laugh softly.

"Maybe. But you do intimidate pretty much every

other person I've ever seen you meet. People don't wonder why you are the way you are. They wonder how to get on your good side, because they're scared of what you'll do if they don't."

She laughs softly. I bring her hand to my lips and kiss her knuckles gently.

"How soon after he died did you move here?" I ask her.

"He was born on December 7. I caught the bus out of town on Christmas Eve. I started classes at NYU at the midyear…end of January, I think it was. I had missed the first semester of my freshman year so I did a double course load in the second. I wanted to catch up."

"And no one here knew what you were going through?"

"My grandmother did. Remember Grandma Chloe?"

"Of course."

"I still miss her. I really only came here because of her." She flashes me a look. "I wasn't alone, Jake. Don't you dare feel sorry for me."

"Well, am I allowed to feel empathy?"

She pauses, then nods.

"Okay. I'll allow it."

"It's your story, Jess," I tell her softly. "You get to share it if and when you want to share it. I'm just trying to understand. I feel like you and I have this long, checkered history—but until these last few years, I never doubted we were important to each other. Even long before we were together, even when we were just sometimes-friends-sometimes-verbal-sparring-partners. I just… I guess I wish you'd been able to tell me, but only so I could be there for you."

"You were there for me tonight," she says. Her eyelids are finally growing heavy, and her voice is getting softer. I rest her hand against the duvet, then rest mine on top of it, reluctant to let go of her. "I wish…"

She trails off as her eyelids flutter closed, and I'm hanging on the end of that sentence, waiting for her to speak again. Just when I think she's fallen asleep, she shuffles a tiny bit closer to me and, eyes closed, whispers, "I regret what happened, Jake. I really wish we'd found a way to have more time together."

There's a painful contraction in my chest, and in a heartbeat, I relive the last few years. I've told myself that I loathe Jessica Cohen—that she treated me so badly, and that I could never forgive her. In this moment, I know that's all untrue.

"Me too," I whisper back, and she rolls away from me, but I know it's an invitation to spoon her. I pull her into my arms, breathe in the scent of her hair and finally let sleep pull me under.

CHAPTER SIXTEEN

Jess

THERE'S A DISTANT buzzing that sounds on and off—a phone vibrating, I think, although I'm not sure if it's Jake's or mine. I rise from the sound, and find I'm completely enveloped in man-mountain.

I've never been a fan of sleepovers, even less so with snugglers. And Jake is definitely a snuggler, even in his sleep, so in theory this should be my worst nightmare.

Everything is different with Jake—even, apparently, sleep snuggles. I'm lying on his chest and his arms are locked around me, even though, when I glance up at him, I see that he's still deeply asleep. Some stubble has grown in overnight, and the skin around his eyes is puffy. I know, when he wakes up, his eyes will be rimmed with red from the late night and the lack of sleep. I've seen him like this before. When we were together, he'd get a call at some ungodly hour and he'd rush to the hospital to be with a patient who was dying.

If I loved Jake, I loved him because he'd always go. If I loved Jake, I loved him because when I saw him the next day, exhausted and sometimes more than a little sad, the one emotion I'd never see in him was resentment. He told me once he didn't have to go for those moments. There were palliative care teams who supported families and, for most of his patients, a whole health care mechanism that kicked into place in the final hours.

He didn't go because he had to. He went because he wanted to. Cancer care is personal to him, and he makes no secret of that. Besides, Jake Winton is that kind of guy and he's that kind of doctor. Maybe that's why I don't regret talking to him about Tristan last night. I told him because I needed him, and I knew I could count on him to carry me through the memories. Even now, the scent of antiseptic clings to our skin in a way I probably couldn't have coped with before yesterday.

I inhale tentatively, reflecting on that scent, this time focusing on something else in the air. Yes, I can smell the hospital, but I can also smell Jake and there's no better scent in the world. Even on a cellular level, I'm drawn to him in a way I've never been drawn to another man. I lie still, counting the minutes. I want to store this memory with all of those other memories I hold so dearly, despite the distance between us now.

Jake shifts suddenly, bringing me with him as he rolls to view the alarm clock. He sighs, and his arms contract around me.

"I slept through breakfast with Mitch," he says, voice rough with sleep.

"Someone's phone has been ringing," I tell him. "Probably Mitch looking for you."

"Or Marcus or Paul," Jake says, and then we both sit up with a start. Everything feels uncomfortable— bleary eyes, the crick in my neck and even the ridiculously large shirt I'm wearing. I reach for my phone. The battery is on 4 percent.

11:00 p.m. Mitch: How are you doing?

12:15 a.m. Mitch: I hope you're okay.

2:00 a.m. Mitch: If you need to talk, come round anytime and wake me up.

10:00 a.m. Mitch: Jake hasn't showed up for breakfast with me and you aren't answering my texts and I'm trying to be gentle with you today because I'm sure last night was really rough, but if you break that man's heart again, I will write you into a book and kill you off.

12:15 p.m. Mitch: Jess, it's noon now and I'm seriously worried about you. Call me.

12:30 p.m. Marcus: Are you coming to visit us today? Abby has just graduated from the ICU to maternity. There are two beautiful girls waiting to meet you.

1:00 p.m. Abby: Jess! Please come see us ASAP. We

have a surprise! Well, two surprises. And we'd all love to see you.

"It's almost 2:00 p.m.," I say, eyes wide as I turn back to Jake.

"Well, we didn't really go to sleep until five, so that's about right," Jake mutters. He scoops his phone off the dresser.

"What time were you supposed to check out?" I ask him.

"I paid for a late checkout. My flight isn't until tonight."

He holds the phone close and then at length and then close again as he tries to read something. I burst out laughing, and he laughs in spite of himself and reaches for his glasses, which are folded up beside the bed.

"Marcus asked me to come in and meet the twins," he murmurs.

"Me too," I say as I draft a text to Mitch.

Jess: You're a good friend, Mitch. I'm fine. So is Jake. He was just being a good friend too, and nothing happened. I'll call you later.

"Should we go together?" Jake asks. There's no undertone to the question, but I glance at him anyway, trying to assess.

"I won't freak out," I say lightly. "I've seen newborns before. It's all good."

He frowns at me.

"That wasn't what I meant, and you know it. I just meant because we're here together, going to the same place."

"I need to go home and change," I say, motioning down toward the ridiculous shirt. "God. I don't even have a pair of shoes."

"Okay. Go home and change. I'll swing by and pick you up on the way to the hospital," he says, with a shrug.

It's on the tip of my tongue to argue with him, because I don't need an escort and I'm independent enough that I really don't want him to think he's rescuing me. The problem, of course, is that I kind of want an escort. It's not that I'm afraid of seeing Abby's babies—I actually can't wait for that and I'm sure I'm going to be fine.

I just want to prolong this time with Jake. And if I argue with him just because that's what I always do, then I might miss out.

"Okay," I sigh. I scoop my dress up and head toward the bathroom. "I'm starved too. I'll get some breakfast delivered to my place and we can eat it before we go."

CHAPTER SEVENTEEN

Jess

AN HOUR LATER, we're together again in the back of an
Uber, on our way back to the hospital. We travel in near
silence. I hate that I feel so close to him right now—
not just physically, emotionally. I hate that I'm going
to have to say goodbye to him all over again soon.

"When do you fly out?" I ask.

"9:15 p.m.," he says, looking out the window.

"Do you miss it?"

"New York?" He turns back to me, and when I
nod, he shrugs. "Sometimes. I don't miss the pace…
the endless noise and activity. I do miss the friends I
have here."

"Did you move because of me?"

I didn't mean to ask the question. As soon as I do, I
panic a little. Somehow, in the intensity of last night,
we fell into an unspoken truce and, apparently, we
both assumed we wouldn't address us any further. Jake
turns back to the window, and for a minute I think he's

going to ignore my question. Well, I'm not about to
take it back, so if he wants to leave things hanging—

"It was a great job offer," he says, staring out at
the street. "Working at the Stanford clinic means my
patients get access to some of the most exciting drug
trials available. It's good work, and it will help a lot
of people." I'm satisfied by this and more than a little relieved. Right up until he turns to face me and he
shrugs. "All of those years we danced around one another, and then the time we were together have changed
the way I see this city. New York will always mean Jess
Cohen to me. I moved because I knew that whenever
I was in this city, I'd want to be with you."

I inhale sharply. He's staring right at me, his gaze
sad but accepting. I swallow hard, then nod, and he
finally looks away.

It's a relief when we arrive at the hospital—and *that*
is a thought I never expected to think. We walk side by
side toward the gift shop, closer than friends would,
but not actually touching. I'm already thinking back
to those moments when I woke up and I could touch
him. I'm missing the privilege.

Jake buys Abby flowers. I buy two enormous green
teddy bears, prompting him to raise his eyebrows.

"Not pink?"

"These kids are going to have to get used to two
things," I say pertly, then I hold up a finger. "One,
Aunt Jess spoiling them. Two, Aunt Jess helping them
smash all stereotypes of what little girls *should* do,
think and like."

He laughs softly and helps me carry the second teddy bear. Now the man-mountain is walking along the corridor carrying an oversize teddy bear that, in his arms, looks like a regular teddy bear, along with a giant bunch of flowers. It's possibly the cutest thing I've ever seen, although that photo of Jake with his tiny, fugly dog is definitely a close second.

At the entrance to the maternity ward, Marcus greets us with tight hugs and bleary-eyed excitement. He's still wearing his suit pants and the button-down from last night, and his cheeks and chin are covered with dark stubble.

"Did you get any sleep?" I ask him gently. He grimaces, shakes his head, then tells me, "I got to hold one this morning, but the other is still not quite strong enough. It might be a few days for her."

"'One' and 'the other'? Please tell me that isn't their names, Marcus," I laugh softly. He grins at me.

"You'll have to see for yourself."

Abby is lying in bed, pale and still connected to all manner of machinery. When she sees me, she bursts into tears and opens her arms. I rush at her and give her the hug she obviously needs.

"Jess," she weeps into my hair. "If you hadn't—"

"Don't," I say fiercely. *God, Abby. Please don't say it.* "You don't need to go there. You're fine, and they're fine, and that's all that matters."

She nods, then pulls away gingerly to stare right into my eyes.

"We will never forget that you did this for us."

"All I did was suggest you get help, Abby," I say, more than a little uncomfortable now.

"And when I tried to be stubborn, you made sure I got checked out. Which is the only reason we're all going to be okay," Abby says, tears rolling down her cheeks. "You saved our lives. All of us."

"I'll take you guys down to the NICU so you can see them in a minute," Marcus murmurs as he walks to the other side of Abby's bed. "But we need you to understand how grateful we are. To both of you."

"I'm just so glad you're all okay," Jake murmurs.

"Have you seen them?" I ask Abby gently. She nods tearfully.

"The nurses took me down earlier—just for a few minutes. And, Jess, there's nothing like it—I got to hold one, and she nuzzled into me. Like she knows me already! She's so tiny and soft and warm, and I—"

He was warm at first when they placed him in my arms. But he was so still, and all I could think was, could I have saved him if I'd been stronger? Braver? Better?

I open my mouth to speak, intending to say something encouraging or congratulatory, but I'm shocked to find I just can't. All I can think about is that moment back in the hospital room in Georgia—the harsh glare of the lights, the scent of the antiseptic, and how utterly, utterly alone I was with that baby in my arms and a lifetime of grief and regret stretching out ahead of me.

The memory is fierce and overwhelming in a way

I don't anticipate. I think of Tristan every single day, but after so much time, I'm actually accustomed to the sharpness of the emotions. There's a gap in my life that he would have filled—I'd have a seventeen-year-old son now. But my entire life would have been different if he'd survived, and maybe that's why it's generally impossible for me to imagine the way things would be if he was here now.

Today though, right in this moment, the loss splits me in two and for the first time, I suddenly can imagine what it would be like if Tristan had survived and somehow made it here to New York with me. He'd live in one of my spare rooms. The apartment would sound different. He'd probably love awful music because all seventeen-year-old boys love awful music. And it would smell different, because I'm pretty sure all seventeen-year-old boys have awful BO and a serious Axe body spray addiction. He might be just coming out of those awkward teenage years, where our stubborn, hotheaded personalities would have clashed. He might have a girlfriend or a boyfriend. I couldn't work as much as I do and my social life would be completely different. Someone would know me as "Mom," just as two little someones will soon know Abby as "Mom."

I don't resent Abby's joy—I do genuinely celebrate it. Even so, I'm suddenly not sure I can keep my composure. I turn and look at Jake, and in a microsecond, he reads my expression and he takes control.

"When are we going to hear these names?" he says, stepping forward until he's right behind me. Abby and

Marcus can't see, but his hand rests gently on my lower back. I focus on the warmth and gentle pressure of his hand, and the overwhelming tide of emotion passes as Marcus and Abby laugh and tease us about "finding out soon enough." I love Abby and Marcus like they're my siblings—but their excited giggles are making me nervous. While she was pregnant, Abby was calling the twins "Luke" and "Leia," and I swear to God if they've gone with some *Star Wars* theme for these kids, Aunt Jess is going to have a very difficult conversation with their parents.

Jake leads the conversation through safe territory: Abby's lab results—"already improving but I'm going to be in here awhile"; Abby's pain level—"I'm drugged to the gills, don't worry"; Marcus's sleep or lack thereof—"I'll catch up tonight"; and then their parents, who are apparently safely ensconced in a hotel room nearby, catching up on their own sleep so they can come back later.

Soon, Abby is starting to look tired again, so Marcus kisses her forehead gently and suggests the three of us take a trip down to the NICU. Finally, I unfreeze. I kiss Abby's cheek, and promise to return tomorrow.

"It's a workday. You don't have to come."

"Bullshit. I'll see you at lunchtime. Do you need anything?"

She catches my hands in hers and squeezes. Hard.

"Thank you," she croaks, one last time.

My eyes well, and I blink the tears away with some determination.

"Sleep well," I tell her, and then I follow Jake and Marcus into the hallway. Marcus is apparently riding another caffeine wave and he chats animatedly as we approach the nursery. Jake is watching me as we walk.

"I'm okay," I whisper under my breath.

"You weren't a minute ago."

"I'm fine now."

Marcus pauses, surveys us and goes right back to chatting. We're soon at the entrance to the NICU, so he leads us through the process of washing our hands and donning a gown and mask before he pushes open the second door.

And then suddenly I am in a world of tiny, sick babies. I knew where we were headed. I even had a picture in my mind of what it would be like. Confronted with the reality of it though, I'm faltering again…until a big, strong hand slides against mine.

I look at Jake, then at Marcus, and I'm panicking because I don't want Marcus to know anything is wrong and I definitely don't want him to know that Jake and I have ever been more than friends. But I need this support, and that hand is *all* that grounds me right now. Panic threatens again, and as much as I hate my weakness, it turns out I *do* need help to hold the feelings back.

Jake nods toward Marcus, and when I look to my business partner, I realize he's making a beeline for his daughters as if they are all he can see in the world. Jake and I could probably strip naked right now and he wouldn't even notice. I relax somewhat from the realization, and then follow Jake to the crib where Marcus and Abby's daughters are sleeping.

They are so small. Both girls are wearing just diapers, revealing their little bellies and the black stubs of their umbilical cords caught up in yellow pegs, and expanses of red-purple, wrinkled skin. They both have adorable button noses like Abby, and they're both pretty much bald. One of the twins has a tube in her nose, but otherwise looks pretty robust there in the tiny crib. The other is obviously weaker—she has a mask fixed over her lower face, an IV strapped into her and cords everywhere around her.

"They're in a cot together," I whisper. Marcus looks up at me, tears in his eyes even as he smiles.

"Well, they've been roommates for a while. I guess it makes sense for them to have each other's company."

"They're so completely beautiful, Marcus," I say. Marcus probably assumes the emotion in my voice is caused just by being overwhelmed by his gorgeous children. He's staring down at his daughters too, his gaze shining with pride and relief.

"Jess and Jake, let me introduce you to my daughters." He points to the stronger of the twins, and announces, "This one is Clementine Jade." He winks at Jake. "The Jade is for you. We couldn't figure out how to make 'Jake' work, so we had to go with something close."

"What? No way!" Jake is visibly delighted. "I've never had a kid named after me before. That's so great.

You guys didn't have to do that. I didn't really do anything."

"You got her here. Then jumped the line for us. We're so grateful. And, Jess, please meet Jessamine Rose. We assume you're going to do a lot of babysitting, so we thought we'd call her Jessie for short. That way it won't be confusing."

I open my mouth, but I don't know why, because I have no clue what to say. A noisy, confusing sob bursts from me as I stare down at that tiny baby in the crib.

"Hey," Marcus says, coming around to hug me. Jake quietly, carefully releases my hand. "She's a fighter already, our little Jessamine. Tough and determined—not even a day old and she's already exceeding everyone's expectations. Even if you hadn't saved her life—which you did—she actually reminds us of you. The name is totally perfect."

"And their prognosis is good?" Jake asks quietly. I have a feeling he's trying to distract Marcus so I have time to compose myself. It's not going to work. I simply have to get out of here.

"They'll both need care for a while," Marcus murmurs. "Jessie especially might need a bit more support. But their outlook is great. And Abby…well, you saw. They're monitoring her liver and kidney function closely, and it might take her a while to get her strength back, but the doctor sounds positive."

"They're beautiful," I tell Marcus, then I raise a hand to my chest. "And I'm honored. Truly. Thank you. I'm just so glad everyone is okay." I draw in a breath, then smile as brightly as I can. "Now you, my friend, look exhausted. So we'll leave you be so you can get some rest."

Marcus's eyebrows knit, but he doesn't say anything. Maybe he knows I'm cutting this short. Or maybe he's deliriously tired, too overwhelmed and sleep deprived to even notice anything is wrong. In any case, we say goodbye to him at the entrance to the NICU, and Jake and I are once again walking in silence along the corridor.

As we reach the entrance to the hospital, a wave of pure impatience and irritability comes over me. I'm just done. I need to go home, cry a little and get some more sleep.

Most of all, I need to be alone.

"Mitch and I are catching up for an early dinner now before I fly out," Jake says suddenly. "Why don't you join us?"

"Since when are you two so close?" I ask him, snippy even though I don't want to be.

"Well, I've known him almost as long as you have," Jake says. That's true—Mitch and Jake met at my place a few months after Mitch and I met. But they were friends in the same way that Abby or Paul are friends with Mitch—friendly enough to say hi in the street, not friendly enough to call one another up and organize brunch. I like to keep a little distance between Mitch and my other friends. Maybe I am too good at compartmentalizing my life these days, but at least there's a good reason for it when it comes to Mitch.

He's safe from any drama that might arise at work or within my work-friendship group. Mitch is my backup plan for any and all emotional turmoil.

"You always knew him a bit, but you didn't *know* him," I snap. Jake is still watching me closely.

"You might not have noticed this, but you and Mitch are all but joined at the hip, so when you and I were spending every spare minute together, that meant Mitch and I spent a lot of time together too," he says, apparently unperturbed by my bitchiness. "He's a great guy. We're pals now."

"I just…" I don't even know how I'm going to finish that sentence, but the tone of it is altogether too sharp. I stop, draw in a breath and try again. "Thanks for the offer, but I already have plans." Plans of a hot bath and a bottle of wine and donning my PMS pajamas as soon as I step through the door.

"Do you really want to be alone tonight?" Jake asks me gently, and I try so hard not to snap his head off, but once again fail miserably.

"Yes," I say flatly. "That's exactly what I want."

Jake sighs and shrugs.

"Okay." He bends and plants a gentle kiss on my cheek, and I pause while he's close, suddenly battling tears again. I catch his hand as he moves to rise, and squeeze it, hard. He pauses, close enough that when I breathe in, his scent fills my lungs one last time.

"Thank you," I whisper, closing my eyes briefly. "Thanks for being there for me."

"Take care of yourself, Jess," he says somberly as

he rises. I pin my most brilliant smile onto my face as I nod and step away.

"I always do."

CHAPTER EIGHTEEN

Jake

"Yikes. I hope the airline doesn't charge you excess luggage fees for those bags under your eyes," Mitch greets me as I take my seat opposite him at the trendy Upper East Side bar he picked for this meetup. There's a beer waiting for me on the table, and I nod toward him as we knock our glasses together. It's early on Sunday evening and this place is freakishly quiet.

"I got close to seven hours of sleep in the end. It was just the wrong seven hours and yeah, I'm feeling it now."

It'll be the middle of the night before I get back to my house in Old Palo Alto, but I can sleep in tomorrow. I don't have anywhere to be. I have a permit for some parts of the trail so there are only specific dates when I can walk those segments, but luckily, I left a buffer so I could organize my gear. As long as I'm on the road by Wednesday, I'll be fine.

"And is she okay?" Mitch asks me quietly.

He isn't talking about Abby, and there's no need

for him to identify the "she" in question. It's the same woman he was worried about last night. The same woman who slept in my arms. The same woman who is so stubborn she still drives me crazy just about every time I speak to her.

"She had her moments, but in the end, she was amazing." I clear my throat, then look at him, signaling that I *know*. "Considering everything."

"Did she talk to you?"

"Yeah. Some."

"Stubborn mule, that woman," Mitch mutters. I tilt my beer toward him.

"That is the understatement of the century." I glance at him curiously. "When did she tell you?"

"I'm not even sure. Six or seven years ago?" he sighs, scratching his cheek. "Maybe longer. My agent's Christmas party, I think. I was drunk and babbling about my college girlfriend. Jess was drunk and babbling about some dude she was with back in Georgia—just...babbling shit about what an asshole he was, I guess. I don't think she meant to tell me about the baby, to be honest. I think it all just spilled out." He sighs heavily. "Turns out the party was on her son's birth date. I don't even know why she agreed to come with me. I guess she didn't want to let me down."

"That sounds like Jess," I murmur, thinking of last night, and her stubborn determination to be there for Abby, at significant cost to herself. I hadn't even wondered about her baby's father. If Jess was eighteen when she had her son, it was probably her high school boyfriend. I take another sip of the beer, pondering this.

"Has…" I hesitate, then glance at him. "Has she been okay otherwise? Since we broke up?"

"Jake Winton, I've told you before. You won't breach the impenetrable no-man's-land that is my relationship with you and Jess, so stop asking."

I laugh softly. Poor Mitch has had a starring role in the drama of Jake and Jess over the years. He was one of the only people in the world who even knew we'd fallen in love in the first place. And I have asked him that very same question more than once over the last two and a half years. He always deflects it the same way, but now, he sighs and says, "She's been kicking ass at work with your brother. She's dated a bit, but not nearly as much as she wants people to believe. Says she has a reputation to uphold but I'm not really sure what that means. How about you?"

"I just don't understand her," I mutter, then I exhale. "I never have."

"I mean, how have you been? Because I didn't actually invite you to dinner so we could cry into our beer and talk about Jess all night," Mitch says, eyes twinkling with mirth.

I laugh and scoop up the menu. I'm suddenly ravenous, so hungry I want to order everything on the menu and devour all of it.

"Sorry, I've been good. Surfing, hiking, a bit of mountain biking. Work is good."

"Jess said you're living with someone?" Mitch says, eyebrows high.

"I am living with someone." I shrug, then I grin. "Her name is Clara."

Mitch bursts out laughing.

"She thought Clara was a human female?"

"I may have accidentally deliberately given her that impression at Paul's rehearsal dinner."

"You two are as bad as each other," Mitch laughs softly. "Are you dating?"

"Not since Vanessa," I say, then I try to change the subject. "By the way, I figured out your pen name."

Mitch quirks an eyebrow.

"Did you, now?"

"You're George R. R. Martin, aren't you? You don full movie-style costume for public appearances."

He throws back his head and laughs.

"Dude, not even close."

"Right genre, though?"

"I'm not answering that."

"Are you ever going to tell me?"

"I'll tell you after I tell my mother."

"But Jess knows."

"Of course Jess knows. She manipulated it out of me because she's an evil mastermind, which you, Jake Winton, are not."

By 5:30 P.M., I'M in a car on my way to JFK, trying not to think about the miles that will soon stretch between me and Jess.

I have to pick up a new sleeping bag before I leave tomorrow.

I wonder what she's doing now. Fuck, I hope she's okay.

I'll make a list of supplies on my phone on the flight.

Did she really say she regretted what happened between us?

I can't wait to wind down once I get out there.

She did say she regretted that we didn't have more time. She said she missed me.

Did I remember to organize Reba to stay with Clara for the whole time?

I regret it too, Jess. More than anything. There's nothing I wouldn't do for another chance.

Traffic is a bitch even on a Sunday night, and Jared, the driver of this Uber, is apologizing profusely as we crawl toward JFK, as though he's personally responsible for the dismal state of New York City traffic. I dismiss his apologies a few times, but then he mentions he's driving the car to put himself through community college because he wants to be a teacher. The next thing I know we're in a full-on conversation, and he's almost distracted me from the fact that it feels *completely fucking wrong* to be leaving Jess behind and flying home.

Jared pulls the car into the drop-off lane and as I put my hand on the door handle, I have a stunning, startling moment of clarity.

She misses us. I miss us. She wishes we'd found a

way to keep seeing one another. Maybe that means
we still can.

"Jared," I say as he reaches to pop the trunk so I
can get my suitcase out. "Change of plans. I need to
go back to Manhattan."

"Don't you have a flight?"

"I just realized that I have unfinished business
here."

I slide my phone from my pocket. Five minutes later
I've spoken with Reba the dog behavioralist, booked
a hotel for two weeks and let my dad know I've decided to stay.

I load Jess's contact onto the screen of my phone,
and my finger hovers over the call button. I'm impatient to talk to her and to tell her I'll be in town a little
longer, but I'm exhausted, and I can only assume Jess
is feeling even worse.

This conversation needs to take place in person,
tomorrow when we're both rested. I slide the phone
back into my pocket, and despite my exhaustion, I'm
suddenly feeling a renewed sense of hope.

CHAPTER NINETEEN

Jess

I HATE MONDAY mornings as a general rule but this one feels particularly brutal. Maybe it's because I'm now staring down the barrel of two weeks with Paul out on his honeymoon, and at least eight weeks with Marcus working at a reduced capacity. We'd planned that he'd take a week off after the birth and then basically do his best until he was ready to come back full time, but no one expected that his welcome to fatherhood would be quite so dramatic.

It's not like the company isn't ready for all of this upheaval. Paul's promoted Audrey so she's going to run his department while he's out, Marcus has prepared his team to pretty much run itself, and Kiah, my operation's manager, is ready to step up and take on even more responsibility if I have to leap over and get stuck in the weeds of what's happening with their teams.

But in the midst of all of this, I still have to figure out what the fuck to do about our Silicon Valley office. It's a smaller team, and our corporate strategy calls for it to scale the fuck up. I've been reluctant to do that for far too long because the staffing and the culture just aren't right and I'm nervous that expanding things there will only make the problem worse.

I've been working with some top-tier consultants over the last six months, trying to get our company ready to list it on the stock exchange. That engagement ended a few weeks ago with a very disappointing presentation from their consulting team.

You have 8 percent of the market share in corporate America, but less than 1 percent of tech companies in North America are using your software. That's a problem, because when a financial adviser wants to know how hot a tech stock is, she's going to call her tech clients, and when she asks about Brainway Technologies, the chances are her clients aren't going to know who you are, let alone add to the buzz you need to get an optimum initial share price. If you try to go public before you fix that problem, you'll be throwing millions of dollars down the drain.

I threw their very expensive report into the bottom drawer of my desk because I had the takeaway committed to memory: *we're close, but Jess needs to woman up and get her ass to Palo Alto to fix the West Coast office and do some networking because until she does, the whole company is stuck treading water.*

We need the initial public offering to raise funds to expand into the Euro market, which is the logical next step for us. And networking is definitely my superpower, so this problem should be easy to solve.

If Jake had moved to Chicago or to Denver or to the moon, I'd already be in Palo Alto. His new address is the sole reason I've spent the bare minimum time there in the last two years, and the sole reason I haven't been working at least part-time from that office since the consultant's engagement began. I've always put the company above my own needs but this time, I just couldn't convince myself to do what needed to be done.

I don't think Marcus and Paul even realize how badly I'm letting them down, but I do. The knowledge of it sits in my gut like a stone every fucking day.

"Now you look like a woman who needs some caffeine," an all-too-familiar voice announces as soon as I step out from my apartment building's lobby onto the street. I startle and turn to find Jake standing right there on the sidewalk, with a large take-out coffee cup in each hand. He's wearing the T-shirt I wore on Saturday night with a pair of jeans. In the cool morning light, the silver in his hair is a little more obvious.

"What on earth are you doing here?" I ask him blankly.

He offers me a coffee, and I take it greedily, even as I'm staring at him in disbelief. Jake shrugs.

"I canceled my hike. Decided to stick around so I can spend some time with Dad and Elspeth."

"So…if you're in the city to see your dad and his girlfriend, why are you standing in front of my building like a creeper at 7:45 a.m. on a Monday morning?" I ask him. He grins, the smile transforming his features in a way that makes my heart dance. God, that blunt jaw and chin still get to me, even after all of this time.

"You're unpredictable in every way except one— you always leave your apartment at exactly this time."

"I do," I concede. "But that doesn't explain why you're here."

"I miss you," he says simply.

Shit, Jake. Don't make me put us both through this again.

"We both know it's for the best," I say, raising my chin.

"Dad's getting older, and I see him for maybe a week a year at the moment. What happened with Abby and Marcus really reminded me that life is just too short, you know?"

I drag my gaze back to him and nod, my throat tight.

"I get that."

"Well, before we were...whatever we were...we were friends."

"Frenemies," I correct him, and he laughs softly.

"Yep, that too."

"And are you a creeper to all of your frenemies?" I ask him, motioning toward the pavement with my spare hand. It's only two blocks to my office, which is exactly why I bought this particular condo. But I like to be at my desk by 8:00 a.m., so I need to get going. Jake gets it—he falls into step beside me, walking in slow motion with those incredibly long legs, which is just about normal pace for me.

"It might surprise you to hear this, but you're my only frenemy," Jake tells me.

"I feel so special."

"Let's hang out while I'm in town," he says, and I knew this was coming the minute I saw him standing there, but even so, my heart does a triple somersault, then sinks to my toes.

"Are you doing this because you think I'm emotionally fragile and need to be babysat?"

Jake nearly chokes on his coffee. He gives me an incredulous look.

"Jess. No one—ever in the history of the world—has ever thought *you* were emotionally fragile."

"Well, now," I scold him lightly, "you know that's not exactly true. You were there on Saturday night."

"I saw vulnerability. I didn't see an ounce of fragility," he murmurs, voice low.

"Please, Jake." I roll my eyes at him. "I'll forgive you for being a stalker because you brought me coffee, but you can cut the bullshit."

He grins, and we walk in silence for a moment while I try to wrap my head around this latest, shocking development in the apparently never-ending saga of Jake and Jess.

"What exactly are you proposing here?"

"I enjoy your company."

"And I enjoy yours, but—"

"Let's just spend a couple of weeks together," he interrupts me. "I'm here. You're here." He drops his voice. "We both regret the way things ended. So let's just enjoy a few more days together. It's doesn't have to be any more complicated than that."

I stop walking and turn to him, frowning.

"Are you sure you want to do this? To randomly spend two more weeks with me?"

It's what *I* want. Two more weeks with Jake? *Yes please*. But I hurt him once before, and I'll be fucked if I'm going to do that again. If he really wants to do this, he has to be sure he's okay with a hard full stop on the end of this new dalliance.

He shrugs nonchalantly.

"I'm here anyway. Paul's away on his honeymoon and Dad goes to bed at 8:00 p.m. Someone has to entertain me."

"So what, you're just going to turn up at my building every morning with a coffee delivery, then walk me to work?" I ask skeptically. Then I pause. "Actually, you know what? That does sound pretty good."

Jake laughs. God, I love that sound—deep and mellow, carefree and strong.

"I was thinking we could hang out a bit when you're not at work, and just…you know. Play it by ear." Well, that's a euphemism if I ever heard one. I am surprised that Jake would suggest a temporary reunion like this, but I'm not at all unhappy about it. I feel something light inside—like he's just suggested we take a vacation together.

Which he kind of has. The next few weeks will be

stressful at work, but I know just the way to relieve some of that pressure and there's never been anyone who can push my buttons in bed the way Jake can. I shiver a little in anticipation, then flash him a grin.

"Well, aren't you full of surprises?"

"I'll pick you up at eight for dinner?"

We pause at the entrance to my office building. I glance around, just to be sure none of my staff happens to be passing by, and then I reach up on my tippy-toes and kiss his cheek.

"See you tonight, then," I say, smiling to myself.

The day has taken an unexpectedly fantastic turn. After all, he's just offered pretty much everything I ever wanted: Jake Winton, with no strings attached.

When I get to my floor, I find my assistant, Gina, is already at her desk. She smiles at me.

"I heard the news. Big weekend for the company directors."

"You have no idea," I mutter, but I have a mental to-do list, and I need to get started if I'm going to be done by eight. "Gina, I need you to do something for me—drop everything else on your schedule, and do whatever you have to do to get me on the phone with Cindy Lang."

I'm a woman who keeps her promises, and no one messes with my friends. By 10:00 a.m., I've had a very enlightening conversation with the CEO of Abby's hospital, and Doogie Howser the Second is about to have a very bad day.

I TAKE A lunch break—not part of my regular day, given Gina usually brings a salad to my desk at 1:00 p.m., but today, I promised I'd visit Abby.

"Hey there," I greet her as I stick my head into her room. Marcus is asleep on a sofa in the corner, and Abby is sitting up in bed, looking down at her phone. When she sees me, a big grin transforms her face.

"Well, well, well. If it isn't the lady of the hour."

"Uh, pretty sure you're the lady of the hour," I say wryly as I take the seat beside her bed.

"I had a visit earlier from the manager of the emergency department, who came to apologize and let me know that that idiot resident is being disciplined for what happened when we first came in," Abby says quietly. "But I'm sure you don't know anything about that."

I shrug.

"It had to be done and you guys have enough to juggle without fighting bigotry too."

"Thank you. We haven't even had time to think about making a complaint. I really appreciate it."

"Anytime. You know that bitching at people is my specialty. I'm glad I could put my skills to good use."

"Also, random question," Abby says suddenly. I look at her, and she gives me a confused smile. "You and Jake. I asked you in the car on Saturday morning and you said nothing was going on."

"Nothing is going on."

"You're sure there's nothing you want to tell me?"

"Why do you ask?"

"Let's call it a mother's instinct," Abby tells me sagely, and I roll my eyes at her. "I was pretty out of it yesterday, but I distinctly remember a vibe between you two. Also, Jake just came to visit us and let slip he's skipping his hike to stay in town for two weeks. Oh, and Marcus told me he saw you two holding hands down in the NICU."

I scowl at my sleeping business partner. It's hard to be mad at him when he looks so exhausted and vulnerable, but I manage.

"Your fiancé is a dreadful gossip."

"You don't have to tell me if you don't want to," Abby says, shrugging, then wincing as she tenderly rubs her stomach.

"Are you trying to make me feel sorry for you?" I ask her skeptically. She grins.

"Well, I did nearly die on Saturday so…"

"Too soon, Abby. Way too soon. And nothing is going on. Jake and I do have a weird vibe. I'm not surprised you're confused."

"And the hand holding?" She's looking at me suspiciously, but my emotions are nicely under wraps today—even so, I'm not really sure what I'd do if she expressed disapproval at the idea that Jake and I might be together. I can hardly blame her for that comment on Saturday—she had so much going on, and she must have been feeling like crap.

But I adore Abby and knowing that she does think Jake is too good for me stings. Best to cut her off at the pass before she rubs salt into that wound.

"It was a strange weekend, babe. He was a godsend, to be honest, but that's all there is to it." I layer my tone with finality, hoping she gets the hint. She does not.

"If…if you and Jake were ever to…" she starts to say, so I raise my chin and try a blunter approach.

"Abby, *stop*. Jake and I are not happening. Now, tell me everything. How are our little Jessie and Clem?"

Abby releases my hand and, in a heartbeat, she's reached for her phone again.

"Brace yourself. I have ten thousand photos, and as aunt, you have a moral obligation to look at every single one and oooh and ahhh at the appropriate times."

CHAPTER TWENTY

Jake

I DIDN'T THINK I'd get to catch up with Isabel and Paul again this trip, since they'd locked themselves away to celebrate their new nuptials yesterday, and they fly out for New Zealand tonight. But once Paul heard I was still in town, he texted me and asked me to have lunch with them before they leave.

They've just come from the hospital and they're both giddy with excitement for Marcus and Abby, as well as, I suspect, giddy with dreams of their own. It's an unexpected bonus to spend this time with them, but I'm startled to find that, maybe for the first time ever, I'm actually jealous of Paul.

I know that he feels about Izzy the way I once felt about Jess. They're just lucky enough to be in a place where they are able to promise one another forever.

From there, I go shopping so I don't have to wear the same two shirts all week, then head over to Chelsea and visit Dad and Elspeth. They've recently moved into Dad's apartment together, and they drag me along for their regular Monday afternoon walk along the High Line. I've met Elspeth over Skype during my regular calls with Dad but spending time with her in person is a genuine bonus.

My mom got sick when I was a senior in high school, and she died when I was in my second year of college. I still feel her with me sometimes, and I still think about her all the time. I remember most her brilliant wit, her commitment to her career and her incredible generosity of spirit. I'd had my sights set on med school since I was a kid, but Mom's suffering and the helplessness we all felt as she battled breast cancer inspired my choice to specialize in oncology. And I don't doubt that the beautiful relationship she and Dad shared has shaped my own thoughts on relationships. I know a lot of young guys go through a commitment-phobic phase, but that was never me. I always wanted to meet the right person—I always craved the kind of devotion my mom and dad shared to one another.

But despite a few long-term girlfriends over the years, I never experienced a patch on that kind of connection until Jess and I started dating. I know that if she was willing to give a relationship between us a real shot, we could share the kind of love my parents shared. The kind of love I've always wanted to find.

It's taken my dad decades to love again after Mom—as far as I know, he hasn't even dated since she died. Not until now. But he's clearly besotted with Elspeth, and it's actually pretty great to see him so happy again.

"Did you meet my little darling, Jake?" Elspeth asks me as she and Dad file back into their apartment after the walk. I'm not going to stick around this afternoon, so I linger in the doorway, watching as a blue-gray, shorthaired cat saunters across the living room. The cat surveys me, then turns its tail as if it's going to walk away. Elspeth chases after it, then scoops the cat into her arms and beams. "Say hello to Jake, Meowbert." I chuckle at the name, and Elspeth explains, "My grandchildren named her. But it suits her, don't you think?"

"Hello…Meowbert," I say, reaching to pet the cat's head. Meowbert raises a paw as if she intends to scratch me, and I hastily drop my hand.

"That's not nice, Meowbert," Elspeth scolds.

"Meowbert is our guard cat," Dad explains. He gives the cat an affectionate head scratch. The cat glares at him. "The downside is, she thinks my drapes are her scratching post." I glance to the drapes and my eyes widen—the bottoms have entirely been shredded. Dad's a fastidious kind of guy when it comes to his apartment, and I'm stunned that he's seemingly so at ease with the wanton destruction of his homewares.

"I'll bet your Clara would never be so naughty," Elspeth sighs ruefully. I laugh weakly and assure her, "Then you'd be surprised."

"I was never a pet person, was I, Jake?" Dad muses, scooping Meowbert from Elspeth and nestling the furiously protesting cat high in his arms. "Funny how things change."

Dad's gaze drifts to Elspeth, and the two share a quiet smile.

"It sure is," I say softly.

"Come for lunch tomorrow," Dad says. "I expect to see you at least once within every forty-eight-hour period before you leave. If you average ninety minutes with us every second day for your extended visit here, we'll have had about 7 percent of your effective daytime hours during the visit. That's an appropriate ratio of parental to free time, given how rarely I see you in person."

It's fair to say Dad and Paul are pretty similar. Elspeth rolls her eyes at him.

"Jake, you just visit us when you can. We don't need to keep a detailed timesheet. If you do want to come for lunch any day, just let me know an hour or two in advance and I'll get Martin to whip something up."

"I'll see you guys tomorrow," I tell her, chuckling. "Try to get him to make us bologna sandwiches. That was his favorite meal to 'cook' when we were kids."

I leave and head back to my hotel to get ready to pick Jess up. I really don't have a plan for these weeks in New York, beyond spending time with her and hoping she'll see our potential. In the back of my mind, I am a little nervous that I haven't thought this all through—it really was a wild impulse to miss that flight. It's just that if there's one thing my job has taught me, it's that life is brutally unpredictable. I've seen countless patients die over the years, and over those sad moments, I've heard more than my share of stories of regret.

People rarely regret the chances they took, even if the chances don't pay off. Those deathbed stories are almost always about the times they failed to try.

Looking back at my life so far, the one regret I have is that Jess and I couldn't find a way to make it work. I don't believe in "love at first sight" or "soul mates," but for years I've felt like Jess and I were meant to be. Maybe I need to give this one last shot, even if just to prove that's nonsense.

Still, now that I'm officially in the city for longer, I am a little nervous. I mean, Jess did break my heart two years ago. The way we ended hurt in a way I'd never experienced before, and although I convinced myself I was over her, that might not be the case.

I have to be smart about how I do this. The last thing I want is either one of us getting hurt again and leaping feetfirst into a full-on physical relationship with Jess is a recipe for disaster. A superfun, superpleasurable disaster, but a disaster nonetheless. I just have to figure out how to avoid it. I don't want to announce straight out of the block that I won't be sleeping with her, because her next logical question will be why, and then we'll have to have a chat about the future right away. That's obviously not going to work. I need another plan, and fast.

I arrive at her building just before eight and the guy at the security desk calls up to let her know I'm there.

When she appears in the lobby a few minutes later, my breath catches in my throat. I just saw her this morning and she's been at work all day, so she looks tired, and her black suit and cream silk shirt are a *tiny* bit crumpled. Even so, she looks stunning. Jess is wearing her hair down today, styled in loose waves around her face, and her makeup is flawless as it always is.

I love you.

I've never said the words to her, but I've thought them countless times. They've danced on the tip of my tongue on all kinds of occasions—every time she made me come, every time she spontaneously showed me affection, every time she put me in my place and I adored her for it. I might never get to say those words to her, but I'm pretty sure that I still know them to be true, even after all of this time.

"Hey. Do you mind if we eat in at my place tonight?" she asks as she approaches. "I can cook, or we can get takeout. I'm just beat."

"Do you have the stuff for that tarragon chicken I used to make? If you like, I can cook, you can drink wine and put your feet up."

She loops her arm through mine and we start walking back toward her apartment as she laughs softly, "You trying to get into my pants, Winton? If so, you're going about it just the right way."

Yeah, I'm going to have to do some rapid-fire thinking about that, and if the gleam in Jess's eye is any indication, I'm going to have to do it sooner rather than later.

"You still work eight to eight, huh?"

"Most weekdays," Jess says, then pauses. "Some weekends too. But I do still like to let loose on Friday and Saturday nights, so my weekend work is often around a scheduled hangover."

She's sitting up on the bench top sipping a glass of wine while I cook us dinner. The suit is gone, and now, she's wearing skin-tight jeans and an equally tight tank top. The new outfit doesn't look much more comfortable than her work clothes did, but I'm just relieved she didn't emerge from her room in that tiny dress she was wearing when I came here Friday night.

I *want* Jess. Desire throbs under our every interaction. But even as I cook in her kitchen and we hang out together innocently, I'm convincing myself that I can't give in to the magnetism between us. She actively tried to avoid emotional intimacy with me on Saturday night by trying to seduce me, and emotional distance is the last thing I want over the next two weeks.

Besides, if we tumble back into bed together right now, sex will mean very different things to each of us. That's an awful footing to start a relationship on, and a relationship is ultimately what I want.

"I really thought you'd scale your crazy hours back once Brainway had taken off," I tell her. "And it's definitely taken off, right?"

"I have big plans so I have to work big hours, Jake. And I love my job. It's my life." She shrugs.

"I get that better than most, but even so, it's rare for me to work those kinds of hours these days."

"Good thing for Clara," Jess laughs softly.

I stretch to pick my phone up from the bench, unlock it and load a photo, then slide it toward Jess.

"Reba the dog-sitter sent me the cutest photo of Clara today on their walk."

"Oh God, not you too," Jess groans, but she's reaching for my phone anyway. At my curious glance, she explains, "Abby. I visited her at lunchtime and she made me look at two hundred photos of the girls. They're two days old! They can't do anything yet! How does she have *two hundred photos* already?"

"You went by yourself today?"

"Jake," she sighs quietly. "I'm fine."

"I know," I say. And I do believe she's okay—she's tough as nails. But I saw the pain on her face when we were at the hospital yesterday. It was palpable—the kind of psychic agony a person doesn't just swipe away in a day. "I'll come with you while I'm here, if you want me to."

"I knew you were staying in New York just to babysit me," she mutters, but then she sees the photo of Clara and she bursts out laughing. "I wouldn't say that's cute, but it is funny."

Clara is wearing her harness, and she's lying flat on the sidewalk, legs on the ground, looking up at Reba's camera and flatly refusing to move another inch.

"She saw a truck," I explain. "Clara has canine anxiety. She's scared of pretty much everything—trucks, mice, when the TV is too loud, being left alone too long. The shelter staff thought she was probably abused by her previous owner."

"What on earth inspired you to adopt a dog? Especially…" Jess sets the phone down and says delicately, "Especially one like that?"

"Ah, it was a particularly impulsive decision, to be honest," I admit, a little self-consciously.

"You? Impulsive?" Jess says, eyebrows high, and then I frown at her, and she bursts out laughing. "Remember when you bought that convertible? You didn't even have anywhere to park it."

"It was a total bargain. Besides, I had some good times in that car."

"You only owned it for two months!"

"They were a glorious two months, Jessica," I chuckle. I don't remind her that I had to sell the car purely because I had nowhere to park it. Total impulse decision—I was thinking about ways to get out of the city on my days off, saw an ad for the car the next day and bam! The rest was history.

"And what about when you let that guy from the hospital move in with you."

"He was a radiographer. A medical professional. He holds people's lives in his hands every day. It seemed safe enough to let him stay in my spare room."

"You met him for two minutes and didn't even get references." Jess is laughing so hard she's nearly in tears now. "If I remember correctly, you woke up the first morning and he was in the process of stealing your wallet from your nightstand."

"Are you enjoying this?"

"So much," she assures me. "And then there was the time you decided you'd get dual tattoo sleeves."

"You have to admit, tattoo sleeves would totally have suited me. I'm tough and manly. And edgy."

Jess is howling with laughter now. She holds her stomach with one hand and wipes at her eyes with the other.

"Tattoos are for men who smolder. You don't smolder, Jake. You *smile*. And besides, as I understand it, people traditionally get a single tattoo before they commit to a whole sleeve, and then maybe a sleeve on one side before they do both. You were booked in for twelve hours in the parlor for four fucking days in a row! If I hadn't made you wait a week to be sure it was what you wanted, you'd look like Adam Levine by now."

"Isn't Adam Levine hot?"

"He *was* hot," she corrects me. "But that was four hundred tattoos ago. There is such a thing as too much ink, and on someone as clean-cut and virtuous as you, one tattoo would have been 'too much ink.'"

I grin at her. The tattoo sleeves were an insane idea. I can't remember what inspired that particular venture, and I'm very relieved she talked me out of it.

"So what was the story with the dog? Just you being impulsive again?" Jess asks me.

I wince, then turn back to the stovetop. We've been laughing together for a few minutes, but my answer to that question will change the tone of this chat completely.

"Something like that," I say. I'm hoping she'll leave it at that, but I'm not surprised when she pushes me for more.

"What happened?" she asks. Jess has read something in my body language. Her tone is immediately serious, and when I turn back to her, I find she's watching me closely. I sigh and give her a sad smile.

"I lost a patient. He was seven years old... He had a type of tumor called a glioblastoma."

"You lose patients all the time," she says, not unkindly, and, of course, she's correct.

I turn my attention back to the stovetop before I explain, "I care about my patients. Too much sometimes."

"I know you do."

"Rafael was particularly special. He had recurrent brain cancer...glioblastoma. His prognosis was terminal but no matter how sick he was, no matter how much pain he was in, he was always hopeful. His spirit was so vibrant. That day, I saw him on morning rounds, and we had a long chat about his two favorite subjects... dogs and baseball." I chuckle softly at the memory, but then tense at what came after. "I fist-bumped him and told him I'd see him the next morning. A few hours later, he suffered a massive brain hemorrhage...just a freak incident, no one could have seen it coming, nothing I did or didn't do could have changed the outcome."

"I'm really sorry, Jake," I hear Jess murmur from behind me, but I don't turn to face her yet. Instead, I stare down into the pot I'm stirring. Dealing with death is a part of my job, but losing Rafael hit me hard. His innocence and his optimism had worn off on me. I'd almost convinced myself that his meds regime would buy him time, and with time, I'd somehow find a miracle for him.

"When a nurse of Rafael's ward called to tell me what had happened, I had just enough energy and composure to go and spend some time with his parents and brother, then I took the rest of the afternoon off. I was driving home when I found myself at the dog rescue center, and when I left there half an hour later, Clara was in my back seat." I turn back to Jess at last, and add with a sad smile, "She chewed through a seat belt on the way home. Clara definitely began her life with me as she intended to continue."

Jess is staring at me thoughtfully.

"Surely every time you lose a patient like that, you're thinking about your mom."

"Not always. But…well, sometimes. Sure."

"Why do you do this job?" she asks me, bewildered.

"It's a calling, Jess," I tell her gently. "I know exactly what it feels like to wish and pray and hope for just one more good hour…one more good day. My mom died too young, but I know she would have wanted some good to come from her death, and it really has. I love my job. I make a difference to people's lives. Sometimes my patients recover. Sometimes I've bought them precious time, and believe me, in these situations, time is *everything*. The day Rafael died was just a low point, and yes, adopting Clara was probably impulsive, but I don't regret it. She's a handful, but she also brings me a lot of joy. And… It's hard to explain, but knowing she's waiting for me at home is actually a comfort."

Jess gnaws her lip. I tilt my head at her, surveying the concern in her expression. Concern for *me*. She might not even realize it herself, but she still cares deeply for me. That realization encourages me to open up a little more.

"I almost called you that day," I admit. She raises an eyebrow at me.

"Why? That's a shit thing to have to deal with and I'm notoriously insensitive."

I laugh weakly.

"That's why, Jess. Because everyone else would have given me platitudes, told me it was natural to be upset… But they wouldn't have understood or really cared. You and I had broken up, I was pissed at you and we weren't even speaking. But despite all of that, I knew you'd give a shit. And I also knew you'd give me the perfect blend of a reality check and sympathy."

"I would have answered if you called," she says, after a pause.

I glance at her.

"I know you would have."

"I really didn't realize you were so angry after we broke up. I felt like we were both sad about it, but I honestly thought we both understood it was for the best."

"I wasn't angry at first. We wanted different things, it almost made sense that we'd part. But you know I was never thrilled about the secrecy, and after we went our separate ways and I started to think about that some more, that's when I started to get angry."

"On Friday you accused me of hiding what was going on between us because I had secret plans the whole time to treat you like shit. That wasn't the case at all. I really did just get caught up because of how intense things were between us."

The thing is, I actually believe that now. Maybe I'm even counting on it, given I'm hoping she gets caught up all over again in the next few weeks. Without the heartbreak part, this time around, of course.

"I feel like sometimes I build walls in my life," she says softly. "I wall off Mitch from my other friends. I walled off my relationship with you from everyone. I wall off work from Mitch. I even wall off my thoughts about Tristan from my day-to-day life sometimes. It's probably an old coping mechanism, but it's not always a healthy one."

"You realized all of that this weekend?"

"It's not easy to talk about Tristan. But I do kind of wish Abby and Isabel knew, and especially now that Abby is a mom, I don't know how to talk about him."

"If and when you're ready, Jess, you just tell them. And if I can help you in any way when that time comes, you know where I am."

Jess is comfortable with me. She might not know how to share her burdens, but she trusts me not to add to them. She's spoken so freely about Tristan tonight that I could almost forget we're talking about a secret she's buried for half of her lifetime.

The connection we share is deep and enduring—despite the way we bicker sometimes, despite the breakup and the years of silence between us. It's still real, it's still here, and I'm suddenly very glad that I didn't get on that plane last night.

"Thanks, Jake," Jess says softly.

"Anytime," I murmur, and I mean it.

CHAPTER TWENTY-ONE

Jess

I ALMOST FALL asleep on the sofa after Jake and I eat his ridiculously delicious chicken, and he kisses me gently on the forehead, then begs off to go home and catch up on sleep too. I'm surprised he didn't stay over— but I am exhausted, so I don't complain too much. I figure he'll stay over tomorrow night instead. We still have eleven days together. We'll make up for lost time soon enough.

When I step out of my building at 7:45 a.m. Tuesday morning, I half expect Jake to be waiting there with coffee, and I'm pained to realize I'm actually a little disappointed when he isn't. But then at 9:00 a.m., Gina lets herself into my office and sets a take-out coffee and a doughnut on my desk.

"Thanks?" I say blankly. I look at the doughnut. "But... You know I don't do carbs."

Let me be very clear about this: I definitely *do* carbs. I just avoid them in food, because I save all of my daily sugar allowance for alcohol, like a sensible person.

"Special delivery from Paul's brother," Gina says, giving me a bewildered look. "Apparently it's a keto doughnut. Almond flour and stevia, I think he said."

She leaves my office and I scoop my phone up off the desk.

Jess: You didn't have to do that.

Jake: I didn't? I'll come back and pick the coffee and fake doughnut up, then.

Jess: Ha, ha. Why didn't you stop and say hi?

Jake: I didn't want to interrupt your workday. Just wanted to let you know I'm thinking of you.

Oh, I am going to give that man the blowjob of his life tonight.

Jess: Do you want to catch up tonight? I was thinking I'd take off early. Say nine?

Jake: Sure. Let's go out for dinner this time.

Jess: It's a date. See you at my place at nine.

And I figure it's going to be a date that ends in sexy times back at my place, so I leave the office at

8:00 p.m. and race home to shower and change. I do some lady-scaping, redo my makeup and hair, and slip into a barely there black dress with sky-high nude heels. By the time Jake arrives at my door, I'm feeling like a sex goddess, and when I throw it open to greet him, I know I've nailed the look.

"Oh," he says. He swallows hard. "Jess. My God. You look stunning."

"Guilty as charged," I say cheerfully. I scoop my bag up from the hall table and join him in the hall, then skim my eye over his jeans and white button-down. The way that shirt pulls across his shoulders is a thing of beauty, but even so, I cannot wait to peel it off him later. I'll undo the buttons slowly while I stare right into his eyes, and then I'll push the shirt off his shoulders, and then maybe drop to my knees and go for his jeans. "You don't look so bad yourself. Are you sure you want to go out?"

"We have reservations," he tells me lightly, then he glances down at his watch. "Actually, we better get going if we're going to make them."

JAKE HAS MADE us a reservation at a restaurant near his hotel, and I figure that's code for *stay with me tonight*, so I mentally update my expected itinerary for the evening.

Dinner.

Back to Jake's hotel.

Time for dessert, because it's on.

I have to admit, I'm a little surprised by his restaurant choice. It's noisy and brightly lit, with red-and-white-checkered tablecloths and silk flowers as centerpieces. There's a somewhat limited wine list and the menu isn't great, but the atmosphere is what really gets to me. It's just…lacking. I don't really need candlelight to get in the mood when it comes to Jake, but it's just not what I expected. When we were together, he was forever taking me to places with extensive wine lists and real flowers on the table between us. Romantic places, I suppose.

This place hardly screams *romance*. Actually, it screams *this is not the place you take a woman if you're trying to woo her*, but then again, maybe that's a good thing. Maybe this is just a sign that Jake really is thinking about these weeks with me as a temporary thing. I suppose I should be reassured by that… But even if I am reassured, I'm definitely also confused.

"What did you do with this beautiful vacation day in this super relaxing city?" I ask Jake as I sip my wine. I had so many choices: I could have had sweet or dry, and red or white.

"I had lunch with Dad and Elspeth," Jake tells me.

"I met her briefly at the reception on the weekend," I tell him. "She seems nice."

"She's great for Dad. They're really working on staying active together, and she's so accepting of his…"

"Quirks?"

Jake smiles at me.

"Exactly. She's just a good woman, I think. The only thing is, I discovered yesterday that she has this crazy cat named Meowbert. It's got serious issues—I mean, it's torn Dad's drapes to shreds. But Elspeth seems to worship that thing." Jake looks bewildered. I burst out laughing.

"So, let me get this straight. The man who adores his crazy-ugly dog is confused by the woman who adores her crazy cat, is that what you're saying?"

"It's hardly the same, Jess." Jake frowns at me. I can't tell if he's joking. "Clara is a *dog*. Dogs are loyal. Man's best friend, you know? Meowbert is basically a destructive shelf ornament."

"If I was going to get a pet, I'd get a cat," I tell him. He gasps.

"I thought you were the perfect woman!"

"I am the perfect woman. As is evidenced by my correct thoughts on the matter of dogs versus cats, and by that I mean, I know that cats are the far superior animal."

Jake clutches playfully at his chest.

"You're breaking my heart right now."

"I'd give my cat a novelty name like Meowbert too. Or maybe I'd get two cats with matching names—like Kitty and…" I pause, searching for the right word, then shrug and go with, "Smitty. I don't know. Something like that, but better."

"So why don't you have a cat, then, if you're such a fan of all things feline?"

"Are you kidding me? That white sofa in my apartment cost me thousands of dollars. I'm not risking its health and safety by letting a *cat* in the apartment."

Jake pulls a face.

"Yeah, we need to talk about that sofa."

"We do, do we?"

"Did you order it from eBay?"

"I most definitely did not," I say, horrified. "Why would you ask that?"

"I thought it might be one of those situations where someone orders what they think is furniture online, but when it arrives, they realize it's actually built to go in a kid's dollhouse."

"It's not that small," I protest, laughing. He gives me a pained look. "Well, when I bought it, I wasn't expecting any giants to visit with me. Next time you come over, you can have the wing chair."

"Your throne, you mean?"

"It's my throne now, is it?"

"Well, when I came by after the rehearsal dinner, I did think you looked almost regal sitting on it," he says, the corner of his lip quirking upward.

"Did you imagine me sitting there stroking a cat on my lap? Plotting world domination or something?"

"Did you think Dr. Evil from the *Austin Powers* movies was 'regal'? Because that's literally the scene you just described." We both burst out laughing, and then he sobers and his gaze is steady on my face as he clarifies, "I just meant that you looked so perfect sitting there. So elegant and poised, like a queen on her throne—completely in command, totally in her element."

"That's so sweet," I say, my voice a little husky.

"I mean every word," Jake murmurs. "You're still the most beautiful woman I've ever known."

Our gazes are locked, and heat radiates between us. The noisy, too-bright restaurant fades away, and it's just he and I because there is no one else in the whole world right now—

"Are you ready to order?" a waitress asks us abruptly, and Jake and I both startle.

I recover quickly and smile to myself as I glance up at her to order, but I notice that when I glance back to Jake, he's wearing a look that's pure guilt, as if he's been caught doing something he's just not supposed to be doing.

JAKE WAS QUIET after we ordered, and it only got worse once the food came. We've finished eating now and I'm bewildered as I try to read his mood. I'd assumed we'd be going back to his hotel, but the longer we sit here sharing this muted conversation, the less likely that seems. I'm disappointed. Actually, that's an understatement.

I'm gutted, and completely confused.

"Should we get out of here?" I ask him cautiously.

"Actually," Jake says apologetically, "I've um…" He waves toward his head. "I have a bit of a headache."

I look at him blankly. I guess that makes sense, given how quiet he's been, but it's just… I mean, it's just such a cliché, isn't it? Isn't "I have a headache" exactly what bored spouses say to one another to avoid advances?

"A headache?" I repeat uncertainly.

Jake winces.

"Yeah, sorry." He waves toward his wineglass. "Maybe some weird preservative reaction or something. Plus, it's kind of echo-y in here. Noisy, you know?"

"Yeah. I noticed," I mutter, but then I tilt my head at him. "Are you sure you're okay?"

"Just need another early night, probably. I'll bring you a coffee tomorrow?"

"You really don't have to do that," I say, which, of course, means *please do*. I let him pick up the check, promising I'll get it next time, and then we walk out onto the street.

"At least let me get you home," he says, glancing up and down the traffic as if he's looking for a cab.

"Jake, I can catch a fucking car on my own," I laugh softly, then I stretch to kiss his cheek. *Holy shit, that scent is heaven to me.* I want to stay here on my tippy-toes in my agonizingly uncomfortable heels just so I can breathe him in. I guess that would be a bit weird. I force myself back down onto my flat feet and give him a sad smile. "Sleep well."

He catches my hand, then stares at me. I'm so confused. I can see that he wants me, but his gaze is also strained. There's reluctance in his eyes…reluctance to let me go, maybe, but a definite reluctance for me to stay. Maybe he's just in pain. I feel a pang of concern for him, so I squeeze his hand.

"It's okay," I say softly, then I quirk an eyebrow. "Rest up, Jake. You're going to need it."

He opens his mouth, then closes it, but doesn't say a word. I laugh softly and walk away, sashaying my hips as I go, knowing his eyes follow me until I disappear around the corner.

CHAPTER TWENTY-TWO

Jess

It's 7:45 a.m. Wednesday morning, and it's pouring rain. I pause at the awning in front of my apartment and struggle with my umbrella.

"Allow me," Jake says, and I glance up at him in amusement as he swaps the two coffee cups for my umbrella. He pops it open easily, then takes his coffee back from me. "Good morning."

Jake doesn't have an umbrella. He's standing in the rain in a light jacket, the hoodie up over his hair. There are water droplets all over his shoulders and resting on his stubble. Apparently, he's one of those "no shaving on vacations" guys now.

I don't mind at all. At this rate, he's going to have a salt-and-pepper beard in a few days, and it turns out I wouldn't mind seeing that.

"Thanks for the coffee, and good morning."

"Good morning to you too."

"Do you want to try to squeeze under this umbrella?" I ask hesitantly. Jake laughs.

"Thanks, but that's not going to work. I'll walk in the rain. It's been dry back home. It's a nice change to see water actually falling from the sky."

"What do you do if it rains when you're hiking?"

"Exactly what I'm doing right now," he says, shrugging. "I put a jacket on and keep going."

We start to walk toward my office, and I sip the coffee, then ask, "How's the headache?"

"Much better, thanks. I'm really sorry about last night."

"You don't need to be sorry," I chastise him lightly. "I came home and finished myself off—I mean, I finished the night off alone."

Jake groans softly as he gives me a tortured look. I laugh.

"You know what I was thinking we should do Saturday morning, if you're free?" he says. "Remember that diner near my old apartment that makes the pancakes you like?"

"The zero-carb cream cheese pancakes? God, I haven't had them in years."

"We could have brunch there. I'll pop in this afternoon and book our old table. For eleven?"

"That sounds amazing." For two reasons: One, zero-carb pancakes are the bomb. And two: 11:00 a.m. is definitely late enough for us to fuck like rabbits on Friday night, get some sleep, go another round in the morning and then head out to eat them. "That's all well and good, but it's two days away. Do you have plans tonight? Mitch wanted to get a drink. I didn't mention to him that you're still in town, but I know he won't mind you tagging along."

"Sure. Where are we going?"

"Just this bar I like," I say. He frowns at me suspiciously.

"Not…that stupid place with the weird drinks."

"That's the one." I grin. "Meet me at my office at 8:00 p.m.?"

Jake grimaces.

"Do I have to?"

"Of course not." I shrug. We walk in silence for a few moments as the rain sprinkles down over him. When we reach the awning over the entrance to my building, he slides one hand into the pocket of his jeans and gives me a pained look.

"Do they have beer? I can't remember."

"They have plenty of beers. Glitter beer and coffee stout and milkshake IPAs and all kinds of other delicious oddities."

"Jesus Christ," Jake sighs. "You could talk me into anything."

I grin.

"Now that sounds promising." I rest my hand on his shoulder, then rise up to brush my lips against his as I whisper, "You have yourself a great day, Jake Winton. Make sure you're thinking of me, okay?"

"I doubt I'll think of anything but you," he whispers back. I grin and leave him to walk inside my office.

Am I disappointed that we've been hanging out for two days and Jake and I haven't managed any naked time as yet? Absolutely. But I'm also more than confident that tonight, we'll finally break that streak.

JAKE AND I are sitting side by side in a booth at Betsy Jane, which is a particularly fabulous bar a few blocks from my office. Mitchell sits opposite us, and since he came in and found us both here two minutes ago, he's been staring at us in silent horror.

"We're just hanging out," Jake says suddenly, apparently *totally* guilted by Mitchell's theatrics.

"Once upon a time…" Mitch says dramatically, and I groan and drop my head down onto my arms on the table.

"Jake, go back to California, a few weeks of fun with you is not worth Mitchell going all wise-storyteller on me."

"…there was a little boy. A *handsome* little boy. Some may have said a *brilliant* little boy. His name was Mitchell C—no, I'll call him Master Cole," Mitch continues, undaunted, even when I half laugh, half groan. "He was a happy boy. He was a content boy." His gaze narrows on my face. "And then his mommy and daddy got divorced and everything went to shit. Mommy cried into her low-carb ice cream."

"I didn't cry," I mutter.

"We both know you did. And Daddy panic-moved to California."

"I did not 'panic-move.' What does that even mean?" Jake mutters.

"It means you were sad and you panicked and you

moved across the fucking country on a whim, Jake. And after that, poor little Master C had to split his time between them. He had to avoid Daddy's incessant interrogations about how Mommy was."

Jake glances at me, then tries to assure me, "I did not—"

"Master C had to lie to Mommy and tell her he was seeing a movie exec in LA when he actually went to visit Daddy in Palo Alto on his vacation."

My gaze flies from Jake's face to Mitch's.

"You lied to me?"

"You left me no choice. Every time I said his name, you got this…" Mitchell waves his hand in my face "…this look on your face, like I was betraying you. And finally, one day Master C came out for a nice, innocent drink with his bestie and was shocked to discover Mommy and Daddy had been spending time together again, apparently forgetting the utter emotional wasteland of their past, and not considering poor Master C's welfare *at all*."

"We get it," I sigh, glancing at Jake, who shrugs at me. "But we really are just hanging out while Jake is in town. No need for Master C to be such a drama queen."

Mitch sighs and scrubs his hand over his face.

"I need a drink."

"Well, good thing we're at a bar, then," I say brightly.

"Allow me," Jake says, sliding out of the booth. "What can I get you, Jess?"

"An elderflower and pomegranate martini, please."

Jake shudders, then glances at Mitch.

"Anything alcoholic that doesn't feature obscure fruits or nontraditional pairing of perfectly innocent ingredients who deserved a better end than a hipster cocktail," Mitch mutters. "Oh, and no foam. Foam isn't a drink and it's not a food. It's what you have in bubble bath. It's not meant to go in your mouth."

"Get Grandpa here a deconstructed Long Island iced tea. Mitch *loves* mixing his own drinks in bars," I tell Jake, laughing when Mitch glares at me.

"I'll get you one of those weird-ass beers," Jake mutters as he walks away.

"Why do I ever agree to meet you here?" Mitch asks me, shaking his head.

"Well, obviously it's because I'm irresistible."

Mitch nods at Jake's retreating back, then says quietly, "Apparently you are. But have you really thought that through?"

"It was his idea to stay." I shrug.

"Jess."

"Seriously, it was. Just two weeks together, hard deadline at the end, no one gets hurt."

"You know I love you."

"You should. I'm amazing."

"So I say this with love."

"Whenever anyone says 'I say this with love,' what they actually mean is 'I'm about to offend you.'"

"I am about to offend you," Mitch sighs. "You aren't good for each other, Jess. Not unless…" I glance at him. Mitch gives me a sad look. "Not unless you're willing to think about something longer term than two weeks. Jake isn't like you and me. He doesn't do casual, and honestly? I'm not even convinced you can do casual when it comes to Jake."

"Two weeks," I repeat. "Hard deadline. No one gets hurt."

"Keep saying it, Jessica," Mitchell sighs. "Maybe then you'll convince yourself it's true."

I can hear genuine anxiety in Mitch's tone, and I bristle a little. This is that awful conversation with Abby all over again, and I hate to think that my friends think so little of me.

"I'm not a fucking monster, Mitchell. I won't hurt him," I say flatly, all playfulness gone now. Mitch gives me a sharp look.

"It's not just him I'm worried about. You hurt each other last time and seeing you like that nearly killed me."

Now I feel like shit. Of course Mitch wouldn't judge me for the way I live my life—he lives his in exactly the same way. This is all just a bit *sensitive* for me right now. But I really didn't mean to bring the tone of the evening down, so I try to turn things around.

"You do realize you're a total buzzkill when you're in wise-storyteller mode?" I say lightly.

"Just be careful, okay?"

"There's just one thing I have to say, Mitchell."

He sighs and gives me an expectant look. I nod toward the bar, where a blonde woman sits with her drink. She's been watching him since he came in. He follows my gaze, then looks back to me.

"You're distracting me with a gorgeous woman. That's a low blow."

"Or is it just me doing my job as your official wing-woman? Want an introduction?"

"Do you even know her?" he laughs softly, and I grin at him as I slide out from the booth.

"Networking is my superpower, Mitch. Give me ten minutes."

BY 10:00 P.M., MITCH is all but sucking face with the blonde woman in another corner of the bar, and Jake and I are still in the booth, now several drinks down and following up our heated debate about the correct way to eat popcorn—Jake, who is wrong, has decided he likes to mix M&M's into his in the years since we last hung out—with an equally heated debate about the correct way to eat Oreos. Jake is now suggesting they are best separated first.

"Then you can scrape the cream off and eat that on its own, and you get two delicious cookies to chase it down with."

"Or, you could not be a monster, and eat them whole the way nature intended."

"I don't think nature has anything to do with Oreos. In fact, I'm pretty sure that Oreos are 100 percent non-natural."

This ridiculous debate reminds me of the four months I spent with Jake, and how once we finally got naked together and diffused that angry tension, every single minute was full of something delicious. If we weren't having lighthearted, hilarious debates like this one, we were talking about shit that mattered—like the job I love, or the job he loves, or our friends or politics or even, from time to time, ethics. We weren't the kind of couple who had to agree, because we do both love to argue, and I'm pretty sure that some of those heated discussions were actually intense foreplay.

Speaking of…

"You want to get out of here and come back to my place?" I ask quietly. There's a flash of something across Jake's face, but he finishes his drink and nods.

Thank fuck.

We're silent in the back of the car, and I feel the anticipation rising with every minute. By the time we reach my apartment, my excitement has reached a fever pitch, and maybe that's why, as soon as Jake closes the door behind him, I pounce on him.

CHAPTER TWENTY-THREE

Jake

I'M NOT AN IDIOT; I did know this was going to happen tonight. I'm not even sad about it—how could I be? The most beautiful woman I've ever known is up on her tippy-toes, arms around my neck, her gorgeous lips against mine, her extremely talented tongue making all kinds of delicious promises right into my mouth.

I still wasn't sure what I'd do when this moment came. Even today, I told myself I'd figure it all out when the moment of inevitability actually arrived. But here we are—at the crossroads where Jess is clearly *very* keen to get naked, and we still haven't had anything like a discussion about the future.

The path of least resistance would be to let her have her wicked way with me. I mean she obviously wants this, and I want it too. This kiss is everything I remembered—scorching hot and urgent. Jess is so bold and so determined. No wonder that even when I thought I hated her, I still wanted her.

Just once, to see if it's as good as I remembered,

my dick begs me, and just a second later, Jess has her hands on the zipper of my jeans and I am this close to just going with it. But I can't kid myself—there's no way once would be enough. Nor would twice, or even several dozen times. If… Hopefully *when* we are together again, we have to be on the same page about the future.

I groan and catch her shoulders gently in my hands.

"Jess," I say, tearing my mouth away from hers.

"Enough talking," she says, immediately reaching up for me again, but this time, I hold her back with a little more determination. Her eyebrows knit. "What?"

"This isn't…" I can't say *this isn't what I want*, because her hand is literally on my groin now and she's got very convincing evidence right beneath her fingers that it is. She's worked the zipper down now and her hand slides inside. She's running her palm right over the length of me through my briefs, and the pressure is so perfect that my knees just about buckle. I close my eyes and pray for strength. "I… Jess…uh… we need. Talk."

"Talk later. Sex now," she suggests huskily, because apparently Jess too has been reduced to caveman-speak. I open my eyes and stare down at her. Her gaze is hazy. Her cheeks are flushed. I want to throw her over my shoulder and carry her into the bedroom and see if we can beat our record for how many orgasms I can give her in the one night. For the record, it was four, and I was keen to keep going but she fell asleep immediately after the last one.

"Jess," I whisper, and I see a little of the haze clear from her eyes at the serious tone of my voice. She's starting to look…irritated. She drops down from her tippy-toes—regrettably away from my mouth—and crosses her arms over her chest. At this point, I realize she'd already undone her shirt—and I'm not at all sure how she managed to get that done without me noticing, but I have to admit, I'm impressed both with the view and her skill.

"What the fuck is going on?" she asks me flatly.

"I…" I run my hand through my hair, then motion toward the sofa. When Jess doesn't move an inch, I zip myself up and lead the way, taking my seat on the Lego-sized mini-sofa, assuming she'll take the wing chair. After a minute, she sighs and joins me on the sofa. Is this because she wants to be near me, just as much as I want to be near her? I hope so, and a desire for closeness feels like a good sign, like an expression of her fondness for me. Unless she's just biding her time so she can leap on me again after we get this conversation out of the way…

Actually, that's probably it. I better just get this over and done with.

"I can't sleep with you," I say.

"Uh…" She seems bewildered. My penis completely understands her confusion. "Why? Is…" She hesitates, then motions toward my groin. "Is everything okay down there? I mean… Everything seemed fine five minutes ago…"

I wince.

"No, that's not… Physically I'm more than capable of getting the job done," I clarify hastily. Jess's gaze narrows.

"Explain."

I turn toward her, then take her hand in mine. She's gazing at me with obvious suspicion.

"I just want to take it slow, Jess. See where this leads us."

"What the fuck are you talking about?" she says, blinking at me. "*Where this leads us?* Where this leads us isn't a mystery. It leads us to a few nights of fun, and then it leads you back to California next weekend. That's the only place this can lead us."

"Is it?" I ask her, gently challenging. "We both regret the way things ended between us. Let's see if we can rewrite the script this time."

"Jake," Jess says, then she draws in a deep breath. She has a strange expression on her face—she's not quite angry, but she's also visibly displeased with this turn of events. "Okay, let's pause for a minute and rewind just a bit. Let's go back in time two and a half years. Pretend for a second that we didn't break up. Where are we now, if things went exactly the way you'd hoped they would have gone?"

I frown at her, because I don't at all understand her accusing tone.

"We'd still be together, obviously."

"Be more specific. What would that look like?"

"Well, we'd probably be—"

She makes a sudden, loud, very harsh buzzer sound and shakes her head.

"Game over. I'm never getting married and I know you've heard me say that. It's not negotiable at all and never has been and the fact that you even thought I'd marry you shows you think you know better than I do what I want for my own life."

"Wait a minute." I frown, and it's my turn for my gaze to narrow on her face. "You knew what I was going to say."

"Of course I did," she snaps. "You're not that hard to read."

But something has slipped into place in my mind. The timing of our breakup always seemed a bit odd. We'd been speaking on the phone every day while I was away, and even the night before I came back, she still seemed warm toward me.

It was quite the shock to get back to my apartment to find that she'd completely made up her mind to end things. Maybe the timing wasn't so random after all.

"You realized I was going to propose?" I surmise grimly.

"I…well, I just figured…"

I peer at her incredulously. "Are you blushing?"

She clears her throat, then looks away.

"I found the ring."

"The ring—" My eyes widen, and I gape at her. "But how?" I try to think back to where I stored it. Surely I wasn't foolish enough to leave it out in the open somewhere?

Jess covers her face with her hands for a moment, then sits up straight, having apparently pressed right through the momentary embarrassment.

"I was staying at your place after I moved out of my old apartment. While I was waiting for this place to be painted. Remember?"

"Of course." It's pretty hard to forget when your girlfriend asks to stay with you for a few weeks, then immediately tells all of your mutual friends she's in a hotel. I was already increasingly frustrated with the secrecy, but that moment just about broke me. It was probably the point where I should have put my foot down and said no more lies, but I was so into her, it was hard to figure out where the line was.

"You were in California doing whatever-the-fuck you did at the college before you got this job."

"I was helping design a clinical trial but go on."

"Well, I was in your bed, and I was horny and un-satisfied," she says easily, then she gives me a pointed look. "Much like I am tonight, for the record."

"I picked up on that."

"I had one of my toys in my suitcase—remember that purple vibrator we liked to play around with?" I groan at the memory, a rush of blood immediately diverting south again, and Jess shrugs as if I deserve to suffer right now. Maybe I actually do. "But I'd run out of lube. I went to help myself to some of yours, which I remembered was in your nightstand. You can guess what happened next."

She's right: I can guess. I'm imagining she reached

into that drawer, pulled out the engagement ring, flipped out and then abruptly broke up with me the day I got back.

"When you ended things, you said you'd just been doing some thinking," I say slowly.

"I did do some thinking. I thought *holy shit, Jake has an engagement ring in his drawer but we said we'd keep things casual and he's clearly got other ideas so I better end things right now*," she snaps.

"Why didn't you tell me this?"

"I was embarrassed! I thought you'd assume I'd been snooping!"

I groan and exhale. That sounds about right. Jess would be happy to speak openly about masturbating in my bed but mortified that I might think she'd been riffling through my things. She crosses her arms over her chest again and glares at me.

"I had heard you say you never intended to marry. But the night of Paul and Izzy's first wedding, I also heard you say we'd just have one night together," I remind her.

"Right."

"And one night became one weekend. Then one weekend became a week. And four months later, we were pretty much living together." We still had our own places, sure, but we used only one of them at a time. From memory, right from the night of Paul's wedding, we didn't have a night apart unless one of us was away for work.

"We weren't living—" She starts to scoff, but I give

her a pointed look, and she sighs. "Okay. Yes, things got out of hand."

"Things changed," I counter. "You were every bit as into me as I was into you. We agreed it would just be one night, but when that went out the window, I assumed that meant the rules had changed too. You wouldn't sleep over at my apartment at first, and by the time I left for that work trip, you'd helped yourself to half of my closet."

She opens her mouth, then closes it again, and scowls at me.

"Jake, I made mistakes two years ago. I didn't mean to give you the wrong impression. I did get caught up in how good things were between us and—" A shadow crosses her face, and she widens her eyes. "Wait a fucking second. You were hoping that would happen again, weren't you? This whole 'let's just hang out casually for a few weeks' proposal was actually a ploy to trick me into agreeing to something more permanent!"

"Of course not!" I exclaim, frustration lacing my voice. "I wanted to *show* you that there's still something special between us. We missed each other. I thought if we spent some time together—"

"You thought you could mansplain to me what I want for my own life," she finishes incredulously. "You think that just because you want some fucking white picket fence Stepford wife that all you had to do was wave your penis around in front of me and I'd change my mind."

"The whole point of this discussion right now is that

I won't 'wave my penis around in front of you!'" I ex-claim. "Sex is never casual to me, and it sure as fuck isn't anything like casual when I'm with you. That's the whole point, Jess. And do you seriously think if we got married I'd expect you to behave like a Step-ford wife? You haven't been compliant for more than a single second in your whole damned life! I wanted to commit to you, not give you a lobotomy!"

"Let me say this in simple terms so it will sink in through your thick skull. *You cannot trap me. I do not want a future with you*," Jess snaps. She stands, her shirt falling open, revealing a delicious sneak peek of skin I desperately want to touch, but won't. And can't, because she points furiously to the door. "Get out, Jake. You don't respect my wishes, you don't get to be here."

"Jess—"

"Get out!"

She sounds angry, but I can see in her gaze that it's more than that. *She's disappointed.* Disappointed in me.

And the worst thing is, I realize she's absolutely right. She told me she regretted the way things ended— she did *not* say she'd changed her mind and was sud-denly willing to give me a long-term commitment. I arrogantly assumed I could convince her to change her mind.

I considered it "wooing" her…reminding her. But in truth, I was actually just trying to convince her to give me what I want.

More of her.

"We'll talk tomorrow," I start to say as I rise, but she snorts incredulously.

"No we fucking won't. I don't want to see or hear from you ever again."

Okay, I know I fucked up, but that seems like an overreaction. She's really angry—maybe angrier than I've ever seen her. I have to fix this—I just have to figure out how.

"Jess…"

"Get the fuck out!"

I sigh and leave her apartment—not because I want to, but because she told me to, and maybe it's time I start listening to her.

CHAPTER TWENTY-FOUR

Jess

THAT ARROGANT BASTARD isn't going to get tears out of me this time.

I wanted this extra time with him. I needed it.

Goddammit, I'm going to have to tell Mitch he was right and he's going to gloat for years, and that isn't even the worst of it. The worst part is that I thought I had more time with Jake, and now I don't, because he was trying to control me and that's number one on Jess's list of unforgivable sins.

I strip and crawl into bed, and in the darkness, try to figure out if he actively deceived me about what he wanted out of these weeks with me, or if I just wanted an excuse to spend time with him so I heard what I wanted to hear.

And why is that, Jess? Why were you so desperate to claw back one more time with him?

"Shut up, brain," I mutter into the darkness, and roll over, determined to sleep.

THURSDAY PASSES IN a blur. It's still raining. This kind of endless rain sucks the color out of the city and usually makes me feel depressed, only I like it today, because the weather actually suits my mood. I snap and snarl my way through my day at the office and swing wildly between thoughts of blocking Jake's number and secret wishes that he'd reappear with a low-carb doughnut.

I really could go for a low-carb doughnut. My emotions are all over the place, and the idea of comfort food sounds pretty fucking good right about now.

I haven't seen Abby for a few days, so I visit her at the hospital after I leave the office. I stay awhile, but her parents are there so the room is crowded. Besides, while Mrs. Herbert fusses over Abby, I feel like an intruder. I'm not really sure I should be there at all while she has her real family in town.

"It is a bit cozy in here with us all here," Marcus chuckles, when I say I should probably go. "Why don't I take you down past the NICU on your way out?"

Oh, hell no. Not today.

"Uh." I scramble for an excuse and come up with nothing. When the moment stretches too long, I raise my chin and just say, "Not today, Marcus. Thanks."

I almost run for the exit after that. Fuck, I wish I'd told Abby about Tristan before. It really does feel too hard now, but sooner or later, she's going to get offended by my lack of enthusiasm to visit the twins. I actually can't wait to see Jessie and Clementine again, but I'm painfully aware that the NICU isn't the place for me to do it. The second those babies graduate to less intense accommodations, I'll make up for lost time, but for now, I might just have to keep myself away.

It rains again on Friday. No one helps me with my umbrella or passes me a coffee when I step outside—and that caffeine would have been super helpful this morning because I've hardly slept.

Also, I'm genuinely pissed off that I miss Jake, but I really do. There's a six-foot, six-inch hole in my life, and I can't believe I became attached so fast, without even hitting the sheets with him. It's beyond irritating, especially when I catch myself constantly watching my phone. It's been a day and a half now. Surely he's going to make contact soon.

As the hours pass, it gradually begins to dawn on me that I did tell Jake I never wanted to hear from him again. Maybe I meant it at the time. Or maybe I just assumed he wouldn't listen.

I'm in a horrible mood all morning, and as she leaves the office after she brings me my lunch, Gina closes my office door behind her and keeps the rest of my staff away for the rest of the day.

Smart woman, that Gina.

Just after 4:00 p.m., my phone sounds and I nearly drop it in my haste to check it.

Mitch: I assume you're busy playing Russian roulette with your emotions tonight—aka hanging out with Jake, in case you didn't get the brilliant analogy. But if you aren't, I'm going to one of those stupid publishing parties you hate and you're welcome to join me.

My heart sinks. I really was hoping it was Jake, and even that hopefulness pisses me off. The last thing in the world I want to do is go to one of Mitch's literary engagements. There's always plenty of free booze, but Mitch is *ultra*-protective of his pseudonym and I always find it all a little ridiculous. I don't even know why he goes to these things given that no one knows who he is or why he's there and he spends a lot of time ignoring the awkward silence after he introduces himself as a writer and then refuses to answer any questions about his books.

I've come to the conclusion he either enjoys the mind-fuck of having this immense secret, or he's trying to keep his own ego in check by forgoing all of the hero worship of his fans. Either one is entirely possible. Mitch is a complex kind of guy. I met him just before his first book deal. I've watched his evolution from barista-living-in-a-shitty-apartment-with-two-other-dudes to Park Avenue penthouse dweller with a penchant for designer clothes and money to burn.

Our long history isn't why I know his pen name. I actually know his story only because in the aftermath of my admission to him about Tristan, I guilted him into telling me. And holy shit, wasn't that a shocking day? I think I gave Mitch emotional whiplash when I told him about my son, but then he dealt that same treatment right back when he told me what he wrote. I'd already read three of his books without even realizing it. Clearly, I'm victim to my own small-mindedness, but never in a million years would I have guessed a guy wrote those stories.

Anyway, I really don't feel like going to something like this tonight, but by the same token, I'm just going home to sulk, and I really hate to let Mitchell down. He doesn't like to take real dates to these parties, so it's one of the duties I've taken on as his official wing-woman slash keeper of all of his secrets.

Jess: I'll come. What time?

Mitch: No plans with Jake?

Jess: I'm definitely not saying you were right to be concerned, but no, no plans with Jake.

Mitch: Siri, remind me to buy bulk Kleenex and Xanax.

Jess: You're so funny. Not.

Mitch: I'll have the driver swing by your place about 8:30 p.m. Wear something fancy.

APPARENTLY, THIS IS one of the swanky parties, because Mitch arrives in a fully stocked limo.

"You look ridiculous," I say, sweeping my gaze over his navy suit. He opens the car door for me, then joins me after I slip inside. The limo pulls out into the traffic. And for the record, Mitch so does not look ridiculous; he looks fantastic and he knows it. But Mitch and I have developed the kind of dynamic I always wished I had with my brother—we constantly give one another shit for no apparent reason.

"I'm so glad you could make it," Mitch says. "I'm genuinely worried about my irresistibility leaving the house like this. Pretend to be my girlfriend if I get mobbed by women, please. Also, what happened with Jake?"

"No comment."

Mitch reaches toward the bar, pours me a glass of wine and hands it to me. I sip it greedily.

"Given I know wine is basically your truth serum, I think I'll ask again when you finish that," Mitch decides. I nudge him playfully with my foot, then sigh.

"He wants forever."

"And the sky is blue," Mitchell says. At my blank look, he shrugs. "Oh, sorry. I thought we were saying things that are fucking obvious."

"I honestly thought he wanted a fling. I'm still not sure if he outright lied to me or if I just heard what I wanted to hear, because I really did not realize he was hoping I'd agree to keep seeing him after he goes back next weekend. I know we've agreed I'm an insensitive cow, but believe me, Mitchell—I'd never have agreed to spend time with him if I knew he was angling for more."

"Sorry, Jess," Mitch murmurs. I give him a pointed look, waiting for the *I told you so*, but he surprises me.

"I really am sorry. I know things with you and Jake are complicated, but I like how happy you are when he's around. And vice versa, I guess. I was really hoping you were right and you two could spend these weeks together without anyone's emotions getting shredded."

"We only had a few days together this time. I'm fine. Frustrated and a little pissed off at him, but I'm fine."

"He means well."

"Of course he does. He's Saint Jake, he always means well. But that doesn't make this any less shitty. What's this dumb party we're going to tonight?"

"It's a book launch."

"What book?"

"My new one."

My jaw drops. For just a split second, he looks a tiny bit self-conscious.

"Mitch, are you fucking kidding me?"

He shrugs and sips his whiskey.

"Why didn't you invite me earlier?"

"I wasn't going to go. I changed my mind this morning, decided it should be a lark."

"But… How does this even work?" I ask him. I'm genuinely confused.

"Well, because the last book did so well, the publisher wanted to throw a party." He shrugs. "It's like a birthday party. But for a book."

"That's not what I meant, and you know it. Do people know it's your book? Are you actually admitting it's you now?"

"Oh, fuck no," he laughs softly. "I think the publisher likes the mystery around my identity as much as I do. My editor is doing a reading. And the crowd will be authors and publishing people, so I'll just mingle and drink like everyone else. When Petra finishes the reading, I'm going to start a standing ovation, and then when we're mingling after, I'm going to constantly say how brilliant this mysterious B. W. Garrison really is."

That's right, Mitchell Cole, my best guy friend, is one of the most successful romance novelists in the world. His books are steamy and emotional and wildly popular—straddling the line between literary fiction and genre romance, read by men and women alike... although, I get the impression his female readership is particularly wild for them. Several of his books have been blockbuster movies, his last release sat on the *NYT* list for months, and if I have to read another fucking article or internet forum speculating about who might be hiding behind the pen name, I'll barf.

The only people in the world who know who he really is are his editor, his lawyer, his agent and me. His family and other friends do know he's a writer, but despite many attempts to convince him to spill the details, they still don't know the genre or his pen name. Despite his ridiculously oversize ego, Mitch is still determined to keep it that way.

"You're such a weird fucker, Mitchell Cole," I say, shaking my head.

He grins at me.

"Guilty as charged. That's exactly why you and I get along so well."

MITCHELL DOES KICK OFF a standing ovation after the reading. He rises, slow clapping with an intensely awed expression on his face, and before I know it, the entire party is on their feet. We mingle afterward, with Mitch introducing himself with a vague reference to working "in publishing," then sidestepping further questions by sparking intense discussions about how brilliant "B. W. Garrison" is. At one point, he even tries to start a rumor that his romance novels are actually the work of a previous winner of the Nobel Prize for Literature, and I nearly spit my drink all over the poor journalist he's chatting with.

As the night drags on, I find myself hanging on Mitch's arm, inadvertently acting as his security guard to ensure he doesn't accidentally spill the secret. Despite his antics, I'm certain that Mitch doesn't give away his real identity because no one would assume this rolling drunk, pretentious idiot is sensitive enough to write the kinds of books B. W. Garrison writes. And when the party starts to wind down, I pour him back into the limo and take him home.

"Are you...sober?" he asks as I unlock his apartment door and help him inside. Even through the thick slur, he sounds shocked about this turn of events. I slip my shoes off, and sigh in relief as my bare feet hit the carpet.

"I am," I admit. Two glasses of wine all night does not a drunk Jess make.

"Why?"

"I didn't feel like drinking."

"There has not been a day when you didn't feel like drinking in all the years I've known you."

I crack a reluctant smile, then admit, "Well, I kind of wanted to look after you, given you have been incredibly drunk since about half an hour after we arrived at the party. Plus—" I sigh heavily, then shrug "—I was scared I'd drunk dial Jake."

"Ah," Mitchell says wisely, then he trips over his sofa and ends up sprawled on the floor of his living room. I walk quickly to his side, then stare down at him. Once I've ascertained that he's not actually injured, I laugh. Loudly. He peers up at me, but his gaze grows sad.

"What's wrong?" I ask him.

"I want you to be happy," Mitch says. He looks like he's going to cry. Oh God. I've seen super emotional Mitch a few times over the years. It's not my favorite side to him at all.

"I am happy," I say stiffly.

"Happiness isn't always uniform across all of the spheres of a life. You can be very happy with your job and your apartment and your lifestyle and your life in general, and even then, still miss someone enough that there's a part of you longing beneath the surface. You say you don't want to be tied to anyone, but whenever Jake Winton enters the picture, you light up like a Christmas tree. Joy radiates out of you. It's beautiful until it ends and then you have to pick up the pieces and I don't understand why you won't consider settling down with him. You two are so beautiful together when you aren't breaking one another's hearts. It's like music, Jess. Like an orchestra is playing in your soul just because he's in the room with you."

"Do you want me to get your laptop?" I ask him impatiently. "If you wrote that down, it would be a great opening paragraph."

"I just love you. You're my best friend."

"No, Mitchell, we are not doing this," I groan. "I love you too but if you get all mushy on me now I'm going to leave you there to sleep."

"Here is fine, actually," he says, and he closes his eyes.

I soften just a little, and crouch to brush his hair back from his forehead as I murmur, "At least let me help you up onto the sofa. You'll have a sore back tomorrow otherwise."

"I feel no pain."

"I'm sure you don't. But you're going to sober up sooner or later, and then trust me, you *will* feel pain if you sleep down there."

He lets me pull him up onto the sofa and then I leave to retrieve a duvet and pillow. By the time I come back to him, he's snoring like a buzz saw. I tuck him in like he's a vulnerable child, then scrawl him a note.

You're an idiot. Text me when you wake up.

Since I'm obviously not going to brunch with Jake now, I decide to sleep in on Saturday morning. My brain does not get the memo, and I'm wide awake and lying in bed staring at the ceiling by 9:00 a.m. when Mitch texts me.

Mitch: Kill me now. Did I embarrass myself last night?

Jess: You sure did. I have the videos to prove it.

Mitch: Can you get your programming team to develop a sarcasm font for texts? I can't tell if you're joking.

Jess: I am joking. You drank the party dry, convinced a few dozen people that you're B. W. Garrison's biggest fan, and then I dragged you home, where you fell over the sofa, soliloquized about all the ways I'm miserable without Jake and then passed out.

Mitch: Sounds like a great night. Wish I could remember it.

Jess: Coffee?

Mitch: I will love you forever if you bring me coffee right now.

Jess: I'm on my way. Just know that if you start that drunken "I love you" shit again, I'm going to pour the coffee on your crotch.

I let myself into Mitch's apartment half an hour later

to find him right where I left him. He's lying on the sofa, eyes closed, but when I approach, he cracks his eyelids open just a little.

"Marry me," he says as he sits up and reaches for the coffee. I groan.

"Not you too."

"Did he propose?" Mitch asks, eyebrows high. There's a crease down the left side of his puffy face from the seam on the sofa and he looks ridiculous, but also miserable enough that I can't tease him about it. Instead, I sigh.

"No. But it was only a matter of time."

"Does he know you never want to get married?"

I glare at him.

"Every person who's ever met me knows I don't want to get married."

"So what makes you think Jake was going to propose?"

"Because I found the ring, remember?"

"I remember that happened two and a half years ago. What's that got to do with you two arguing on Wednesday night?"

"Well, he admitted he stuck around for these weeks because he was hoping to trick me into staying with him long-term," I snap. Mitch tilts his head at me.

"I'm so hungover I can't even remember what day it is, I wasn't actually there for the conversation, and even I know that's not how it went down."

"Maybe *trick* is a strong word," I mutter. "But he was trying to convince me."

"Correct me if I'm wrong, but what I'm hearing is, he told you that he wants to be with you and he wishes you'd give it another shot and then admitted he stayed in the city to spend time with you, hoping you'd feel the same."

"Exactly."

"So what did *you* want out of these weeks?"

"Time with him," I croak.

Mitch gives me a sad look.

"Did you tell him that?"

"Not exactly."

"What did you say to him?"

"I told him I never wanted to speak to him again."

Mitch stretches back out on the lounge, balancing his coffee cup on his chest and closing his eyes.

"And do I correctly guess he's harassed you incessantly ever since, despite your demand that he leave you completely alone? I mean, that would be the logical reaction from a man who's determined to trick you into marrying him. I'm sure he's not doing anything sane like actually doing what you told him to and leaving you alone."

"Shut up, Mitchell."

"I think my work here is done. Thanks for the coffee." He waves his hand toward the door. "You may leave."

"You're an ass," I say, but my gaze is already drifting toward the door.

"You're going to see him now, aren't you?"

"Smugness is not a good look on you, Mitchell." I bend and kiss his cheek.

"Text me later and let me know how it goes!" he calls after me.

"Go fuck yourself!"

I HAIL A cab as I step out of Mitchell's building. When the driver asks me where I'm headed, I rattle off the diner's address.

Jake won't be there anyway. I did tell him I never wanted to speak to him again. We've argued in the past, but I've never said that *before.*

I step out of the cab at the diner just as the sun finally peeks out from behind the clouds. I see Jake immediately—he's sitting at the table in the window. We used to come here when we were together, almost every weekend. We always sat at that table because I like to people watch. Now that I think about it, I can't believe Jake even remembered that.

He's resting his elbows on the table, staring down at the menu as if it's fascinating. His shoulders are slumped, and that new beard doesn't hide the way his lips are turned down.

"So… You assumed I'd come this morning?" I surmise grimly, when I finally walk inside and approach him. Jake raises his gaze, his expression hollow.

"Actually, I was pretty sure you wouldn't come, but I didn't want to risk getting it wrong." He swallows and looks away. "Again." Remorse and regret radiate from him in waves. Even before the apology comes,

I know he means it. "I thought I saw a chance, and I went for it. But I can see that I wasn't listening to you, and I'm sorry."

"You look like shit," I say. Jake looks back up at me, and our gazes lock.

"You don't."

Of course I don't. I'm wearing half an inch of concealer beneath this foundation.

"I can't offer you anything more than this week," I tell him flatly as I slide into the seat opposite him.

"And I can't..." He shakes his head. "Jess, I can't do casual sex. Especially not with you."

"So what do we do, then?" I say. I bite my lip, then say hesitantly, "Maybe we really should say goodbye today."

"I miss you," he whispers. Our hands are both resting on the table, but he makes no move to reach for me. I know it's for the best, but I want the warmth of his skin against mine. In some impossible way, Jake and I have always been connected. Our connection has somehow persisted as emotional and personal, and when there's a physical aspect to it too, it feels complete. It feels perfect.

Maybe it was never just about sex, even for me. It pains me to admit that even to myself and I'm a long way from being able to admit it to Jake. I am, however, ready to make another painful admission.

"I miss you too," I say heavily.

"Is there really no middle ground?" he asks me.

"Such as?"

"We spend this week together. But just this week. And we don't…"

"No fucking?"

"No fucking," he sighs. He looks miserable about it, so I remind him, "It's your rule, Jake. I'm down for it. We can go back to my apartment right now."

"I didn't say I'm thrilled about it," he said wryly, but then he sobers. "I want you. I've never wanted anyone the way I want you. But I can't be with you like that and not want more. Sex means too much to me. You mean too much to me."

"I get it," I sigh, then groan. "Plus I'd be a total ass-hole if I pressured you for sex."

"Like I'm a total asshole because I pressured you for more?"

"No," I admit reluctantly. "Your execution could use some work, but you don't deserve to feel guilty for wanting to build a life with someone."

"So what do we do now?"

I raise my gaze to him. He's staring at me with something magical in his eyes that I wish I could embrace. It's warmth and passion and affection and admiration, and in another life, I'd give him everything he asked for, and everything he wants. More than anything, I want this man to be happy.

But I won't compromise my values, and that means the one thing I cannot give him is me. I've fought too hard to get to where I am, and I simply will not share the controls to my life.

I reach across the table and grab his hand. Jake immediately turns it over and links our fingers together. We are completely still, staring at one another, but the gap between us seems to be shrinking.

"I want to spend time with you," I whisper. "Jake, I want next week with you. But when the time comes for you to fly home, that has to be the end of it. That's all I can give you."

"And you want this even if we don't make love?" he whispers back.

"Even if we don't have sex," I agree, then I exhale and straighten my posture. "Yeah. Okay. Maybe this is the solution. We hang out this week, but it's really just us hanging out. Nothing more than friendship."

Our gazes meet again, then lock. It's a painful compromise for both of us, but it's the only way we can have more time together.

"One more week," he says softly.

"One more week," I agree.

CHAPTER TWENTY-FIVE

Jake

WE FIND OURSELVES in the odd position of not having plans, but not wanting to part, and so Jess and I automatically head back to her apartment together. I can see that we're both still feeling a little uncertain, and even once we're inside, neither one of us seems to know what to do. After a few nervous bouts of laughter, Jess suggests we head up to the rooftop courtyard of her building.

I'm more than happy to enjoy the good weather after a miserably wet week, so we sit on the Adirondack chairs in the shaded area of her courtyard. I know Jess is always extra cautious about sun exposure given her pale complexion, but we probably would have chosen this spot even if she wasn't, because now that the sun's come out from behind the clouds, the direct light has some serious bite to it. But there's a nice breeze blowing up here twenty-five stories in the air, and the temperature is perfect in the shade.

For a while, Jess and I chat about nothing much at

all, about Dad and Elspeth and whether they'll marry, about Marcus and Abby and how they'll find life with twin girls, about Clara's latest antics—specifically, taking a dump in Reba's suitcase while she was in the shower on Thursday. After a brief lull in the conversation, Jess rolls toward me.

"You said you don't do casual sex."

I glance at her hesitantly.

"I don't."

Jess looks a little confused.

"How does that work?"

I laugh softly.

"You make it sound like I've achieved some feat of astounding skill."

"Forgive me for being indelicate, Jacob," Jess says, and then we both laugh, because we're both well aware she's indelicate more often than not. "But I'm familiar with your sex drive. I think it is a feat of astounding skill if you're managing on your own between long-term relationships."

"It's a preference thing," I tell her quietly. "I could probably find hookups if I wanted them."

"You could," Jess interjects. I laugh dryly.

"Thanks. But I don't want them, so I cope."

"Well, how many women have you been with?"

I give her an amused smirk.

"There's no one like you in the whole world, Jessica Cohen."

"Does that mean you won't answer the question?"

"It means that most of my ex-girlfriends don't sit around asking me about my other ex-girlfriends."

"Was I your girlfriend though?" she asks me, wincing. I blink at her.

"Yes. You definitely were."

"Hmm." She doesn't seem entirely pleased by this, but she doesn't argue either. "So there was me...and who else?"

"Are you sure you want to have this conversation?"

"I do. I'm curious. How many?"

"Seven."

"Seven...in total?" Jess sounds aghast. I raise my brows at her.

"Wait, are you actually judging me for what you perceive to be a lack of sexual partners? I didn't hear any complaints about my inexperience when we were sleeping together."

Jess winces.

"Yeah. I'm a hypocrite, sorry. I'm just shocked. Who were they? Who was your first?"

"My high school girlfriend, who then became my college girlfriend."

"Was that Mina? I think I met her once."

"You probably did. We're still friends."

"Of course you are. How did you break up?"

I shrug.

"What works when you're kids doesn't always work when you're adults. We just grew apart. Our breakup was more of a whimper than a bang."

"Who was next?"

"You're really going to ask me about every one of them?"

"There are six other than me, Jake. This isn't exactly going to take long."

"This is so weird."

"You seem surprised that I've surprised you. Honestly, sometimes I feel like you don't know me at all," Jess says, laughing as she stretches her legs out.

"Next was a woman I met at a party my first year of med school. That was my one and only one-night stand. It wasn't for me."

"Why not?"

"I like sex as much as the next person. Hell, I love it. But I love what goes with it just as much as the act itself—the deep and meaningful chats, the cuddles, the sense of partnership. For me, sex without that just isn't the same."

"Hmm," Jess says, then she ponders this for a moment before she asks, "Well, who was next?"

"Quinn, whom you also met."

"She was in your cohort at med school, right?" When I nod, Jess smirks. "Let me guess. You're still friends."

"We are still friends."

"How did you break up?"

"Quinn fell in love with a guy at her gym. She didn't cheat—she was honest about it and ended things with me before anything happened."

"And you're still friends?"

"It's hard to be angry when someone sobs and begs

for forgiveness even when she's breaking up with you."
I shrug. "She married that guy from the gym, by the
way. His name is Andy. We all had dinner when she
was in California a few months ago, so I guess we're
still friends."

"Who was next?" Jess asks. She looks enthralled,
and I'm bewildered.

"This isn't even a little uncomfortable for you,
Jess?"

"I actually hate it when people get possessive about
sex. I can't stand the idea that being with you for any
length of time would give me *any* kind of right to feel
I owned you before or after that. Jealous just reeks of
controlling bullshit to me." She shivers, then shakes
her head. I'm fascinated by this, because she seems le-
gitimately uncomfortable with the idea that she might
have felt jealousy. "So no, I'm not uncomfortable. Who
was next?"

"Anita. She lived in my apartment building when
I was a resident."

"I don't think I met her."

"It didn't last long. We weren't great together."

"And you're not friends with her now?"

That makes me laugh.

"What's with the questions about me being friends
with these women?"

"Saint Jake," she says, smiling softly. "I know the
answer is going to be yes every time."

"Well, it's not 'yes' with Anita," I tell her, bewilderingly triumphant since we're actually talking about the end of one of my relationships.

"Are you Facebook friends?" Jess asks me slowly.

"Yes," I admit. "Does that count?"

"That depends. Are you 'comment on each other's posts' Facebook friends, or 'silently stalk one another when you're bored' Facebook friends?"

"Ah…the former, I think."

"Then yes, it counts. Who's next?"

"Becca."

"Oh, yeah." Jess gives me a thoughtful look. "She was great. I actually thought you two would have been married with a couple of kids by now. I really liked her."

"Really? She hated you."

Jess gasps, and an outraged hand flies to her throat. "She did not."

"She was convinced I was in love with you," I explain, smirking. Jess's indignation fades a little.

"Oh."

"I'm pretty sure I was, by the way," I add, just in case she's still somehow not getting it. "Even way back then."

"Jake."

I shrug. No point pretending otherwise, especially now, when it really is inevitable that we're going to part next week forever.

"Who was next?" she asks me.

"That leaves Vanessa. And, of course, you."

"Who's Vanessa?"

"I met her on a hike out west. We didn't last long."

"Why not?"

"It's complicated."

"Well, Jake, you prefer relationships to hookups so you're always going to have to deal with complicated," Jess informs me. She slides her sunglasses down her nose to peer at me over the top. "Are you and Vanessa still friends?"

"I'm not really sure, actually. She was hurt when we broke up."

"What happened?"

"I think she was in love with me. And she's great, but I couldn't love her back."

Jess finally falls silent. I'm sure part of the reason she actually stops asking me questions is that the next logical one is *Why couldn't you love her back?* and she's probably scared of what the answer might be. After a while, she asks, "Do you want to know how many people I've slept with?"

"No."

"It's more than you."

"I figured."

"A lot more."

"I don't care."

"Plenty of men would. Especially because the truth is I've lost count."

I straighten, impatience rippling over my skin.

"I don't believe that you'd waste a second of your life with someone who judged you for having the sex you wanted and enjoying it. You're fucking incredible in bed because you know what you like and you know how to give, so any guy who's in a position to judge you is probably benefiting from your experience anyway and—" I pause, then frown. "Wait. I am 100 percent certain that you'd tell any guy who made any comment about your sex life to go fuck himself."

"Accurate. On all counts," Jess says, and she slides her sunglasses back up, then stretches her legs out again. I stare at her incredulously.

"So why did you even say that shit?"

"Truthfully?" She turns back to flash me a surprisingly soft smile. "People *have* tried to make me feel shitty about my sexuality in the past. It's been a sore spot lately and I just knew you would never do that. I guess I just wanted to hear you say it."

"Who?"

"Who what?"

"Well, you just pumped me for information about my sex life for ten minutes, and while I have no interest in doing the same to you, I am interested in hearing who tried to make you feel shitty about yourself. So who tried to slut-shame you?"

Suddenly, I see Jess's guard go up, and that reaction is fascinating. I feel like even now, even after all of these years, I'm still collecting data to try to understand her.

Happy to talk freely about sex. Shivers in disgust at the idea that someone might feel jealousy or possessiveness. Not at all happy to talk about the times people have made her feel shitty about her sex life.

I decide that she's going to clam right up on me because I've accidentally taken a conversation where she was completely in her element and shifted it to an area that leaves her feeling uncomfortable. It seems I'm still a long way off from being able to predict her though, because Jess sighs and tucks her hands beneath her head to stare up at the roof again.

"Most recently a friend. It was an accident, I think, but it still hurt. But probably the worst was my parents," she says.

"That's literally the first time I've ever heard you admit you actually have parents," I say, somewhat stunned. I lean forward now, resting my elbows on my knees, fascinated. She gives me an irritated glance.

"Of course I have parents. Everyone has parents."

"I assumed you just willed yourself into existence somehow."

"Ha, ha, Jake."

"So, can I ask about them?"

"I'd rather you didn't."

"You literally just interrogated me about every single sexual partner I've had in my entire life and not once did I refuse to answer you. You know pretty much everything about me. You know my mother and father were both academics. You know Mom died when I was finishing high school. You know it was cancer, you know that's why I chose my career. You're in business with my brother. You know where I went to college and where I did my residency and which brand of toothpaste I use. Until last weekend when you told me about your son, I knew nothing about your life before I met you when you were twenty-two."

"That's not true. You always knew I grew up in Georgia."

"Okay, so now I know two things about your life before you were twenty-two, and one of them I figured out just because of your accent."

"You know I went to college here."

"Jess."

"Jake."

"Are they still alive?" I ask her gently. Her nostrils flare.

"I have no idea."

"You don't speak to them?"

"Never."

"Since when?"

"Since a few weeks after Tristan died."

"What happened?"

She's visibly uncomfortable. Jess adjusts her posture a few times and crosses then uncrosses her legs. Finally, she stares out over the courtyard, looking stubbornly away from me.

"His autopsy results came in. I was a mess, still trying to figure out how I was ever going to live with myself if I couldn't know why I lost him. I overheard my mother and father discussing him while I was out of the room. They were convinced that Tristan died because of my 'loose morals'…that the death of my son was a punishment I brought upon myself. Like his death was just a trial sent to make me turn my life around."

I feel physically ill. Jess glances at me, surveys my expression, then suddenly sits up and shoots the full force of her glare toward me. The space between us feels fraught.

"Don't you dare, Winton," she whispers fiercely. "Don't feel sorry for me. I won't have it."

It's all I can do to stop myself from reaching across and pulling her into my arms. All I can do to stop myself hunting down those bastards to make them apologize. All I can do to stop myself from throwing myself at her feet and worshipping her strength and the way she's built such a successful life after such a rocky start to adulthood.

"Jess," I whisper thickly. "That is just unforgivable."

She shrugs and sinks back onto her chair.

"And that's exactly why I will *never* forgive it."

ON SUNDAY AFTERNOON, Jess and I are walking through Hudson River Park. The afternoon sunlight is golden and warm, and Jess is wearing a huge straw hat and oversize sunglasses, carrying an air of old-school glamour. We're walking in comfortable silence when her phone sounds. She fishes it from her pocket, reads the screen, then lets out an excited squeak and grabs my arm.

"Jake," she squeaks. "Abby is home."

"That's great news."

God, she's beautiful when she's happy. I'm pleased that Abby's been discharged too, but something about Jess's joy right now is particularly infectious. I want to sweep her up in my arms and spin her around. Then I'd lower her to her feet and I'd kiss her until she was breathless. Then I'd throw her over my shoulder and spring back to her apartment, and as soon as we closed the door behind us, I'd strip those little shorts off her and I'd probably go down on her right then and there.

I'm glad we're not sleeping together right now, but that doesn't mean I'm not thinking about it a million times a day. Jess touches me so freely, so affectionately. Every single fucking time she makes contact, I come up with a whole new fantasy. It's a necessary torture, but it's exhausting.

"It will be a while before the twins come home though." Jess's hand falls from my arm and she sighs. "She said they're at a bit of a loss being at home without the babies and since she's supposed to be resting, they can't go out, so she wants me to come for dinner."

"Oh," I say, surprised. "Well, sure, I'll—"

"Come with me?"

"Um…" I clear my throat. "If we go together like this, they might…"

"Make wild assumptions? They probably will. If they dare to broach the subject directly, which they won't, I'll say something exceedingly awkward about the superhot sex they'll assume we're having and then no one will ever, *ever* ask us again."

"So when we were having superhot sex, you didn't want them to know. And now that we're not, you want them to think we are."

"Meh. Whatever works."

We've already turned around and we're walking back toward Marcus and Abby's apartment. So it seems we're doing this, and I'm bewildered by how blasé Jess is about the idea of our friends assuming we're together.

"Let me ask you a question," I say slowly. "Let's say we go to Marcus and Abby's place right now, and they ask why we're there together, and I tell them it's because we dated a few years ago but we're still friends."

Jess doesn't say anything. When I glance at her, I see her face is set in an expressionless mask.

"Fine," she says suddenly. I gape at her.

"Seriously?"

"Sure. It was a dick move of me to insist you keep it a secret in the first place."

"Why did you insist on the secrecy?"

Jess shoves her hands into the pockets of her shorts.

"At first I really didn't intend for that night to become a whole thing," she mutters. "And then even once it did, I was genuinely worried that things would get messy and it would be complicated for me and Paul at work. Mostly though, I wanted to keep it a secret because I knew they wouldn't approve."

"Of us…?"

"Of Slutty Jess and Saint Jake being together, yes," she says impatiently.

"You've got to be fucking kidding. These are your best friends in the world."

"Last Saturday, after you and I had our…disagreement at the rehearsal dinner, Abby made it pretty clear that if our…mutual tension was…" Jess is uncharacteristically lost for words. She gives up and shrugs. "Anyway she just made it clear she did disapprove. So, I was right to be worried." She raises her chin. "Everyone adores you. If they knew how much I hurt you, they'd be pissed. That's the main reason I'm glad they don't know now, but it's a weak reason for me to insist you keep what happened a secret from them. They're your friends too. That was never fair."

"We hurt each other."

"Well, you didn't do anything—" she starts to say, but I cut her off impatiently.

"I didn't listen to you. We've established that. I won't tell them, Jess. Not because I'm ashamed of you or what happened between us, but because I don't want anyone to misinterpret what happened. You fucked up, I fucked up, we fucked up together. But I think maybe…" I nudge her gently with my elbow. "I think maybe we wound up friends anyway. Right?"

"It would seem that way. Friends with a limited-run season, but sure. We're friends now."

"If they ask, we'll just tell them we've finally graduated from frenemies to actual friends. Okay?"

"I *hate* how perfect you are," Jess sighs, shooting me a sideways glance. "It's so annoying."

"I've tried to stop," I say dramatically. "It's just hopeless. Perfection is who I am."

"Want to watch a movie after dinner?"

"Can we eat popcorn while we do?"

"Will you bastardize it with fucking M&M's?"

"I absolutely will."

"Then I'll think about it and let you know."

When we get to Marcus and Abby's place, Marcus opens the door, glances between us, then gives an exaggerated sigh of relief and pretends to wipe fake sweat from his brow.

"Thank God you're both here. I was going to have to be on both teams for Pictionary and I was really not looking forward to it."

"No one said anything about Pictionary," Jess says, feigning alarm.

"We've exhausted the whole Netflix catalog, Jess. Board games are *all* we have left until those babies come home to fill our days."

"Um, we could just get drunk or something?" Jess suggests hopefully.

"Abby can't drink. Pain meds, plus she's expressing breast milk for the girls. It really has come to this."

When Jess and I step into the living area, I see the surprised expression cross Abby's face. She glances from Jess to me, and her gaze grows thoughtful.

She was incredibly ill on Saturday. Whatever she said to Jess, she does deserve a bit of grace, but...

...the idea of anyone making Jess feel less-than makes me furious, but especially knowing it was Abby. Jess was willing to put herself through hell for this woman and her family last week. She simply deserves better from her friends.

The urge to say something to Abby is almost overwhelming, but I know that Jess wouldn't want me to.

Partly because Abby's been through a lot and she's likely still a little fragile herself, but mostly because Jess is more than capable of fighting her own battles. She'd hate for me to intervene here, so I won't.

When Marcus and Jess get distracted in the kitchen ordering takeout, Abby waves me over to the sofa where she's resting. I sit opposite her, and she says hesitantly, "I can't believe I'm saying this, but I think I might have hurt Jess's feelings last weekend, before everything went haywire with the twins. When Marcus tried to take her down to the NICU the other day, she didn't even want to go."

"You should talk to Jess about this, Abby," I say gently.

"I tried," Abby says unevenly. She blinks rapidly. "I mean, I tried to apologize for... I said something, and I think it hurt her. But when I tried to say sorry, she cut me off, and now I just really don't know if I should raise it again or leave it. I think that maybe the reason she doesn't want to see the girls now is that she's angry with me."

Ah, hell. Looks like I'm doing this anyway.

"Jess would do anything for you," I tell Abby quietly. "I think she's proven that."

"She has," Abby murmurs.

"She's the *best* woman I know, Abby."

Abby's gaze lifts to mine.

"I know that too." She gnaws her lip. "It kills me to think I might have hurt her, Jake. How do I make it better?"

"I'm not brave or stupid enough to get involved in Jess's business when I know she wouldn't want me to," I say carefully. "But… I will say this—I'm just glad that you know she's a marshmallow underneath all of the bluster."

"I really need to just apologize and make her hear it," Abby sighs, then flicks a glance at me and asks curiously, "*Is* there something going on between you two?"

"No. We're just friends." My gaze gravitates back to Jess, just like it always does.

"But that's not what you want, is it?" Abby says gently. I turn back to smile at her sadly.

"It's the best Jess can offer me, and I guess I'll take her any way I can get her."

CHAPTER TWENTY-SIX

Jess

"COME SEE THE NURSERY," Abby blurts as we finish eating. She looks nervous so I'm wary, but then again, any diversion Abby might want to take would buy me a few more precious Pictionary-free minutes, so I rise to follow her anyway.

Has it really come to this? My friends have kids and suddenly I'm spending my weekends playing fucking Pictionary? Given Mitchell has often accused me of being lame and boring on weekends when I hit the clubs with him only once, he must never know how far I've fallen.

I walk beside Abby as she leads the way to what used to be her bedroom. She and Marcus have obviously put a lot of effort into redecorating the space. Now, it's painted in soft yellow shades, there's a mural of frolicking woodland animals on one wall and two precious little baby beds set up in the center of the room. Abby walks gingerly, no doubt still healing from her surgery, but as soon as we're in the room she pushes the door closed behind me.

"I'm sorry," she blurts. I frown at her.

"What for?"

"In the car on Saturday on the way to the hotel to get ready for the wedding. About Jake and you. I think maybe I hurt you, and I really didn't mean to."

"You didn't hurt me," I say stiffly, even as my gut twists, but I try to laugh it off. "Honestly, Jake and me? What a ridiculous idea—"

"Jessica," Abby says, and she gives me a pained look. "Don't do that."

"What?"

"You're the most confident woman I know."

"Well, of course I am. I'm amazing." I'm not even playing. I believe this to my very core. Someone wise once said that there's nothing stronger than a woman who has rebuilt herself. I like to think I'm living proof of that. Just as I love the life I've worked so hard for, I love the woman I've become.

"Exactly. So don't for a second suggest you're some-how not good enough for a guy like Jake."

"That was definitely not what I was doing. But surely you can see we're mismatched. Mr. Perfect out there and…" I shrug, then open my arms wide before I point back to myself. "Me. It would definitely end in tears." As it already did, and probably will again next week. But speaking of tears, Abby's big brown eyes are suddenly full of them. I'm going to give her the ben-efit of the doubt and blame postbirth hormones. She reaches for me and brings me close for a hug.

"I wasn't trying to say you and Jake weren't a good

idea. I really just meant that the timing would have been off, given it was the night before the wedding. I can't stand the thought that my stupid, careless comment made you hate me."

"Abby," I laugh softly, pulling back from her. "I could *never* hate you. Why would you even say that?"

"You didn't want to go see the girls after you visited on Thursday," she says, gnawing her lip.

"Abby." I close my eyes briefly, then force myself to explain. "Hospitals are tough for me, okay? I don't want to talk about why, but that wasn't because of anything you said about Jake."

"Promise?" I can see she's curious, but she doesn't press the issue.

"I promise."

"You just deserve every good thing, Jess."

I pull away to look right into her eyes as I reassure her, "My life looks exactly the way I want it to. Exactly the way I always dreamed it would. Jake has been a good friend to me, but that's all he is."

"And all he'll ever be?" Abby looks so sad about this I'd almost marry Jake just to bring her smile back. Almost. But not quite.

"Yeah," I tell her softly. "That's all he'll ever be."

AFTER A GAME of Pictionary that might actually almost be fun, Jake and I came back to my place and now he's microwaving popcorn. There's a bag of M&M's on the counter beside it and a cup of melted butter beside that. I'm sitting right on the counter, watching him warily.

I'm still hoping to find a way to make sure those three things do not mix because I'm not at all convinced it's the magic formula for happiness Jake thinks it is.

"Jake. What did you say to Abby?" I ask him suddenly.

"About?" Jake prompts me.

"About what she said to me on Saturday."

"Why?"

"She apologized. When she dragged me in to see the twins' nursery."

Jake is silent for a moment. He's folded himself pretty much in quarters to bend low enough to watch the bag of popcorn as it circulates in my microwave on the countertop. When he glances back at me, I see the truth in his eyes.

"Before you rip me a new asshole, she asked me about it. I just told her to talk to you."

"If I wanted her to apologize, I would have asked her to apologize."

"I know."

"So why did you—"

"I told you, Jess. She brought it up." He links his hands behind his head and exhales. "I love Abby like a sister and I'm very conscious that she's been through a lot but knowing that she hurt you made me crazy. I wanted to talk to her. I wanted to make her apologize. I've got your back, and I always will. In fifty years' time if I hear rumors the nursing home isn't giving you the good pudding, I'm going to want to shuffle over there on my walker to get it for you myself. But I won't, and do you know why?"

"I feel like that's a rhetorical—"

"Because I know that you don't need or want me to fight your battles for you. So even when I want to, and even when I'm tempted to, I won't do it. But what I will do is mix these delicious M&M's in with this popcorn so you can experience the next best thing to sex you'll find in this lifetime."

He snatches the M&M's off the bench, dumps them into the bag of popcorn, then pours the melted butter over the top. I faux-gag, and Jake takes advantage of my open mouth to press a buttery, salty, chocolaty kernel of corn right on in there.

His finger is in my mouth. I catch it, and suck it gently, ignoring the popcorn altogether. He doesn't move his finger, so I suck again and then twirl my tongue around it, because apparently, I can't help myself. Jake groans, and gently drags his finger away.

"Wench," he mutters.

"You stuck it in there," I remind him, around the mouthful of popcorn. I chew, then stare at him. "That's it? That's what all of the fuss is about? It's gross."

Jake grabs his chest in false horror.

"Jessica! How dare you! That's the love of my life you're talking about."

"You're welcome to it, then." I grimace as I swallow. "Yeah, that's far too salty *and* too sweet *and* too buttery for me. All kinds of wrong. No thanks."

Jake grins and starts to walk past me toward the

couch. I hook my ankles around his waist and he stops, then turns back to me.

"Thanks," I say softly. "For talking to Abby. And for not talking to Abby too."

He nods, and maybe I want to kiss him in this moment more than I've wanted anything else in my life. I want to taste the salt and the butter and the chocolate right out of his mouth just because sometimes he just gets me. I do feel for him—I feel affection and gratitude and something that's already bordering on adoration. I want, more than anything, to find a way to express that to him. I even lean forward and lick my lips, but then I groan and unlink my feet from around his waist so that I can gently nudge him away.

"I just want you to know that not having sex with you sucks," I mutter as I slide off the bench. Jake laughs and slides his arm around my shoulders, then places an innocent kiss against my forehead.

"I actually think that's the nicest thing you've ever said to me."

THE WEEK THAT follows is awful and amazing all at once.

I start off thinking I'll play it cool, but quickly wind up devoting every second outside of my working hours to Jake. For the first time in memory, I even skip the gym. I am *all* Jake, *all* the time. Now that we've done it once, there seems to be no reason for us not to visit Abby and Marcus, so we even do that together.

When Abby hesitantly asks if I want to come visit

the girls with her on Wednesday, I say yes, despite her fifteen awkward reminders that it's okay if I don't want to.

I kind of do want to see the girls again. Besides, it's going to be some time before Jessie is discharged, so if I want to see my little namesake, I'm going to have to learn to deal with her temporary environment. I arrange to meet Abby there in the afternoon after Jake is done having lunch with his dad. That's partly because I want the buffer just in case the NICU gets to me again, but it's also because I'm carelessly, greedily soaking up every second of his presence before he goes home.

And in the end, the NICU seems far less overwhelming. Maybe it's because I'm well rested. Maybe it's because the first shock of all of the tiny, sick babies has passed. Maybe it's because talking to Jake about Tristan has made me strong. Whatever the magic elixir is, I'm grateful for it.

Two drums beat beneath the music of my week with Jake. One sounds that our time is running out, and that makes me feel frantic and urgent to be with him. The other sounds a warning; that this has to be the last time we flirt with danger like this. We both need to move on, and this time around, we have to do so in a way that gives us both closure. Maybe I've spent at least some of the time since we parted still pining for him, but I'm pretty sure he's done exactly the same, given what he said about this Vanessa woman.

But enough is enough, this has to be the end.

Every minute we spend together is going to make

our inevitable separation harder. And yet, I want every minute I can steal with him. I'd prefer it if some of those minutes were spent beneath my sheets, but even when it comes to that, I get where Jake is coming from.

Because I feel it too—the way our contact is about more than just skin against skin. Even when we hug now or our hands brush, I sense the way that our souls strain toward one another.

Besides, maybe the reason our relationship ran so out of control last time was the potent combination of great sex and this great camaraderie we've developed. Maybe, if we keep our clothes on, we can keep cooler heads too.

Then again, I'm not sure how cool our heads are, given it's now Friday and we had breakfast before I came into the office, we've been texting all day and we already have plans for dinner. The week has flown by in a blur of shared meals and light chats and moments I know I'll be replaying in my memory for years to come.

I'm trying to concentrate on clearing out my chaotic inbox, but I see that Jake has sent me a text, so I pick my phone up and open the image.

Jake: I don't care what you say. Dogs are definitely better than cats, and this is why.

The image below the message is of Clara, who is sleeping in a dog bed, using what I have to assume is Jake's sweater as a pillow.

Jake: She dragged this sweater out of my closet and put it in her bed. She obviously misses me. If she was a cat, she'd probably be busy staring out a window and wouldn't have noticed I'm gone.

Jess: If she was a cat, she wouldn't be slobbering all over your sweater. So there's that.

I suddenly wish it was winter. If it was, Jake would have brought sweaters with him for this trip, and then he might accidentally leave one at my apartment. I'd do exactly what Clara is doing. I'd keep that sweater forever, and it would join my PMS pajamas and low-carb ice cream in my comfort routine.

I scroll back up through our text history. It's two weeks now since he walked into that rehearsal dinner and turned my world upside down. Twelve days since we started texting again. There's humor in our digital chats, but there's also a fierce undertone of affection.

Jake knows me. He knows parts of my messy history. He knows I'm a deeply flawed individual. He likes me anyway, and I believe that right to my very soul.

I set the phone down and try to look at my monitor, but my vision is blurry. I rise and quickly shut my office door, then sit back down at my desk and let a few tears leak out as I acknowledge the coming storm.

I'm a woman who knows grief. It's defined so much of my life so far.

I can smell it in the air... I can *feel* it coming. Tomorrow night, Jake is going to get on that plane and leave me, and I'm going to have to mourn our connection all over again. It was unbelievably difficult the first time. This time around, I'm not entirely sure how I'm going to survive it.

We've shared a single kiss since his return, but I feel closer to him than I ever did. I'm entrenched in intimacy with Jake again, only this time it's on an emotional level.

But I have to stay true to the promises I made myself when I was eighteen years old. And so even as I dread the grief, and even as I fear it, I know I'll have to accept it, because Jake and I were simply never meant to be.

CHAPTER TWENTY-SEVEN

Jess

OUR ORIGINAL PLAN was to go out for dinner for Jake's last night in town, but I suggested we order in instead. I'm glad he didn't ask why, because I didn't have an excuse ready, and never in a million years would I want to tell him the truth. I wanted to stay in tonight so we could just be together, alone. I wanted him to myself. I wanted the intimacy of an empty room—the freedom to just be myself in a way that I don't have anywhere else...except when I'm alone with him.

Now, Jake is sitting on one end of my sofa and I'm lying across the rest of it, my feet in his lap. This afternoon, I planned out how we'd sit on my "mini-sofa," just so we could wind up touching one another like this—it's such innocent contact, but important contact. If I can't have him inside me, I'll soak up how it feels to have my skin against the warmth of his body. I didn't even want a glass of wine tonight. I didn't want to numb the feelings or blur the memories. Twenty-four hours from now, he's going to be on his way to the airport. I have no idea how I'm even going to function next week.

He's massaging my feet now, casually, as if he doesn't even realize he's doing it. Actually, I'd believe that; I'm certain that Jake gives without conscious thought sometimes. We've been chatting for a few hours, and I'm doing that rambling, relaxed thing I hardly ever do with other people. I'm speaking without thinking. I'm too at ease with Jake. That's partly what brings me undone.

"...initial public offering of our shares. We just need to sort out—" I break off, and Jake turns and raises his eyebrows at me. Shit. I didn't mean to tell him about this. Inevitably, I'm going to have to bite the bullet and spend more time over there, and I didn't plan on clueing him in to that arrangement. It would be unforgivably cruel to give him false hope. "There are just some issues we have to resolve first," I finish. Jake releases my foot and waves toward me, indicating I should go on. "We've got a lot of corporate customers now and that pays the bills, but our take-up within the tech industry is still too low and that means our reputation isn't where it needs to be to float shares."

"So how do you fix that?" Jake asks me, quietly curious.

"Marketing. Advertising. Focusing on sales. And... networking," I say. "Mostly the latter. We just need to do more networking, that's all."

"Networking in...New York?" he asks cautiously. "You have another office, don't you?"

Shit. I should have known he'd connect the dots. Jake is smart—like freakishly smart. Not that a person even needs to be a genius to figure out that the major tech center in the United States is likely no more than twenty minutes from his house.

"Yes. We have a West Coast office."

"So… What are you saying?"

"One of us will just have to spend some more time on the West Coast."

I shrug the question off, then try to find a way to change the subject, but I miss the opportunity because Jake immediately asks, "*Where* on the West Coast?"

I swallow and look away.

"Silicon Valley."

"Well, obviously Marcus can't go."

"No. Not now."

That was my plan twelve months ago. I was trying to figure out how to convince him to go. I already knew he'd have resisted, given Abby and his family are here, but when he and Abby fell in love, I had to give up the plan altogether.

"And it won't be Paul."

Jake's brother *is* a card-carrying genius, but there's no denying that he's awkward as fuck.

"No."

"So *you'll* be spending some time on the West Coast in the…what? The long-term future?"

"I don't know," I say, dismissively. I sit up and reluctantly lift my feet away from Jake. He tilts his head at me.

"Jess. Are you seriously telling me you'll be regularly visiting *Palo Fucking Alto* in the near future? You do realize I live there, right? My house is in a suburb that's literally called *Old* Palo Alto. Your Silicon Valley office must be…what? Fifteen minutes away?"

"I know," I say, croaking the words out. I'm waiting for Jake to do one of two things: get angry with me for not mentioning this sooner, or leap on what looks like an opportunity for us to continue to see one another. He surprises me when he draws in a deep breath, then says quietly, "I won't say it, Jess. You've made your decision clear."

I squeeze my eyes closed.

"Thanks. You know our problem isn't even geography," I croak. "Our problem is us. You want things I can never give you."

"Can I ask you something?"

"You may as well."

"You've missed me, right?"

"You know I have."

"And the last few weeks?"

"Have been magical," I say unevenly. "But nothing has changed, and that's exactly why we put a hard full stop on things tomorrow."

"I honestly don't get you, Jess," he says, a hint of frustration in his voice now. "You don't want a relationship, but you miss me when I'm gone. You don't have to miss me, you know. You don't have to miss us."

"What does it look like?" I croak. He stares at me, his gaze impenetrable. "Two years from now. Say we didn't go our separate ways on Sunday. What does it look like?"

"We're busy but we're happy. Clara drives you insane, but you love her. You've tried hiking just to make me happy and you secretly loved it but you won't admit it. I stopped eating Oreos the proper way because it started grating your nerves after a while, but I still enhance my popcorn with delicious M&M's because a guy has to eat. We sleep in on Sundays and when I get home at 4:00 a.m. because I left our bed to say goodbye to a patient, you ask me to wake you up when I get home so you can make sure if I'm okay."

God. It's beautiful. It's everything I never thought I wanted.

"And where do we live?" I whisper. Jake's gaze is soft.

"Wherever you want."

"Together?"

"Definitely. Assuming that's what you want too."

I close my eyes.

"Jess. If you want to be with me, you can be with me. I'm already yours," Jake whispers. I feel him shifting closer to me on the lounge and then he tucks a lock of hair behind my ear.

"You need this to be more serious than I could ever allow it to be."

"When we're apart, it feels like my heart is beating outside my body," Jake says, sighing sadly. "I don't know how things could be any more serious than they already are."

"I just mean that you want more from me than I can give you."

"All I want is to be with you, Jess."

"But you'd want more eventually," I say, suddenly impatient. I open my eyes and my gaze is hard on his face. "You'd probably want more from me by the time we finished this conversation if I gave you any indication that I was weakening on this. You want to tie me down. And that's the last thing in the world I will ever allow you to do."

"You make it sound like I'm trying to control you," he says, confusion flickering across his features. "Now, that's the last thing in the world I want—"

"It is what you want!" I exclaim. God, I want him and I adore him but right now he's just sitting way too close to me and I feel crowded. I stand, but only so I can turn to stare down at him. "You want to own me. The kind of commitment you need would be suffocating to me."

Jake stares up at me. He makes no move to rise, and he doesn't seem angry or even frustrated. He's just staring at me, thinking. Then he nods, almost to himself.

"Last week, when I decided to stay, and I hoped I could change your mind, I had it all planned out in my mind," he says quietly. "We'd spend two weeks together. You'd fall back in love with me. I'd propose before I left, we'd be engaged and I'd go home to California, pack up my life and come back here to be with you. I even had Reba send the ring over, because yes,

I still have the ring I bought you two and a half years ago. I told myself I'd get around to selling it or giving it away, but I never would have. It was *perfect* for you—I love the way green looks against your skin..." His voice drops to a whisper. "The way green looks against your hair. I kept it because I couldn't let go of the dream that one day, you'd let me give it to you."

He rises, and I take a step back. I'm angry because this was exactly what I feared all along, but I'm also confused by a sharp pang of guilt.

"I *knew* it—" I start to say, but he gently rests his hands on my shoulders.

"That ring means nothing. Less than nothing. I saw it in a window, and it reminded me of you and I already knew I wanted a life with you, so I bought it. It was always meant to be a gift, a gesture to show you how I feel about you. But right now, if I thought it would change your mind, I'd go get the ring from my hotel and I'd help you smash the fucking thing. This isn't about a ring or even marriage, Jessica. Whether you're willing to talk about it or not, this is about something else altogether." He sighs heavily, then bends to kiss my cheek. I don't pull away, so he cups my cheeks in his hands, and he stares right into my eyes as he murmurs, "I just wish you could tell me what it is that holds you back from me."

"There's nothing—" The compassion in his gaze is breathtaking. And I'm so tempted to talk to him— just so he understands that it isn't him, it *really* is me. But Jake already knows more than enough about those

days. And when people understand your past, they
know how to manipulate your future. I learned that
the hard way already and it's a lesson I do not need to
learn again. "You should go."

The words are flat and hard. Jake sighs, and drops
his hands form my face. He gives me a resigned smile.

"This is it, isn't it?"

I harden myself. I draw in a deep breath to fill my
lungs and I straighten my shoulders.

"Were you still hoping to change my mind when
you came here tonight?"

"You've made your point more than clear, so I
wasn't even going to ask you again. But honestly? I'll
probably be hoping you change your mind until I die,"
he sighs, raking his hand through his hair. It's sticking
up all over the place now. His gaze is quietly devastated, but his hair is wild.

"Then it's probably best for us not to draw this out
any further. We're on very different pages, aren't we?"

I sound so professional. I actually sound like I do
when I talk to staff or consultants—like I'm only mini-
mally invested in the outcome. Jake scoops his wallet
and phone up off my coffee table and walks to the door.

He pauses, his hand on the door handle, then glances
back at me.

"Goodbye, Jessica."

"Goodbye, Jake," I say.

The door closes behind him, and I'm still standing
in my living room.

I'm alone. I've been alone for a long time—but this

is the first time since my grandmother died that I've really felt it. It's certainly the first time in a very, very long time that alone has felt anything like lonely.

I sink back onto the sofa and reach for the remote. I decide I'll put some trashy reality TV on and tune out, but I don't actually do that.

I just sit staring at the TV, trying to squash the urge to chase Jake, even as time begins to pass and the urge builds and builds. But images flick through my mind—of Jake's kindness to me, of the way he's respected my wishes, of the way he shows his affection to me...of the hurt in his gaze when we said goodbye.

That last one is the kicker. I drop the remote back onto the coffee table, scoop up my handbag and go.

I can't offer Jake anything but the truth, but maybe that truth will bring him some comfort. I've convinced myself over the years that hiding my past behind a wall meant others couldn't control me, but for the first time, it occurs to me that Jake would *never* use my past to manipulate me.

That's just not who he is. When I've given him my burdens, he never once weaponized them—all he ever did was offer to carry them.

CHAPTER TWENTY-EIGHT

Jake

I'M BACK AT the hotel room, lying on the bed staring at the ceiling—which is what I've been doing for over an hour. This moment was always inevitable, but that doesn't take away from the disappointment. I remember how it felt after Jess and I broke up the first time… how deeply I missed her. How sharp the sadness was. We were together for months then, really together, sharing our bodies and our lives. This time it's only been a few weeks of friendship, but I'm just starting to realize that my brilliant plan to keep things casual by staying out of the bedroom has been a miserable failure but losing her all over again is going to be worse even than the first time around.

My phone sounds—it's a text message. I know it's not going to be her, and for a minute, I consider ignoring it. Maybe it's Dad butt-texting me or Paul sending me some random snap from the last few days of his New Zealand trip.

After a minute or two, it occurs to me it might actually be the clinic trying to get in touch about a patient, and I sigh and reach for the phone.

Jess: I'm at your hotel. Can I see you?

I know she's not coming to tell me she's changed her mind. I don't know why she's here, and I don't hold anything like hope that it means we can be together.

But I can't say no to her. I love her too much to turn her away.

She'll need a key to get up to my floor, so I go down to the lobby to get her. Our eyes lock as the elevator opens and Jess silently steps inside, but we don't speak as it travels back up the twenty-six floors to my room. We don't even speak as we walk side by side along the corridor. As soon as we step inside, she rests her handbag on the hook on the wall, then walks to my bed and sits on the edge.

She holds herself with dignity and pride, her chin high, her shoulders back. Even so, I can see that Jess is distressed. It's in the lines around her mouth and the little wrinkle that's formed between her eyes.

"I don't know where to start," she admits. "It's so hard for me to talk about. And…" She raises her gaze to mine. "I just want to explain it all to you so you can understand, but nothing has changed. We still can't be together."

She's agitated and wound up. I don't think she even wants to talk to me about whatever she has to share right now. Or maybe she does, but now isn't the time.

I want to reconnect with her. I want to express my love for her. I want to worship her. I walk to the bed and kneel before her to rest my hands on her shoulders.

"We can be together tonight, can't we?" I murmur, bringing one hand to her face, where I run my knuckle gently down her cheek…to her neck. Maybe I'm completely misreading the mood here, but if I am, I know she'll tell me.

Jess gives a confused whimper as my hand comes to a rest just above the curve of her breast.

"What are you doing?" she whispers thickly. "I thought you didn't want this."

"You *know* I wanted this," I whisper back. "I just thought that we could make the separation easier if we tried to keep sex out of the equation. But that's not going to work, is it? We were apart for an hour and I had a taste of what's coming, Jessica. When I go home tomorrow, I'll be leaving a part of my soul behind— nothing we do tonight can change that."

"Are you sure?" she asks me. I lean forward and kiss her gently but pull back before it can escalate.

"Do *you* want this?" I ask her gently. "We can just talk if you want to. Or we can do both. You're in control here. You just tell me what you need."

"I want you to make love to me," Jess says, her voice breaking. "Jake, I want you to make love to me. Please."

I kiss her properly then, from my uncomfortable position on my knees beside the bed. She's uncharacteristically coy—her mouth soft against mine, her tongue hesitant when she touches mine. I run my hands over her shoulders and her neck and then cup her cheeks, the movements gentle and reverent. Jess tilts her head back, and I know that means she wants me to kiss her neck, so I slide my way down to comply. I kiss her everywhere—along the neckline of her shirt, all across her neck, over her cheeks and even her eyelids. Then I help her back into the center of the bed, and together we slowly remove her clothing. The shirt goes first, then her skirt, and soon she's lying on the bed in just her lacy white bra and panties.

My mouth goes dry. I stare at her for a minute, and she lies beneath my gaze, unashamed. My eyes roam over her abdomen, and I see it now—the collection of faded stretch marks around her belly button, and the trio of scars that I think I remember her telling me were from a laparoscopic appendectomy.

In my mind, Jess's body is perfect—but no one is really perfect. She's scarred, this woman, but when you love someone, you love them scars and all. That's why I bend to kiss her belly, kissing my way across the stretch marks and the tiny, pale surgical marks.

Then I kiss her nipples through the bra, and I kiss her over her panties, but to her obvious frustration, I don't remove her underwear yet. I want to draw this out. Maybe I even *need* to draw it out.

When I glance up to her face, I find her staring at me, her pupils wide and her breath coming in pants. I shift so that I can kiss her lips again, and she's bolder now, much more like the Jess I remember, kissing me with want and need and demands. After a while, she breaks away and says unevenly, "Take your clothes off. I want to see you too."

I do as I'm told, throwing off my T-shirt and jeans and briefs, and I come back to her naked. I cup her breasts through her bra and then kiss the valley between them, then I slide my way down to the junction between her legs.

"I like these," I murmur, running my fingertip over the lace of her panties. She sucks in a breath, then laughs shakily.

"I'll like them a lot better when you take them off me."

"Soon," I say, and then I take my time—touching her through and around the lace, licking and kissing and sucking her. I know I've riled her up when her hands sink into my hair and she's holding me in place.

That's when I slide her panties off to throw them across the room. Jess is wet and swollen, and the shine of her sex is all over her folds. I can feel my dick weeping against my stomach as I bend to bury my face against her, focusing my tongue and my lips over the swollen bud of her clit. She bends her knees on either side of my face, and I shift my hand so that I can slide one…two…three fingers into her. Loosening her up. Stretching her for me. I can't wait too much longer. I want this too much. I want *her* too much. There's something I just need to finish right here, and then I can—

"Jake!" she moans, long and loud, as she suddenly

stiffens and cries out. She collapses on the bed, and I climb up to rest on the pillow beside her, watching as she recovers.

Jess is so beautiful like this: her cheeks flushed, her features relaxed, the curve of a smile on her face. I reach to touch her lips with my fingertips just as she opens her eyes. The haze clears, and just like that, she's already hungry again. I run my finger around the shape of her lips, then dip it inside like I did the other night with the popcorn. When she sucks on my fingertip, my dick jumps.

"Enough of that," I laugh weakly as I reach to kiss her. "I want to be inside you."

"I want that too," she whispers back. I lean away from her to scoop my wallet up off the nightstand so I can fetch a condom, but as soon as I bring it back to the bed, Jess scrambles away and runs to her own handbag.

And just like that, something shifts in my mind and I see a pattern I never really noticed at the time: when Jess and I were together, we *always* used her condoms.

It's smart and it's safe for a woman to provide the protection, given she bears more chance of consequences if there are any mishaps. But Jess and I had known each other for years. And were together for *four fucking months*, but even at the end, she was still the first to reach for her own condoms every single time we made love.

I wanted to broach the subject of finding other contraception so we could be together skin to skin, but I never got around to it. Maybe on some level I knew this was an issue for her. Maybe I even knew that pointing out how long we'd been together and asking for a deeper commitment would freak her out.

Now, she comes back to the bed, condom in her shaking hand. Our eyes meet. There's shame in her gaze. I've never seen this look on her.

"Do you want to talk about it?" I ask her gently.

She looks down at my erection, then shakes her head with some determination.

"Not now. Later."

She throws the condom onto the bed beside me, then rises onto her knees. I'm not expecting this—but there's sudden heat and warmth around me as she takes me into her mouth. She gets me good and wet, and she's working me with her tongue and her hands and *very* quickly, it's almost too much.

"Jess," I say breathlessly. She looks up, my dick still in her mouth, and I groan and gently pull her up toward me. I scoop the condom up from the bed but pass it to *her* to apply it.

Our eyes lock again, and hers fill with tears.

"Thanks," she croaks, and then she blinks the tears away and slides the condom over me.

"How do you want this?" I ask her gently, brushing her hair back from her shoulders. She's still got the bra on, so I sit up and gently unclip it. Jess throws it onto the pile of clothes beside the bed, then climbs on top of me and guides me into her body.

Time is a funny thing. It can play with your memories, making moments feel richer or poorer than they really were. I remembered that sex with Jess was uniquely special—that our connection was vibrant. I thought, perhaps, that my memory was playing tricks on me—romanticizing things.

I realize now that I was wrong about that. In fact, my memories didn't do these moments justice, because I forgot that being with her is transcendent. I forgot how it felt like a union of souls as well as a union of bodies.

I love you. I love you so much.

I can't say the words now. I don't want to upset her...to distract her as she chases her pleasure. But I decide that I will say them tonight. I've never known when to push Jess and when to just let her be, but on this, I realize, I need to say the words, even if it makes her angry...even if it makes her feel uncomfortable.

For now, she's got one hand on my shoulder, and the other resting on my waist. She pauses, letting her body adjust, then she begins to work against me. She stares down into my eyes, that brief moment of shame long gone.

"You feel so good," she whispers thickly. "I love your cock, Jake. I love how hard you are... I love the way you fill me. You stretch me."

I'm way past the point of intelligible dirty talk. Maybe we'll go another round later and I can make it up to her. For now, all I can manage is a strangled groan, and Jess laughs, then bends to kiss me deeply. She leans down onto me, pressing her breasts into my chest, her nipples pulled into tight buds that brush against mine.

I wish this could last all night, but it's just not going to. Jess is already whimpering as she moves, and I'm thrusting up into her, urgency taking over.

"Jess," I whisper. "Are you close? I need—"

"Now," she chokes. "I'm going to come too."

The pleasure bursts over me, sending sensation across my nerve endings through my torso and my spine and into my limbs. Jess cries out, and then after a few violent jerks against me, collapses to lie across my chest. I've all but dissolved into a puddle on the bed, but I wrap my arms tightly around her and hold her close while we catch our breath.

After a few minutes, she kisses me sweetly, then moves to use the restroom. I tie off the condom and throw it into the waste basket, and I turn off the lights and we reunite in the bed. I'm sated and tired and conflicted—so happy to be with her again, so miserable that it's all going to end again tomorrow.

But most of all, I'm ready to tell her how I feel.

CHAPTER TWENTY-NINE

Jess

"I HAVE TO SAY IT," Jake whispers, his breath hot against my ear. "Let me say it, Jess. Just once, and then you can forget you ever heard the words."

I know exactly what he wants to say. He hinted at it on the rooftop that day when we talked about his exes, but he's never said the words to me directly. And although it makes me nervous, it turns out that after all we've shared these last few weeks, I actually want to hear him say the words. I squeeze my eyes closed and nod once.

"Jessica Cohen, I love you. I have loved you... God, probably ever since I saw you in those fucking short-shorts in 'the incubator' in Brooklyn when you were just a tiny baby CEO with the gleam of megabucks in your eye. And no matter what you go and do for the rest of your life, wherever I am in this world, a part of me will be missing you, and all of me will be loving you."

So many emotions bounce around inside me as he speaks. I'm soaring. *He loves me.* I'm drowning. *He loves me.* I'm ashamed. *I let him love me.* I'm sad. *Maybe I even love him too, but we just can't be to-gether.*

"It wasn't just the ring," I blurt. I feel him stiffen a little, but his arms are still locked in place around me. "I didn't just break up with you because I knew you were going to propose. I'd already been thinking about it."

"Why?"

"The… We went to the theater with Paul and Izzy and Abby. Remember?"

"I do," he says slowly. "We saw that stupid play. About the robots."

"God, it was bad."

"*So* bad."

"When we were waiting at the bar that night, you said something about kids."

"I did? I don't even remember that."

"Abby didn't know we were together, obviously. She was teasing you about some girl she wanted to set you up with…joking about how you and this woman would get married and have two-point-four kids. And you said something about 'Why stop at two-point-four? I want a whole football team like Izzy's parents.'"

"So I made a stupid joke about having kids. Why was that such a big deal?"

"I don't want more kids. I've…" I draw in a sharp breath, then motion toward my stomach. "I had a tubal ligation. I'm sure of this, Jake. I'm not having any more children. Not now, not ever."

"The surgical scars?"

"Yeah."

"You said it was an appendectomy when I asked last time."

"I didn't want to explain. No one knows."

"When did you have it done?"

"I couldn't find a doctor to do it when I was in my early twenties. I finally nagged a surgeon into doing it after my twenty-fifth birthday. They kept telling me I'd change my mind, but I *knew* I never would. That they wouldn't let me manage my own body still…" There's tension in my voice. I try to wind it back and fail miserably. "Those fucking bastards. It makes me so angry to think that they felt they knew better than me what I wanted for my own life."

"So that was nearly ten years ago?" Jake murmurs.

"Yeah." I swallow hard. "I didn't want to get pregnant in the first place, but I loved Tristan. I honestly loved that baby more than I knew I could love another human being. But I had my choice taken away from me once, and I'm not ever going to let that happen again."

"We always used your condoms, didn't we?" Jake asks gently. "I don't think I noticed at the time, but tonight… Mine were right here, and your bag was way over there…"

"Yes," I croak. "I never, ever let a guy supply the condoms."

"Can you tell me why?"

He speaks so gently. He's so relaxed, his arms

around me keeping the world out, not locking me in. *He's a good man. He deserves to understand.*

"When I was fifteen, I started sleeping with my high school boyfriend. His name was Garrett, and he was…" I actually smile at the memory. "He was the sweetest kid. We were young and stupid, but we thought we were in love, and it was actually kind of beautiful. But…"

I hate these memories. I *hate* going back there in my mind—to small-town Georgia, to a family that was a vacuum for self-expression. But for Jake, I'll do it. I'm about to give him more power over me than I've given anyone else in my adult life, but he's earned my trust, and he's earned this explanation.

"I wanted to go on the pill. Garrett's parents had given him condoms, but I wanted to be extra cautious. I wasn't sure if I wanted kids or not at that stage, but I knew I wanted to go to college and an accidental pregnancy would make everything so difficult. So, I sat down with my mother and I asked her to take me to the doctor so I could get contraception."

You're sleeping with him? You little slut!

"I take it she said no?" Jake murmurs.

"Yeah, we're talking nuclear-level-meltdown type reaction." I draw in a sharp breath. "They basically grounded me permanently. Drove me to school. Picked me up from school. I snuck out a few times, but it was almost impossible. My paternal grandfather was the mayor of the small town we lived in, and he had been for two decades. He was retiring soon, and my father was planning on running. I honestly believed that our reputation as a wholesome, clean-cut family meant more to my parents than anything. And you have to understand, they weren't deeply religious—but they were conservative to the core. I have an older brother and a younger sister, both of whom were very compliant...very *good*. My brother got married in his late teens, my sister wasn't much older. And then there was me. Defiant from birth, determined to leave Georgia and set the corporate world on fire, mad about boys and then sex and I loved to party and... Basically I was just like I am now. Long before I lost Tristan."

"Jess, I get it. You don't love sex because you're traumatized. You were *always* the black sheep."

"I think I was a different species altogether," I laugh weakly.

"So Garrett was Tristan's father?" Jake asks me.

"No." My throat feels tight. Jake must pick up on the tension because he shifts so that he can rub my back. "I had one friend from school that my parents trusted. Her name was Tansy. Garrett and I gradually drifted apart, as kids do, I suppose. And when Tansy and I would hang out at her place, her brother E-Eric gradually started to pay attention to me." I stumble on his name. I pause to draw in a breath, trying to shake off the vague fear that lingers when I bring him to mind. That he has power over me even now is frustrating and irritating. The deep breathing doesn't work, but focusing on Jake's strong body against mine does. After a minute, I can continue. "He was a lot older—eight years, actually—and he didn't even live with Tansy anymore but he was suddenly at his family home all of the time. But by the time I was seventeen, I was lying to my parents. I'd tell them I was going to see Tansy, but Eric would pick me up and we'd go to his place instead. He was charming and possessive and handsome, and it was a total whirlwind. And it felt so grown-up to have a twenty-five-year-old boyfriend with his own apartment and a job.

"I missed my period just before finals. I was so confused—we'd been *so* careful. I tried to ignore it until graduation, putting off facing the problem because I just had no idea what else to do. Then the morning sickness hit me hard and it all became so much more real. That's when I told Eric.

"He seemed so excited," I whisper. "He was just *so* calm...so supportive and happy. I'd been trying to figure out how to get an abortion, but Eric talked me out of it. He promised me that if I stayed in town and had the baby, he'd help me get to college the following year. My next concern was my parents—I knew they'd lose their minds. But Eric convinced me that my parents wouldn't care...as long as we were married."

My voice breaks. Jake's arms lock around me.

"There's no waiting period for marriage licenses in Georgia, so a few days after my eighteenth birthday, we drove down to Atlanta and got married."

"And how did your parents react?"

"They were furious. They had no idea I'd been seeing Eric, and they were just so angry about the whole situation. And the ridiculous thing was, when he first suggested we get married, I *knew* that they wouldn't give their blessing even if we were married. But Eric was persuasive and so certain that they'd be happy for us as long as we 'did it right,' and I was utterly desperate to fix things. Maybe I was a defiant kid, but I was still a kid and I was terrified. In the end, my parents' panic didn't help, even though I eventually realized that the reason they were so hysterical was that they could see Eric had manipulated me."

"He gaslighted you."

"Exactly. He made me feel like he was the only solution to a mess I had made. And my parents were livid and judgmental and ashamed, while Eric was calm and charming. I stayed with him. I wanted to show my parents that I could manage my own life."

"You were so young, Jess."

"I know. But I could have gone home to my parents, and I didn't. I want you to remember that when I tell you what happened next."

"I will. But even though you chose him, I can already see that none of this was your fault," Jake protests gently. I barely hear him. I'm on a roll now, the words pouring out of me. I couldn't stop explaining if I tried. Maybe keeping all of this locked up inside for seventeen years wasn't the best idea I ever had.

"He'd cut me off from my whole support network. I don't know what he said to Tansy, but even his own sister stopped coming around. And once I was in his house, I was completely vulnerable. He had a good construction job, but I had no income. When I first moved in with him, I wanted to get a job, but he talked me out of that too. He said he wanted me to rest. He kept pointing out that no one would hire me anyway because I was pregnant, and my morning sickness was still pretty bad. It felt like concern, Jake, but over time that concern began to intensify, and I was totally out of my depth before I even realized what was happening. Eric decided where we went and what we did. He started taking the keys to my car when he left for work. He said he loved me and just wanted to make sure I was resting. And then once I stopped protesting about that, it was the phone—he took my cell first. He said he didn't want other men bothering me. His jealousy was constant—all I had to do was look out the window and he'd be flying off the handle. After a while, he was taking the landline to work with him too. I was completely isolated. I had no money of my own. No support. No power, Jake." I'm shaking now, and my voice is shaking too. It's not distress—it's sheer fury. "I was completely fucking powerless."

"Was he physically abusive too?"

"Coercive, perhaps," I whisper unevenly. "The lines became very blurry after a while. I certainly didn't feel like I could say no to sex. He got angry at the drop of a hat, and my whole life became about calming him. And the whole time, he was telling me my family didn't love me. That *no one* loved me. It felt so real."

"Did you have prenatal care?"

"Oh, sure. He'd come with me to my checkups, playing the part of the perfect husband," I say bitterly.

"Did your family try to help you?"

"My brother came one day while Eric was at work. He told me that Mom and Dad would probably forgive me if I came home and apologized."

"Jesus."

"Besides, I was so confused by that stage. I had no idea who to believe. What to believe. I actually felt like this worthless piece of shit who deserved to be where I was. You have no idea how quickly it can happen. One minute, I'm the most popular girl in school, class valedictorian headed for a college scholarship, the world at my feet. A few months later I'm asking that asshole for permission to buy toilet paper."

I break off and take a series of deep breaths. Jake is now massaging my back and neck, his hands kneading me gently, grounding me. I focus on that sensation for a while, until the torrent in my mind has settled. I can tell he feels the relaxation returning to my body.

"What happened to Tristan, sweetheart?"

I'm still not used to hearing that name, but I love the way Jake says it—with respect and care, with love for my son—just *because* he was my son. I blink away tears and clear my throat.

"I was eight months pregnant. Uncomfortable and sore. Tired. I'd just had a checkup at the doctor's and wasn't due for weeks. But I just felt...*off*. Tristan didn't seem to be moving as much. I started to worry."

Eric will get angry if I make a fuss. I can't make a fuss. I'm sure it's going to be fine. It has to be fine.

"You have to understand, Jake," I choke, eyes filling with tears. "My whole life was about keeping Eric calm. I was terrified that if I made a fuss and it was all for nothing, he'd fly off the handle."

"Jess, I'm not judging you," Jake whispers. He shifts me so that I'm lying beside him, staring at him right in the eyes, just like I was the night Abby had her twins and we talked in his bed. He reaches up to stroke my cheek with his big bear-claw hands.

"Eventually I panicked, and I asked Eric for the money to go to the doctor just for a checkup and he lost his shit with me…told me I was being stupid or something. But over the next day, I realized Tristan wasn't moving at all, and so I waited until Eric fell asleep and called Grandma Chloe. I hadn't actually been close with her before that—she was here in Manhattan, I was in a small rural city in northern Georgia. But I'd met her enough times to know that she was nothing like my parents or my siblings, and I couldn't think of anyone else to call. I was so desperate. So terrified."

Not before or since have I felt fear like that. Even remembering those moments now makes me shake. I was on the landline in the bathroom with the shower running to hide my panicked whispers into the phone, convinced that any second now, Eric would smash the door down and catch me and there'd be hell to pay.

"Chloe called my parents and they were at the door with the sheriff within an hour. Eric played dumb when

they asked him about the things I'd told my grandmother. He told them he thought I was having some
mental problems because of the pregnancy. And
they..."

"They believed him?"

"Yeah. They took me to the hospital not because
the baby wasn't moving but because they thought I'd
lost my mind." I laugh weakly, bitterly. "They weren't
wrong—I really felt like I was losing my mind. I was
a mess. And then of course..."

The nurse turning pale.

The ultrasound.

*The doctor with his cold hands and his gaze brim-
ming with sympathy.*

I'm sorry, Jessica. We can't find a heartbeat.

"He was already gone?"

"I was too late," I whisper, my voice breaking. "I
knew for days that something was wrong. I had an instinct to save him. It just took me too long to find the
courage to call for help. I let him down."

"You were in an impossible situation, Jessica."

"I was. But just remember, Jake, I put myself in that
impossible situation," I say bitterly. "In the hospital
after the birth, Eric came to see me. I was sobbing,
petrified of him and grieving and broken. He told me
not to worry. He said I fell pregnant right away when
he tampered with the condoms, so it wouldn't take us
long to have another baby."

Jake sucks in a sharp breath. I can see the fury and
the tension in his expression. His jaw is set hard, and

there's a sheen in his eyes, but he doesn't say a word. He doesn't make *my* painful past about him and his reaction.

If I love Jake, I love him for this moment, when he quietly makes sure I have a safe space to air my pain.

"I've thought a lot about why he did that," I whisper. "He was *always* so possessive… At first, I actually thought it was romantic. He'd call me 'his,' tell me he wanted to keep me forever because I was so special. But soon enough, he was also jealous and insecure, especially about the idea that I'd leave him behind when I left for college. And he was right, you know. I was always going to break up with him and leave town. The only way he could tie me down was to get me pregnant, and once he did that, he owned me."

I've broken out in a cold sweat more than once during a sexual encounter when a guy went to reach for his own protection—I *have* to use my own condoms, so I know they're safe. It's almost a phobia now, and I really thought the tubal ligation would help, but it didn't. Something in my mind is stuck on this. Maybe it always will be.

"You went home with your parents after you left the hospital?"

"Yes. I was virtually catatonic. I wasn't eating or talking much. They gave me some tranquilizers, I think. I don't remember much of his funeral."

"And then your parents said those things…"

"They did me a favor."

"Fuck, Jess. That was *no* favor."

"It snapped me out of my emotional coma. I called Grandma Chloe and told her what happened. She sent me the money to come to New York. Pulled some strings to get me into college midyear even though I hadn't applied. Gave me a room and held my hand while I cried. You asked if I was the black sheep—well, maybe it runs in the family after all, because my grandmother was so much more like me than my mother. She was wild and bold and blunt, and she saved my life."

"Did your parents try to come after you?"

"My brother did. It was basically the same conversation we had at Eric's house. *Come home, beg for forgiveness, they might take you back in.*" I almost spit the words. This, I'm still bitter about, even now. I cut my biological family off, but it's fine, because I'm better off now. I left my biological family because they were assholes, but these days, I have a chosen family of friends around me. I have people who love me not despite of who I am, but because of it.

"What did you say to your brother when he came to talk to you, sweetheart?"

"I swore for a while, then I told him the whole family was dead to me. And then Grandma threw him out of her house—I mean she literally chased him out with her walking stick. That was the last time I ever heard from them, and I divorced Eric and changed my name as soon as I was legally able to."

"What was your name?"

"I grew up Jess Underwood. Then I married Eric

and was Jess West. After I cut ties to my family, I took Grandma's name—my mother's maiden name. That's how I became a Cohen."

"She was your hero, wasn't she?"

"I lived with her for the first two years of college, then moved in with some friends. When I needed my share of seed funds to start Brainway, she offered before I could ask. When she died, she left me everything. Grandma was something of a stock market whiz... Business savvy must run in my blood."

I'm so tired I can barely hold my head up, but I shuffle closer to Jake and then rest my cheek against his chest. He winds his arms around me and kisses the top of my head.

"So that's it," I whisper.

"Thank you for telling me."

"Is that all you have to say?"

"You had this whole other life before we met. And it was brutally unfair and hard. The only thing I don't understand is why you've never let your friends here support you in all of this."

"I told you, Jake. I didn't want to be *that girl*, the one who was defined by the fact that she'd fucked everything up before her nineteenth birthday. Besides, I couldn't open myself up when I met you guys. It was too raw, and I knew that once people knew about my past, they'd know my vulnerabilities."

"You didn't trust us. And I can understand why. It must have been very difficult for you to trust *anyone* after what you went through. Everyone let you down,

Jessica. Eric, your parents, even his fucking family. You were young and vulnerable, and you deserved better from your community."

I think about that for a while, then I roll to face him, lying on his chest.

"But do you see now?" I choke. "I'm not the woman for you, Jake. I'm not having kids, and you want them. I'm never getting married again, and you want that. I won't… I *can't* ever let anyone own me like that. Not ever again."

"I'm forty in a few months, sweetheart," Jake whispers, and he gives me a soft smile as he strokes his finger down my face. "I've always been open to the idea of kids, but I've long since wrapped my head around the idea that I probably won't have them."

"But you said…"

"I made a joke I don't even remember. If anything, I was probably trying to get you to *start* the conversation with me about what our life together might look like. But I wouldn't have come into that discussion with a strong agenda. Kids have always been a 'maybe' for me, not a 'must-have.'"

I bite my lip, then search his gaze as I whisper, "It's not just that. I know I can't give you what you need. What you *want*."

"Monogamy?" Jake whispers hesitantly. I wince and shake my head.

"Trust," I choke. "Commitment. *Control.*"

There's no mistaking the frustration in Jake's gaze

now. He brushes my hair back from my face tenderly, but the gesture contradicts the tension in his voice.

"I do not and would not ever want to control you, Jessica."

"You still don't get it," I whisper sadly. "To me, committing feels like allowing myself to be controlled. It's saying that you own me, isn't it? And you and I both know that if I'd come here tonight and told you I wanted to try to have a relationship, you'd have whipped that ring out before I could get my clothes off."

"I wish I'd never bought that ring," Jake says with a groan. "You keep coming back to it, like the stupid fucking ring is the sticking point here. It's a symbol, Jess. It's a symbol of how I feel about you—not even a symbol about the future I needed us to have. And I bought it before I realized how serious you were about not getting married. I'd never propose to you now that I understand. Never."

"But then you miss out on the future you wanted. If we go our separate ways, you'll meet someone else… someone who wants the happily-ever-after you deserve," I argue. "I want that for you. I want you to be happy with someone. You…" My voice breaks, and I shift so that I can touch my fingertips to his lips. "More than anyone else I know, Saint Jake, you deserve a happily-ever-after."

"Life doesn't work that way, Jess. *No one* gets a happily-ever-after. The best you can do is to find someone who fits you, and then you build the life you want.

Shit comes at you and you deal with it together. Good times come at you and you enjoy them together. There are ups and downs and struggles and blessings, but when you love someone, the only thing that matters is that you navigate them *together*."

I stifle a yawn, and he kisses my fingers, then shifts me so that I'm lying on my side again, close to him.

"Let's sleep," he whispers. "You're staying with me tonight, aren't you?"

"Yes, I'll stay tonight."

I drift off to sleep then, nestled safely in the man-mountain that is Jake Winton.

CHAPTER THIRTY

Jake

JESS IS CLEARLY EXHAUSTED, and she sleeps like a log in my arms. Twelve long hours pass, and in all of that time, she barely moves.

I sleep lightly, and I wake up with a start several times, images dancing through my head of Jessica in the control of that asshole. Of Jessica grieving her son alone. Of Jessica landing in New York, putting on a brave face and building a fucking empire on her own.

I've loved her for a long time. Tonight, I just want to worship at her feet. I'd do it every day for the rest of my life if she let me.

I'm in utter awe of her just because she survived.

You still don't get it. To me, committing feels like allowing myself to be controlled.

I want a commitment from her. That's certainly true, but it's only true because I want her to choose to stay in my life. I'd love a promise from her that she intends to try to be in this for the long haul.

But it's also true that the last thing in the world I

want is to control her. And I definitely don't want to *change* her. I love Jess just as she is—survivor, leader, lover and friend. She's fierce, but she's imperfect. She's just Jess, and Jess is everything I want.

I can't untangle the mess of this. How do I ask her to try with me, when just doing so might feel to her like I'm pushing her, and whenever I push her, she retreats?

The answer comes to me in the early light.

It's in my nature to go after what I want, sometimes the second the thought crosses my mind that I want it. But that isn't going to work with Jess. She's been through too much. She needs to know she's in control.

I never wanted to build any particular life with her. I don't give a shit about kids and marriage if that's not what Jess wants, but it seems like no matter how often I tell her that, she just can't hear it. All I really wanted was the push and pull of our lifelong dynamic, over and over again, forever. I wanted to negotiate with her and debate with her and fight with her. I wanted to compromise with her. I wanted her to trust me to give her whatever she needed to be happy.

If I push her, she runs away. The harder I push, the further she runs. She found the ring, so she broke up with me. She realized I was staying in town to try to rebuild a relationship with her, so she threw me out of her house.

But the inverse is also true. When I respected her wish for me to leave her alone, she came back to me. And even last night, when we argued at her apartment and I walked away, she came here to the hotel.

This isn't some stupid game she's playing—she opens up to me only when I inadvertently remind her that she will be safe if she does so.

I have to listen to her, and time and time again, she's asked me to let her go.

It's actually simple in the end. I finally realize that all I can do is trust Jess to figure all of this out for us. I know she wants me. I know she's scared. But if I wait for her to find a way to choose us, maybe I'll show her that she really can trust me with a part in her future.

CHAPTER THIRTY-ONE

Jess

I WAKE TO the sound of the hotel room door closing, and Jake is there with a tray. He's shirtless, wearing boxers, and this is a view I wish I could wake up to again. He rests the tray over the bed, then crawls across and kisses me. He's cleaned his teeth and shaved this morning. I think he's even taken a shower.

"I really passed out, huh?" I say. I'm actually feeling odd. It takes me a moment to identify the emotions. I'm feeling self-conscious. Vulnerable. More than a little embarrassed that I exposed parts of myself to Jake that he didn't even know were there.

"You were exhausted," he murmurs as he flops to sit beside me, propping himself up on the pillow. He brings the breakfast tray to rest on his lap, and I see that he's ordered me a coffee and some eggs. When I sit up, he hands me the coffee. "Do you have plans today?"

"Thanks. And…no," I say cautiously. "Why?"

He smiles at me.

"Do you want to stay in bed with me this morning?"

I hear the subtext. He's not even talking about sex, although I'm sure we'll manage plenty of that. He's talking about relaxing together. He's talking about pillow talk and cuddles and just *being*.

One last morning. Let's have one last morning together.

"I'd love to."

"THIS IS A bit awkward," Jake says as we finish eating a late room service lunch together. We're still in bed, after another intense round of lovemaking and a morning nap. It's rare for me to just stop like this, and it's actually incredible to do so in the company of the one person on earth who makes me want to stop. I glance at Jake, intrigued and more than a little excited. Hopefully he's going to ask me to do something *really* kinky. I'm disappointed when he gives me a sad smile. "This has been great, but I really need to pack up for my flight soon."

My jaw just about hits the sheets.

"Oh," I say, when I can speak again. *Seriously, Jake? Throwing me out of your hotel room?* I can't really complain though. Not when I know he'd happily agree to continuing this relationship, and I'm the one refusing to have the discussion. "Okay."

Ten minutes later, I'm dressed and standing at his door. He's on the inside, leaning against the door frame. We stare at one another, and it hits me that this is really it.

Another chapter in the saga of Jess and Jake. The last chapter, because we need to let it go now. It's going to break my heart to hear he's met someone and settled down, but at the same time, I hope I do hear that at some point soon. Jake deserves to be happy more than anyone else I know. He's wasted enough of the last ten years waiting for me.

"It's been fun," I say as brightly as I can. Jake chuckles softly, even as my smile fades. "I'm going to miss you."

"Me too," he murmurs.

"But this is really it, isn't it?"

"It seems that way."

"Move on, Jake."

"I'm trying to."

This is where I kiss him and turn away.

Kiss him and leave.

My body just refuses to move.

"When do you fly out?" I blurt. God, this is pitiful. I'm just asking random questions, trying to prolong this last moment. Something flashes across Jake's gaze, but it clears before I can interpret it.

"9:15 p.m.," he says quietly.

Six hours. In just six hours he's going to get on a plane to go home, and I might never see him again.

"JFK?"

"Yeah."

I nod, then turn to walk away. Jake catches my elbow and turns me back toward him, then pulls me close. He cups my face in his hands and bends and brushes his lips against mine. His mouth moves softly over mine, and his hands on my cheeks hold me in place so gently it's almost worshipful.

It's not a kiss intended to arouse me, although maybe it's a kiss intended to arouse *feelings*, and if that's what Jake's trying to do here, it works. Emotionally, I'm about to melt down.

"Goodbye," he whispers after a minute, and then pulls away from me.

I blink away confused tears, then reach up to kiss him one last time.

"I'll miss you," I blurt.

"I love you, Jess."

When I take a step away from him, he gives me one last sad smile and closes the door.

I LEAVE HIS hotel and walk. It's a beautiful afternoon, and I'm enjoying the fresh air—as much as the humid, smelly summer air in New York ever is fresh. It's twenty blocks back to my office, twenty-two back to my apartment. I guess I'm probably headed to either one of those places, although I have no actual destination in mind. I walk because I need to think.

I think about the first time Jake asked me out. We were so young then—so green. He had just started a six-year fellowship. I was at the "make it or break it" part of building a startup. He asked me to get a drink with him after work one day, and I could almost *see* the cogs turning in his mind. Reflected in Jake's eyes,

I saw a white picket fence in the suburbs, two adorable redheaded children and a dog.

And not a dog like Clara. More like a golden retriever, named something unfortunate like Mr. Fluffy by one of those imaginary redheaded children.

I knew right from the start that he was a forever kind of guy. I knew right from the start that the feelings that he had for me, even at that early stage, ran deep. I just told him I couldn't—I didn't explain or offer excuses.

Jake read between the lines. We hung out a lot in the years that followed, but usually in a group. On my birthday a few years later, he bent to kiss my cheek to say good-night and the lust in the air was so thick I nearly choked on it.

God, I wanted him so badly. We almost kissed that night…we came *so* close. He texted me the next day and suggested we go out for coffee. We met up alone, and I told him I couldn't date him. He told me he respected that.

And so set the pattern for the years to come, until Paul and Isabel's first wedding. We'd circle around one another like sharks hunting prey. Neither one of us was pining—we both dated other people. But on some level in my mind, it was always him. And I knew he felt the same about me. Still, I held back because I knew I was no good for him. And Jake?

Jake held back because I'd asked him to.

Even at Paul's first wedding, *I* made the first move.

He probably always wanted me, but he respected that he'd already asked me out and I said no.

And not only can I trust Jake, I already do trust Jake. I would never have explained my past to him last night if I didn't.

I'm nearing my office when I slip my phone from my handbag to text Mitch.

Jess: What are you up to?

Mitch: Writing a sex scene. What's up?

Jess: Are you on a roll? If so, ignore me—I'd hate to leave your characters unsatisfied. If not, do you feel like catching up for a drink?

Mitch: Definitely. I've actually been waiting for this. Fully stocked with Kleenex and Xanax.

Jess: If I needed tissues and Xanax would I propose meeting at that bar across the street from my office?

Mitch: That's what I love about you, Cohen. Impossible to predict at all times. See you soon.

"I'm confused. Was I wrong?"

"Wrong?"

"About you and Jake spending the last few weeks together. I figured you'd both get far too attached again and by now it would have all come to tears." Mitch takes a sip of his drink, then pauses. "I wasn't kidding about the Kleenex and Xanax. I know he flies out today and I'm ready."

"Do you think I'm even capable of having a healthy long-term relationship?" I ask him.

Mitch sets his drink down on the table and frowns at me.

"I remember reading an article about Brainway just after I met you," he says, after a pause. "It basically mocked the very concept of a startup trying to compete in the web browser space. Then it mocked the idea of a subscription model for a software application most business users get for free. Finally, it mocked the idea of a twenty-something *woman* taking on the big boys. Not in so many words, of course, but the subtext was undeniable."

"Newsflash—the tech industry is sexist and small-minded. Any other groundbreaking revelations you have to share before you answer my question?"

"I read another article about you just a few weeks ago. Same publication, might even have been the same journalist. This one speculated about a potential stock market listing down the line and basically suggested that since everything you touch seems to turn to gold, Brainway could be the hottest stock in town one day," Mitch says. He gives me a pointed smile. "You've made a career out of setting yourself an impossible goal and making the naysayers eat their words when you exceed it. Do I think you're capable of having a healthy long-term relationship? I think that when you want something and you're determined to get it, there is *no* stopping you."

"We aren't talking about the corporate world, Mitch," I mutter, staring down into my drink. "If I try and fail, it's not money at stake."

"It's Jake's feelings," he surmises. I nod. He draws in a deep breath, then asks gently, "You were adamant you didn't want anything more. You broke up with him because you were so sure. So, what's changed, Jess?"

"I thought he wanted children," I admit, unable to meet my best friend's gaze. "And last night he told me that's not the case—he was open to the idea of kids, but he's also accepted it might not happen for him and he's fine with that too. It wasn't the only reason I ended things. But it was a factor because I knew that if we were together, I'd never want kids and I thought he'd miss out to be with me. I thought, eventually, he'd come to resent me."

"And that's it? You realize he might be fine with not having kids, so after all of these years of angst and push and pull, suddenly you're open to the idea of a relationship with him after all?" Mitch asks carefully. I bite my lip.

"It just hit me tonight that he's *always* respected my 'no.' Even when he didn't understand it. He's always, always respected it."

"Of course he's respected your 'no.'" Mitch frowns. "What the fuck are you talking about, Jess?"

"If I were to..." I clear my throat. I don't even know how to say it.

"If you were to give a relationship with him a real shot," he prompts, laughing softly.

"Yeah. That." I draw in a deep breath.

"What are you scared of?"

"I *need* to be independent. I need to steer my own ship. I can't sign up for a partnership with someone if it means handing over control of the rest of my life."

"Jesus Christ, Jessica." Mitch blinks at me. "Have you even *met* Jake Winton? Are you seriously telling me all of that drama two years ago was because you thought he had his heart set on having children and you assumed he was going to turn into a controlling asshole the minute he got his mitts on you?"

"No, of course not, I just…"

But on some level, that's exactly what I thought. Not with my head—with my heart. And the only reason I'm really thinking any different now is that there is an undeniable pattern in our relationship. Over fourteen years, time and time again, he's walked away when I told him to.

I say no. Jake backs away, even when it breaks his heart. He has proved to me that he can be trusted to respect my wishes even when they aren't the same as his. And all I've ever done in return is to hurt him.

"Jess," Mitch murmurs. I look up from the table to meet his gaze. What is it with the men in my life making me face my own pain these days? There's heartbreak in Mitch's gaze. I can see he's feeling very sorry for me right now, but I'm far too wound up to even snap at him.

"I promised myself I'd never let a man control my destiny. I made bad decisions and wound up powerless," I croak. "I was eighteen and my life was over."

Mitch knows two things about those days: I had an asshole boyfriend named Eric, and I lost a son named Tristan. It feels fucking stupid that I've never shared the rest with him, and I'd probably explain everything else right now but I'm too emotional to get my head straight enough to do so. This conversation might not have even made sense to him, except that when you've been close for as long as Mitchell Cole and I have, conversation can flow around gaps.

"Eighteen? You were a kid, Jess. Now you're a terrifying, formidable woman talking about a partnership with a good man who worships you. It's not the same."

"But Jake has more power over me than Eric ever did."

"Babe," Mitch whispers, reaching for my hand. "Would he *ever* abuse it the way Eric did?"

When I shake my head, I knock a tear loose. Goddammit. I swipe it away, and down the rest of my drink.

"Just do me one favor," Mitch says. I glance at him again, and his smile is sad as he whispers, "Be sure, Jess. Just be sure this is what you want, okay? Before you even tell him. He's all heart, that man. You hurt each other last time, but I think if you get his hopes up about this and then back out, it'll crush him."

"You're a wise man, Mitchell."

"And sensitive. And handsome. And did I mention wealthy? Far wealthier than you, by the way."

"My life's goal is to make it so that you can't say that anymore, you know," I mutter. Mitch grins.

"And you know what, Jessica? I'm ready to pass on the mantle. You've set your mind to it, so it's only a matter of time now."

I TELL MITCH I'm heading home to think, but I actually find myself in my office. There's something reassuring about this space, even empty, even at 5:30 p.m. on a Saturday evening. Maybe this is, in some bizarre way, my spiritual home. I sit behind my desk, then put my feet up and close my eyes.

Change has been in the air for a while. Abby and Marcus. Paul and Izzy. Even this stock market project. And now...my personal life?

I'm scared. But if there's one principle I've lived my life by, it's that I never let fear hold me back when I know what I want.

I sit up and wake my laptop up, then load the text messages app and open my group chat.

Jess: Are you guys busy?

Replies come immediately.

Paul: We've got the worst jet lag. It feels like 5:00 a.m. to us and we're just waking up.

Isabel: Paul's not kidding. He was just about to order in breakfast.

Abby: We have twin newborns. We're always busy.

Abby: Kidding, they're still in NICU and we've just come home from a visit. Jessie is off the CPAP today! You probably don't know what it means, but it's good. But now we have nothing to do and we're actually bored.

Marcus: Everything okay, Jess?

I pause. Am I really going to do this? But then I'm dialing the video chat, and their faces fill the screen.

"Hey, lunatics," I greet them lightly.

"Are you seriously working from the office on a Saturday afternoon?" Marcus's brow knits as he scans the bookshelves behind me. He and Abby are together in their living room, cuddled up. For the first time, I feel a pang of longing. *I want that. I want to cuddle up with Jake on the couch on a lazy Saturday afternoon. Maybe we'll stay there all day. Maybe we'll wear pajamas. Actually, I'll even show him my PMS pajamas and he'll laugh at me, but he'll also think I'm cute.*

"It's been a weird week," I say, which is possibly the understatement of the decade.

"Hi there, Jess," Isabel greets me. She motions toward the space off camera. "I wasn't kidding about

Paul ordering in breakfast. He's just about done. Everything okay?"

"Yeah. I just wanted to…"

"Sorry. I'm back." Paul joins Isabel, sharing her phone, and I know it's time.

"I need to tell you something," I say. I stare between their concerned faces on the screen. This is my family—a completely safe space, and I'm suddenly not even sure why it's taken me so long to do this. "My life back in Georgia was really different. It's been hard for me to talk about it over the years, but I really want you all to know. When I moved to New York, I'd just come out of an abusive relationship. And I actually had a son. His name was Tristan and he was stillborn."

My four friends all stare into their phone screens with visible shock.

"Jess," Abby croaks, tears springing to her eyes. Her face crumples, and the tears are already leaking out. I know all too well what she's doing—processing how hard the day of her birth must have been for me, and then she'll be imagining the panic and the pain I must have felt when I knew she was sick. "Holy shit. Why didn't you tell us?"

"I couldn't," I say, then I give her a sad smile. "I wasn't ever ashamed of Tristan, but to survive, I had to hit the ground running here and I guess… Maybe I tried to build a wall between that life and this one. The thing is, I've actually realized that I don't need that wall anymore and maybe now it's just keeping the people I love at a distance I don't want."

"Thanks for telling us," Izzy whispers. She wipes at her eyes. Paul tilts his head as he stares into the lens.

"What's sparked this, Jess?" he asks me quietly. "Is this because of Marcus and Abby's girls?"

I shake my head.

"No. This is because I'm in love with your brother and I'm hoping that I'm about to start another new chapter of my life. I don't want to stay in my old patterns."

There's a collective gasp. I sigh.

"Don't be overdramatic. It's not *that* shocking."

"It actually *is* that shocking," Isabel says, blinking. "You and *Jake*?"

"Called it," Marcus says triumphantly, elbowing Abby meaningfully, and she shoots him a look.

"We both called it. You don't get credit for noticing what was right in front of our faces for the last two weeks."

"What have you guys been up to while we were away?" Paul laughs softly.

"I...I need to talk to him first so please don't say anything to him just yet. I just wanted you guys to know. I wanted to be open with you and I had to explain because..."

I'm starting to feel uncomfortable now, but I can't wind the conversation down yet because I need to talk to Paul and Marcus. I clear my throat.

"Actually, Abby, Izzy...can we have a moment of business chat now?"

"Yeah, I'm not going *anywhere*," Abby tells me

pointedly. "Not when bombshells are raining from the sky like this."

"If it's boring, we'll just tune out. Go right ahead," Isabel says. I sigh.

"So, the thing is, you know I've been thinking about ways to build some buzz about Brainway in the Silicon Valley set in the lead-up to an IPO…"

"Holy shit," Marcus says, blinking. "Is this why you didn't want to work from the West Coast office? Because you and Jake…"

I swallow.

"It was a factor," I say, but that's a lie. I sigh. "No. Yes. It was *the* factor. I was avoiding him, and I put my personal shit before the company's needs. I'm really sorry."

"And now…"

"I'm going to work from Palo Alto part-time for a few months. One week of the month there, three back here." I draw in a deep breath. "Starting immediately. I'm going to fly back with him tonight." Paul and Marcus both nod easily. I frown at them. "Seriously? You're just nodding along like this isn't completely out of left field? I'm talking about your CEO working from the other side of the country. *Immediately.*"

"On a business level, it makes perfect sense and one of us should have done this sooner," Marcus says easily. "On a personal level… It's you and Jake. Why would I hesitate? I'm so excited for you both."

"Ditto." Paul shrugs. "He's my brother. I want the best for him. You're the best, so it's a no-brainer."

Stupid, hot tears fill my eyes.

"Thank you," I croak.

"You seem surprised, Jess. How did you *think* we'd react to all of this?" Isabel asks me softly.

"I don't think I was sure I was doing it until you guys picked up the video call."

"We're just happy for you." Paul shrugs. "And we're a tech company, for fuck's sake. Whether you're in Palo Alto or the moon you can still lead the company, and besides, that office is a *mess*. Get in there, crack some skulls. Win-win."

"When are you talking to Jake?" Abby asks.

"In a few hours," I say. My throat is suddenly dry.

"Go get him, Jess," she says softly.

"I have to go," I say, my voice cracking. "Talk to you all soon." At the last second, I point to Abby and Marcus. "Give Clem and Jessie a cuddle for me!"

I RUN HOME to pack. I have some very aggressive butterflies in my stomach. It's an odd feeling; less a gentle fluttering, more of a violent thumping sensation.

What if I've got it wrong? What if he doesn't want me to come? What if he treats me like shit and I can't get out? What if, what if, what if.

The suitcase is soon full, and I look down at it, then realize what a bad job I've done. I definitely do not need four pairs of jeans for seven days in California in late summer, and it seems I've managed to cram the suitcase full...without a single pair of underwear.

On the one hand, I'm going to spend time with Jake

so that's probably perfect, but on the other hand, I am going to be working at the office this week during the day, so I definitely do need panties.

I groan in frustration as I tip the suitcase out onto my bed. Riffling through it, I realize I've managed to pack pretty much everything I don't need.

I draw in a deep breath, then turn to my wardrobe and start again.

BECAUSE IT TAKES me over an hour to pack my fucking suitcase, then another hour to get dressed because I have to redo my eye makeup twice because my hands are shaking, I'm running later than I'd like when I finally slip into the back of a car and head to JFK. I open my laptop and spend the first thirty minutes of the drive emailing my team.

Gina, sorry I didn't get to tell you this in person, but I'm going to be working from Palo Alto part-time for a little while...

Kiah, great news! You're getting a promotion. Now for the fine print... I'm really going to need your help.

The next challenge is getting a ticket on the same flight as Jake, but this proves to be easy when I see that only one airline is flying out to San Francisco at nine fifteen tonight. I also remember that Jake, as a general rule, flies first class. Not because he's flashy,

but because his legs are longer than most human bodies, and modern planes are not designed for legit giants.

I know we probably won't be seated together, but I
figure if we both wind up in first class, I'll be able to
sweet-talk *someone* into swapping, so I load the airline website and try to buy a ticket.

As soon as I hit Purchase, the website crashes. I
curse furiously and swap out of my own browser into
one of the inferior ones that comes with my operating
system by default. I plug in my details all over again
and an error flashes up.

You have already purchased a ticket for this flight.

I figure the ticket must have gone through before
the website crashed, and I check my email, expecting
to find the details there. But there's no email from the
airline, and when I check my credit card, there's no
transaction there either.

"For fuck's sake," I groan, and the driver glances
back at me.

"You okay there, lady?"

"Airlines," I mutter, and he nods.

"Oh, I hear that."

I decide to try again on my laptop. The flight is now
showing limited seats available, so I hastily type in all
of my details again.

You have already purchased a ticket for this flight.

"No I fucking haven't!"

I call the customer service number and I'm warned
that after the recent system outage, the expected wait
time is forty-six minutes…by which time I'll be at the

airport. I hang up in frustration and stare out the window. I'll have to sort this out when I get there and hope
this isn't some kind of sign from the universe that I'm
about to make a god-awful mistake.

Now that there's *nothing* more I can do but sit and
wait, I finally start to think about what I'm going to
say to Jake and how he might react. I know he's going
to be shocked, and I'm pretty sure he's going to be over
the moon, but, of course, there's a tiny voice whisper-
ing to me that maybe he won't be.

Maybe he's relieved to be going home, back to his
quest for a soul mate who can give him everything.

I tell that voice to shut the fuck up and try to plan
my speech.

*Jake. I know you want forever, but that's going to
take me a while to get my head around. In the meantime, can we take it one day at a time? I want to be with
you. It's you—it's always been you. So, I can't promise
you the rest of my life just yet, but I can promise you
this: I choose you today. I will choose you tomorrow.
And maybe if we keep choosing each other day by day
for a while, I'll be able to give you more.*

It's all clear in my head by the time we get to the
airport. But the flight will close in half an hour, and I
don't even have a fucking ticket. I'm wearing amazing
emerald green heels because they match this green-
and-white sundress and I wanted to look my best, and
I do. I'm going to blow his fucking socks off.

The only problem is that I'm sprinting through
what's possibly the world's worst airport in three-

inch heels and maybe it's possible that Jake's impulsivity has rubbed off on me, because I clearly haven't thought this through. Still, I make it to the customer service counter, then groan loudly when I see there's a long line.

"Computer problems," the senior citizen in front of me mutters. I stifle a curse, and the woman turns and glances at me, then smiles. "Special occasion?"

"I'm trying to… There's this guy… I…" I groan and wipe my hand over my face. "God. I've *got* to make this flight. He's been waiting fourteen years for me to get my shit together."

"That's quite the wait. I guess I should stop complaining about this line when you put it like that," the woman chuckles, then glances at me. "What's your name, darling?"

"Jess. What's yours?"

"Yolande."

"Yolande, I *need* to get on this flight," I say desperately. "I'm out of ideas. What can I do?"

Yolande drops slowly and carefully down onto the floor.

"Oh my God," I say, crouching beside her. "Do you need me to call—"

"I need you to shout for help, and then when the airline staff comes to assist me, stay with me. I'll do the rest," Yolande says, and I realize she's helping me. I grin at her.

"Is this going to make you late for something?" I whisper.

"I just flew in from my grandson's place in Idaho. But I left my iPad on the plane and I'm hoping these nice people can get it back for me."

"Right. It's go time. Try to look old and frail."

"I *am* old and frail."

"Please, Yolande, you were scheming evil ways to skip this line the second you met me." I wink at her, and she grins. "Can someone help?" I call, waving toward the airline staff. Two women come running right away.

"Ma'am? Are you okay?" one of them says, crouching beside Yolande. "We'll call the paramedics—"

"I've just been on my feet for so long," Yolande says, throwing her hand against her forehead dramatically. "And I'm so worried about my granddaughter here. She's going to miss her flight."

"Don't you worry about a thing, ma'am. Jenny here will get you somewhere you can sit down and take a breath and I'll help your granddaughter," the other attendant says. She glances at me. "Will she be okay on her own while we go to the computer?"

"Of course I will," Yolande says, voice already back to normal strength, already sitting back up. "Come on, then, Jenny. Help me somewhere I can rest. And Jess—go get your man."

"I want to be just like you when I grow up, Yolande," I whisper to her, just before I rise. She winks at me, and I follow the attendant past the long line to a spare terminal.

"I just need to buy a first-class ticket for the nine-fifteen flight to San Francisco. I tried to do it online but whenever I hit Purchase, I was getting an error."

"The computer went down for about ten minutes earlier but it's all back up now." The attendant smiles at me. I hand her my ID and credit card, and look around impatiently, as if the bustling airport can speed this up for me somehow. The woman hits a few keys on the keyboard and frowns. "Oh, I'm sorry. Our first-class section is sold out for that flight. Can I suggest premium economy?"

"No, I *really* need to be in first class," I say, hands gripping the counter.

"Sorry, Ms. Cohen. Premium economy is the best I can do, and the flight is closing soon so…"

Does it matter if Jake and I can't sit together on the flight? Of course not, and every second I stand here trying to change what can't be changed, I'm wasting precious time. I take a deep breath and nod.

"Okay. Premium economy it is."

The clerk smiles and starts to type, then pauses.

"Well," she says, then she flashes me a smile. "Your purchase on our website must have been successful after all."

"No, it definitely wasn't," I tell her, frowning. "I checked my credit card."

I hear the printer working, and she hands me a boarding pass.

"Maybe the funds will come off later, because you're definitely already booked into first class," she tells me. I open my mouth to argue but as I take the pass, it *finally* hits me.

"Am I seated with Dr. Jacob Winton?"

She glances at the screen, then nods.

"You sure are, ma'am."

"I see," I say slowly. Then I draw in a deep breath and begin my march toward security.

CHAPTER THIRTY-TWO

Jake

I'M SITTING IN my seat on the plane, staring at a medical journal, but I haven't read past the headline. There are two untouched glasses of champagne on the tray below the window to my right. Both are probably flat by now.

The flight will be closing soon and if she's coming, she should be here.

"I can't tell if I'm pissed or impressed," Jess says abruptly. I drop the journal and shoot to my feet, forgetting to duck my head and almost giving myself a concussion in the process. She looks amazing in that green-and-white dress, with shoes so high she almost reaches to my nose. I rub my head ruefully as Jess raises her eyebrows and demands, "Got anything to say for yourself?"

"Do you know how much I'd pay just for the chance to have six hours with you at my side?" I say. My voice is hoarse as I stare down at her. I'm overwhelmed by emotion: relief, fear, anticipation, excitement, anxiety. "Because I can now put an *exact* dollar figure on how much those hours would mean to me. Apparently, I'm willing to buy a superexpensive last-minute ticket that may have gone to waste, just on the off chance you decided you wanted to come home with me."

Jess gnaws her bottom lip.

"It's just… Did you *trick* me into coming here? I can't figure out how you did it."

I reach to take her hand. "If you didn't come, you'd never have even known about the ticket, right? I wouldn't ever have told you. I decided this morning that I'd listen to you and watch you walk away. I just had this feeling that you wanted us, but I knew that if we were going to be together, you had to figure out how to make it happen." I tug her closer, until we're standing chest to chest—or perhaps more accurately, chest to eyebrows. "You're pretty smart, you know. I knew that if anyone could solve the problem of how to make us happen, it would be you."

"I can't give you forever," she whispers, but the sting of those words is softened by the fact that she steps even closer to me. "But I can give you this week. And then… When I'm back in Palo Alto next month, I'll give you that week too. I don't know if I can do this," she says, raising her chin. But then her gaze softens. "But I want to try, Jake. I'm sure it's not going to be pretty and I'm also sure this won't be the last time we crash headlong into my baggage, but I want to give it my best shot."

"That's all I ever wanted. We're going to crash into my baggage too—that's just how relationships work.

But I really need you to know that I don't want to own you, sweetheart. It's your life—you'll always be in control of it. All I ever wanted was to share it with you."

She reaches up on her tippy-toes, and I wrap my arms around her as I bend to kiss her. She's really here, and we're really doing this. As it finally sinks in that we're going to get a real shot to be together, I find myself overcome…completely, hopelessly undone. And so is Jess, because I can feel the tremors in her body quaking in time with mine.

"I love you," I choke out as I close my eyes and run the tip of my nose down over hers, then over her jawline, just breathing her in. "Jess. *Jess.* I love you. I *love* you."

"I love you too," she whispers back, and I think my heart is actually going to stop. I open my eyes to stare at her.

"You do?"

"Oh please," she says impatiently. "You totally already knew that."

I grin at her.

"I mean, I suspected, sure. But it's still pretty fucking good to hear you say it."

She links her arms around my neck and stares up at me. I can see the affection in her eyes. I can see the cautious hope.

She's so fucking beautiful it hurts.

"I think we're going to make it," I say softly. Jess rolls her eyes.

"I think you're going to drive me insane."

I grin, then reach into my back pocket.

"Let me say before I show you this, it will never, ever be an engagement ring," I say. Jess stiffens, so I add pointedly, "I'm never going to propose to you. I don't need to. I don't even want to get married unless *you* change your mind one day." I slip the ring out of my pocket and hold it between us in the palm of my hand. She stares at it as if I'm offering her toxic waste. "So take it. Or don't. But if you do take it, I don't want you to wear it on your left hand."

Jess looks back to my face, finally surprised.

"Why not?"

"It's a gift without agenda." I shrug. "It just reminded me of you. It still does. You're beautiful. It's beautiful. I want you to have it."

Jess reaches out and tentatively picks it up. She holds it cautiously in her fingertips, then glances up at me.

"I do love it," she murmurs. "When I found it in your drawer, I knew it was for me just because it was exactly what I'd have chosen myself. You know me so well."

"If you ever decide that you're ready to call me a boyfriend or partner or whatever the fuck term you come up with, and if you one day want to, you can just move it to your left hand. Whether you take it or not, whether you wear it or not, whether you wear it on your left hand or right hand, this ring will never be a symbol of ownership. But it can be a symbol that we're living our lives, side by side."

"Living our lives, side by side," Jess repeats, her eyes swimming in tears. "I really like that."

"We're going to fight and fuck and then fight and fuck some more, but in the end, I think we're going to keep choosing one another."

Jess reaches down and slips the ring onto her right hand. She holds it against her dress, then holds it against her face so I can see it against her skin. My heart skips a beat.

"Perfect," I whisper.

"I'll tell you this much. You definitely have great taste."

"In women *and* jewelry," I say, then I motion toward the seats behind me and move to sit. Jess dumps her handbag onto the floor beneath the chair in front of her, curls up on the chair beside me, then reaches across my lap to take one of the glasses of champagne.

"Should I make a toast?" I ask her jokingly.

"Let me do it," she insists. I laugh as she raises her glass. "I won't toast our happy-ever-after, because we both agree that such things don't exist. But I will toast to this—to figuring out how to ride the ups and downs of life together. And to you, Jake Winton, my patient, kind love."

I blink away tears, and she touches my cheek gently.

"You're such a fucking marshmallow," she whispers, kissing me sweetly.

"I'm happy," I say.

"Me too," she says as she downs half the glass of champagne in one gulp. "God, that was a day. Broke my heart. Pulled it back together. Packed up and moved across the country. Oh, and your brother says hi."

"Did you tell him?" I say, eyebrows high.

"I told them all. Not just about you. About Tristan and Eric and pretty much everything."

"Jess. Wow."

"It wasn't as hard as I thought it would be. Plus, I do trust them. And I want them to understand me."

"And what did they think about us?"

"They were all sickeningly happy. It was nausea inducing."

"So, how's this going to work for you? Your work schedule, I mean."

"I'll do one week in Palo Alto. Three weeks in New York. Then repeat…for…at least a few months."

"And…" I clear my throat. "Where will you live?"

"I don't have to stay with you," Jess says quickly. "I can get my own place."

"Do you *want* to stay with me?" I ask her gently. She gnaws her lip. "Let me ask a different question. If you stay with me, and it's not working out, what happens then?"

She looks right into my eyes.

"I leave."

"Exactly. I'll even help you pack."

"Promise?" she whispers.

"You know I would."

She nods, then hesitates.

"Is your dog going to drive me fucking crazy?"

"She sure is," I say cheerfully.

"Can we cuddle on the couch on Saturday afternoons and watch movies together like complete losers?"

"Whatever you want, Jess."

"I think that *is* what I want."

"Then that's what we'll do."

EPILOGUE

Jess

JAKE WINTON DRIVES me up the wall sometimes, but I wouldn't have it any other way. He's in our kitchen right now, bastardizing perfectly innocent popcorn with M&M's and butter.

"I got Oreos too," he tells me with a gleeful grin as he brings the whole tray over to join me on the sofa.

"You better eat those Oreos properly," I warn him. He picks one up, cracks it open and gives me a teasing look even as he scrapes the cream into his mouth. "You're a *monster*."

"You love me," he reminds me.

"I must to put up with this shit," I mutter, then I reach across to the tray of snacks on his lap and snatch an Oreo for myself.

It's Saturday afternoon and I'm in my new PMS pajamas—Jake bought them for me for Valentine's Day. I think he got sick of running the AC on high all the time just so I didn't die of heatstroke in my Winnie-the-Pooh onesie. These days, I'm rocking a pair of cotton boxers and a tank top, both adorned with bright green hearts.

Jake loads the movie we negotiated earlier, and I shift closer so he can put his arm around my shoulders, although we're both extra careful not to disturb the drooling creature who's sleeping on my lap. The reality is, if I'm at home and seated, Clara is either on my lap or trying to get up on my lap. I'm pretty sure she thinks I'm just a heated dog bed. She has a set of subservient siblings these days—all of whom live very much under her command, just as Jake and I do. Mickey, our rescue greyhound, is asleep in his bed beside the sofa. And Theo and Cleo, my cats, are predictably sitting on the ledge Jake built them on the front window.

Jake says they love to watch the traffic from up there, but I think they like that spot because it's the only part of the house where they are safe from Clara's torment. We still argue about whether cats or dogs are the superior pet, but privately, I've come to accept that they both have their charms. One thing we agree on: Theo and Cleo do not notice if we aren't here. Unlike Mickey and Clara, who both fret so much that since Mickey came to live with us, Reba has more than doubled her daily rate. She's made a fortune off our motley crew over the past year and a half, but even so, when we told her we were moving back to New York, she actually seemed relieved.

These months in the Californian sunshine have been the happiest of my life, but my skin can't take much more of this climate. I need to get back to New York, where at least winter is a miserable frozen wasteland, so my freckles can fade a bit. And my "one week west, three weeks east" plan lasted exactly one month before I missed Jake too much and I flipped the ratio. I live here now, because I quickly came to realize that *home* is actually wherever Jake is.

But my work here is done, and my Silicon Valley team now works like a well-oiled machine. There's not a tech CEO in the country who doesn't know the name Brainway, and when we floated the company on the stock exchange four months ago, we raised more than enough money to fund our Euro expansion.

Plus, I'm actually wealthier than Mitch these days. I've been gloating about that mercilessly ever since it became official, but the fun has to stop now. He's recently learned he's assuming full-time care of his four-year-old niece. Jake and I were already talking about moving back to New York, but the change in Mitch's situation was enough for us to actively start to plan the move.

Our family is in New York: Martin and Elspeth and Meowbert, Abby and Marcus and the girls, Izzy and Paul and the baby they're expecting next month, and Mitch and now little Savannah. When your family needs help, you move heaven and earth to be there for them. Or, as the case may be, you move a whole menagerie of animals and a house full of our combined belongings.

Jake and I are busy but happy. Clara drives me

crazy, but I love her. I tried hiking just to make Jake happy, but I did not love it. We compromised—I go camping with him sometimes, but never for more than two nights. When he wants to do an endurance hike, he plans it for when I'm in New York working and we run up stupid satellite data bills sexting one another.

We sleep in on Sundays and when Jake gets home at 4:00 a.m. because he left our bed to say goodbye to a patient, I always wake up to comfort him.

Part of the journey for me in learning to live and love Jake the way I want to has been working through the trauma of my relationship with Eric, and since I moved to California, I've been regularly seeing a great therapist. Jake finds a way to be there for my sessions with her whenever I ask him to. He and I talk a lot too, especially if either one of us feels like the ghosts of the past are coming between us. Sometimes, we cry together. This life with Jake is everything I never knew I wanted, and now, I can't imagine my future any other way.

"Uh, Jess?" Jake asks me suddenly. His gaze is on my hand, and I've been waiting for this all damn day, so I know exactly what he's noticed.

"Hmm?"

"Did you lose your ring?" he asks. His tone is carefully neutral.

I look at my right hand, then tilt my head, as if I'm confused. But then I raise my left hand and waggle it in front of him.

"You mean *this* one?"

Jake stares at the ring in its new pride of place on the fourth finger of my left hand. He clenches his jaw. His eyes become suspiciously shiny.

Look, this whole swapping-hands thing is really going to be a huge pain in the ass, because now every person we see is going to ask if we're engaged, and then I'm going to have to explain to them that no, we're not, and we're not going to be, but that we *are* in this for the long haul.

I did this for Jake. He's taught me that commitment is a gift we give to one another, and I'm ready to stop pretending this love we share is temporary or fragile. Jake and I are rock fucking solid. I'm not easy to live with, which he tells me all the time, but he also tells me it's much easier to live *with* me than without me.

"Thank you, sweetheart," Jake croaks. I shift Clara out of the way—despite her growl—then climb up onto his lap so I can kiss him.

Fuck the movie. I have another surprise for him in our bedroom, given I threw the condoms away today.

"Thank *you*," I whisper, kissing him deeply. "I love our life, Jake."

"Me too. And I love you."

"Why wouldn't you?" I sigh happily as he slides his hands up under my tank. "I'm completely fabulous."

* * * * *

*Turn the page for a special preview
of Kelly's upcoming novel,*

Truths I Never Told You

Coming soon from Headline Review

PROLOGUE

Grace
September 14th, 1957

I am alone in a crowded family these days, and that's the worst feeling I've ever experienced. Until these past few years, I had no idea that loneliness is worse than sadness. I've come to realize that's because loneliness, by its very definition, cannot be shared.

Tonight there are four other souls in this house, but I am unreachably far from any of them, even as I'm far too close to guarantee their safety. Patrick said he'd be home by nine tonight, and I clung on to that promise all day. He'll be home at nine. You won't do anything crazy if Patrick is here, so just hold on until nine. *I should have known better than to rely on that man by now. It's 11:55 p.m., and I have no idea where he is.*

Beth will be wanting a feed soon and I'm just so tired, I'm already bracing myself—as if the sound of her cry will be the thing that undoes me, instead of something I should be used to after four children. I feel the fear of that cry in my very bones—a kind of whole-body tension I can't quite make sense of. When was the last time I had more than a few hours' sleep? Twenty-four hours a day I am fixated on the terror that I will snap and hurt someone: Tim, Ruth, Jeremy, Beth...or myself. I am a threat to my children's safety, but at the same time, their only protection from that very same threat.

I have learned a hard lesson these past few years; the more difficult life is, the louder your feelings become. On an ordinary day, I trust facts more than feelings, but when the world feels like it's ending, it's hard to distinguish where *my thoughts are even coming from. Is this fear grounded in reality, or is my mind playing tricks on me again? There's no way for me to be sure. Even the line between imagination and reality has worn down and it's now too thin to delineate.*

Sometimes I think I will walk away before something bad happens, as if removing myself from the equation would keep them all safe. But then Tim will skin his knee and come running to me, as if a simple hug could take all the world's pain away. Or Jeremy will plant one of those sloppy kisses on my cheek, and I am reminded that for better or worse, I am his world. Ruth will slip my handbag over her shoulder as she follows me around the house, trying to walk in my footsteps, because to her, I seem like someone worth imitating. Or Beth will look up at me with that gummy grin when I try to feed her, and my heart contracts with a love that really does know no bounds.

Those moments remind me that everything changes,

and that this cloud has come and gone twice now, so if I just hang on, it will pass again. I don't feel hope yet, but I should know hope, because I've walked this path before and even when the mountains and valleys seemed unsurmountable, I survived them.

I'm constantly trying to talk myself around to calm, and sometimes, for brief and beautiful moments, I do. But the hard, cold truth is that every time the night comes, it seems blacker than it did before.

Tonight I'm teetering on the edge of something horrific.

Tonight the sound of my baby's cry might just be the thing that breaks me altogether.

I'm scared of so many things these days, but most of all now, I fear myself.

CHAPTER ONE

Beth
1996

"What's the place…you know…where is the place? What…today? No? It's now. The place."

Dad babbles an endless stream of words that don't quite make sense as I push his wheelchair through his front door. My brother Tim and I exchange a glance behind his back and then we share a resigned sigh. Our father's speech sounds coherent enough if you don't listen too closely—the rhythms of it are still right and his tone is clear; it's the words themselves he can't quite grasp these days, and the more upset he gets, the less sense he makes. The fact that he's all-but speaking gibberish today actually makes a lot of sense, but it's still all kinds of heartbreaking.

The grandfather clock in the kitchen has just chimed 5:00 p.m. I'm officially late to pick my son up from my mother-in-law's house, and Dad was supposed to be at the nursing home two hours ago. We were determined to give him the dignity to leave his house on his own terms and this morning Dad made it very clear that he wanted to be left alone in his room to pack for the move.

Tim and I promised one another we'd be patient, and for four and a half hours, we *were* patient. He pottered around the backyard doing overdue yardwork— weeding the chaos around the bases of the conifers, scooping up the pinecones, reshaping the hedge that's run completely amok. Dad's house is in Bellevue, east of Seattle. Over the last little while he's been too ill to tend his own yard and we've confirmed my long-held suspicion that nature would entirely swallow up the manicured gardens in this region within just a few months if humans disappeared. While Tim tried to wrangle some order back to the gardens outside, I vigorously mopped the polished floors, vacuumed the carpet in the bedrooms and sorted the fresh food in Dad's fridge to distribute among my siblings.

But every time I stuck my head through Dad's bedroom door, I found him sitting on his bed beside his mostly empty suitcase. At first, he was calm and seemed to be thoughtfully processing the change that was coming. He wears this quiet, childlike smile a lot of the time now, and for the first few hours, that smile was firmly fixed on his face, even as he looked around, even as he sat in silence. As the hours passed though, the suitcase remained empty, save for a hat and two pairs of socks.

"I can't… Where is the…" He started looking around his room, searching desperately for something he couldn't name, let alone find. He kept lifting his right hand into the air, clenched in a fist. We couldn't figure out what he wanted, Dad couldn't figure out how to tell us and the more he tried, the more out of breath he became until he was gasping for air between each confused, tortured word. The innocent smile faded from his face and his distress gradually turned to something close to panic. Tim helped him back into his wheelchair and pushed him to the living room, sitting him right in front of the television, playing one of his beloved black-and-white movies on the VCR to distract him. I stayed in the bedroom, sobbing quietly as I finished the packing my father obviously just couldn't manage.

This morning Dad understood that he was moving to the nursing home, and although he'd made it clear he didn't *want* to go, he seemed to understand that he had to. This afternoon he's just lost, and I can't bear much more of this. I'm starting to rush Dad, because I've finally accepted that we need to get this over and done with. I guess after a day of getting nowhere, I'm ready to resort to the "rip the Band-Aid off" approach to admitting him to hospice care. I push his wheelchair quickly away from the door, down the ramp my sister Ruth built over the concrete stairs, down to the path that cuts across the grass on the front yard.

"Lock the wall," Dad says, throwing the words over his shoulder to Tim. In the past few weeks, I've found myself arguing with Dad, trying to correct him when he mixes his words up like this. Tim's told me not to bother—Dad can't help it, and correcting him won't actually fix the problem. My brother is definitely much better at communicating with Dad than I am. He calls back very gently,

"I'm locking the door. Don't worry."

"Sorry about that," Dad says, suddenly sounding every bit as weary as I feel.

"It's okay, Dad," Tim calls as he jogs down the path to catch up to us.

"No work today, Timmy?" *Tim* hasn't been *Timmy* for at least twenty years, except at family functions when our brother Jeremy wants to rile him up. Forty-two and forty-one respectively and with several graduate degrees between them, my brothers still revert to adolescent banter whenever they're in the same room. Today, I can only wish Dad was teasing Tim playfully the way Jeremy does when *he* slips back into that old nickname.

"I have the day off today," Tim says quietly.

"Are we going to the…that thing…" Dad's brows knit. He searches for the right word, waving his hand around vaguely in the air in front of him, then his shoulders slump as he sighs heavily. "Are we going to the green place?"

"The golf course? No, Dad. Not today. We're going to the nursing home, remember?"

We only realized Dad had dementia earlier this year, and at times like this, I'm horrified all over again that it took us so long to figure it out. He had a heart attack four years ago, and in the aftermath, was diagnosed with heart failure. His deterioration has been steady despite medication and cardiac rehab, and with the changes in his physical health have come significant changes in his personality and, we thought, cognitive function. He'd been losing words the whole time, but his mind seemed intact otherwise. And who doesn't search for a word every now and again? What exactly *is* the tipping point between "not as sharp as you used to be" and "neurologically deficient"?

Tim's an orthopedic surgeon, and given his years of extensive medical training he could probably answer that question in excruciating detail, but his eyes are suspiciously shiny right now as we walk Dad to the car, so I don't ask.

Dad sighs heavily and turns his attention back to me. He's on permanent oxygen supplementation now, the cannula forever nestled in his nostrils. Sometimes I forget it's there, and then when I look at his face, I'm startled all over again by the visual reminders that it's really happening—Dad is really dying. The evidence is undeniable now…the cannula, the swelling around his face, the sickly gray-white tone in his skin.

"Where's Noah?" he asks me.

"He's at Chiara's house." My mother-in-law worships my son—her third grandchild, first grandson. Today, when I dropped Noah off, she barely looked at him—instead she threw her arms around me and hugged me for so long that eventually, I had to disentangle myself to make a hasty exit. I like Chiara and we have a great relationship. It just turns out that I *really* don't like her feeling sorry for me, and that hug today was a strangely awkward experience.

"Visit him?" Dad says, immediately perking up.

"Another day, Dad. Soon," I promise. Between my siblings and our spouses, at least one of us will visit Dad every day from now on. My sister Ruth pinned a roster for the first two weeks of visits to the fridge in Dad's house, but for some reason, she's left me off it. Ruth has a lot on her plate so the mistake is understandable. I noticed it a few days ago. I just keep forgetting to call her to sort it out.

I help him from his wheelchair into the car, but just as I move to shut the door, he reaches up to hold it open. He pauses, frowning as he concentrates. I scan his face—those beautiful blue eyes, lined with sadness, lips tugged down. Tim helped Dad shave this morning and his cheeks are smooth. I'm suddenly besieged by a memory, of snuggling close to Dad for a hug after I'd fallen on this very path rushing out to meet the school bus one morning. I'd skinned my knee pretty bad, and Dad had waved the bus driver away, promising me he'd make it all better then drive me to school himself. I remember his cheeks were rough that day with stubble, but his arms around me were warm, and his gentle kiss against my forehead gifted me instant courage to deal with the blood that was trickling down my leg.

That moment feels like a million years ago. I just wish there was some way I could return the favor, to make him feel as safe as he made me feel so many times over the past four decades. But hugs can't make this better. Nothing can change the reality that our time with Dad is coming to an end.

"Come on, Dad—" Tim starts to say, but Dad shakes his head fiercely and he looks right at me as he says, "Beth."

"Yes, Dad?"

His entire expression shifts in an instant—from determination to a sudden, crippling sadness. His gaze is pleading and his eyes fill with tears as he whispers, "Sorry."

"You have nothing to apologize for."

"I do," he insists, and his gaze grows frustrated, presumably at my blank look. "I...the mistake and of course I didn't. Because I'm sorry and she's gone."

What strikes me first is simply how much I miss Dad being able to speak easily. His speech has been getting worse and worse over the past few months; most days now, it's just fragments of language that are, at best, related to whatever he's trying to express.

"Dad..." I'm trying to figure out what to say, but I can't, and Tim and I just stare at him in confusion for a moment as he tries to explain himself.

"I, when Gracie...alone. Remember? What's it called? When...and *she* came and I tried..." There are tears in his eyes again, and he looks from me to Tim desperately, as if we can help him somehow.

"That's enough now, Dad," Tim says firmly, then he adds more gently, "You're okay. Just relax."

Dad's language issues stem from a form of fronto-temporal atrophy called semantic dementia. His memories are intact, but his language skills have been devastated. Tim sighs heavily and runs his hand over his salt-and-pepper beard, and I belatedly notice how weary my brother looks. For the first time all day, he seems to be struggling more than I am.

This situation is awful and it's been hard on all of us, but I know Tim, and it's not the stress of a sick parent that's giving him anxiety. Tim's habitual over-responsibility is slowly driving him crazy this week. Despite being the one to miraculously win Dad a place in the hospice ward of an amazing new nursing home on Mercer Island, he's still been trying to find some last-minute solution that would enable us to decline the placement anyway.

"We're doing the right thing," I assure him softly. We've been using a combination of at-home nursing care three or four days a week, supplemented with a rostered system of sleepovers for me and Tim and our siblings Ruth and Jeremy on the other days. This has mostly worked for the past six or seven months, but it was never going to be a long-term solution, especially now that Dad is well into the "end stage" of the heart failure process.

Tim's apartment is a forty-minute drive from here, in downtown Seattle close to his hospital. It's a lovely home, but it's on the twentieth floor of a high-rise tower—not at all a suitable place for Dad to live out his final days. Plus, Tim works insane hours, and his wife Alicia isn't exactly a nurturing soul. And Ruth has three children of her own *and* runs the family con-

struction business. Jeremy is an earth sciences professor and when he's not teaching, he's traveling. Right
now he's in Indonesia, reading seismic waves or something, and I know he's supposed to spend the second
semester of next year teaching in Japan.

My husband, Hunter, and I probably were the only
family members who could have cared for Dad given
I'm at home full-time at the moment anyway. We already live nearby too, so we could have just moved
into Dad's house, or Dad could have moved in with
us—either home is plenty large enough to accommo-
date us all. When Jeremy casually tried to hint at an
arrangement like this, I just told him I was going back
to work soon. That's a lie, but it was a necessary one.
I've quietly extended my maternity leave by another
six months, but I have no idea if or when I'll go back
to my position as a child psychologist at a community
center. I do know for sure that I simply cannot take
on Dad's care full-time…especially knowing what's
coming.

"I wish there was a way we could keep him at
home," Tim says, for what feels like the one mil-
lionth time. "Maybe I should have looked into moving here…"

I step closer to him and slide my arm around his
waist, then rest my head on his shoulder.

"Come on, Tim. Be realistic. The commute would
have killed you." The commute or his wife. For the past
seven or eight months, Tim has been here with Dad at
least one night a week—usually on his only day off,

sometimes making the journey straight from a night shift. Alicia came with him a few times, then suddenly stopped helping out. As far as I can tell, she's very busy being a "media personality." Given she hasn't had an acting or modeling gig for at least a decade, "media personality" seems to mean she spends her mornings at the gym and her afternoons with her socialite friends, hoping she'll make it into the frame of a paparazzi photo so she can complain about her lack of privacy.

It's fair to say I was never Alicia's biggest fan, but her decision to sit on the sidelines while the rest of us struggled with Dad's care is not something I'll forgive anytime soon. Jeremy is newly single, but even his ex-girlfriend Fleur made an effort to help out a few times. And my husband, Hunter, and Ruth's husband, Ellis, have gone out of their way to help too. Hell, even Hunter's parents, Chiara and Wallace, have taken their share of turns with Dad, especially after Noah's birth when I just couldn't get myself here.

It's been a team effort: Team Walsh Family and Friends—minus Alicia. And yes, I suppose it's possible I'm a little bitter about that.

"Are you okay?" Tim asks me suddenly. I grimace and nod toward Dad.

"I've been better."

"I don't actually mean about what's happening with Dad. I mean…in general." He says the words so carefully, it's like he's tiptoeing his way through a minefield. I raise an eyebrow at him.

"Do you realize you're deflecting?"

"Do you realize *you're* deflecting?" he fires back. We stare at each other, then at the same time, both break and reluctantly smile. "Look, everyone is busy, and we're all a bit overwhelmed at the moment. But I just need to make sure you know I'm here if you want to talk."

"I'm fine," I assure him.

"I can't tell what's going on with you, Beth. Sometimes I worry that you don't realize how little time he has left. Other times I worry that you're all *too* aware of that and maybe...not really coping with it?"

"There's a lot happening," I say, then I glance at my watch. "We really need to go."

Tim sighs, then gives me a quick hug before he walks around to slip into the driver's seat. I look back at the house one last time, aware that after today, it's no longer *Dad's house*, but *Dad's old house*.

Until this year when his speech started fading, Dad had a saying—*everything changes*. For as long as I can remember, those words have been my father's default response to pretty much everything that happened in our lives. He used the words so much when I was a kid that it felt like a corny, meaningless catchphrase—but there was no denying that my dad genuinely believed in the sentiment. *Everything changes* was his consolation when things were rough. It was his reminder to stay humble when things were good.

And now, as I sit in the back of the car and the house gradually shrinks in the rearview mirror, those words cycle through my brain on a loop—a simple but un-avoidable truth.

The years have been rough and they've been kind and they've been long and they've been short…but everything changes, and the best and brightest era of our family's life has drawn to a close.

Grace
October 4th, 1957

My baby girl turns one today. For some people, a mile-stone like this is bittersweet. After all, a first birthday marks the shift from helpless infant to inquisitive tod-dler, and inquisitive toddler leads to precocious pre-schooler and so on and so forth until that helpless newborn is a fully fledged adult who must leave the nest. A first birthday marks proof positive that the in-nocent days of parenting a child are a finite resource.

I don't grieve the end of the babyhood era. I won't miss the milky scent of her forehead, or the intensity of her gaze on my face as I feed her in the small hours. I won't be one of those mothers who laments the passing of time or coos about being broody, dreaming of going back and beginning all over again. No, I celebrate the closing of this chapter because if history repeats it-self, it means that my life will soon improve again. For the sake of my marriage and my sanity, this day really couldn't have come soon enough.

We didn't have the money for a gift, which I feel so sad about. I'm sure for my first birthday my parents lavished me with toys I would have been too young to understand or appreciate, but my daughter's child-hood circumstances are very different. She's growing up in a modest house in a modest neighborhood. She shares a room with her sister because although they constantly wake each other up, there are only three bedrooms, so in a family of six, everyone has to share.

I grew up in a house so large my sister and I never had to be in the same room unless we wanted to. This *baby is growing up in public housing where just scraping by is the norm, and when she makes friends, many of them will be used to birthdays where a cake is about the extent of the expense spared. I grew up in a place where fathers were bankers and lawyers and politicians, and mothers outsourced the cleaning and cake baking so they could spend their days at the salon. My mother was busy with her charity work and her*self, *and while she was very formal at times, I can't ever remember doubting her love for me. She was steady and dependable in both mood and temperament, strong and capable as a mother and a woman. She wore the titles of* wife *and* mother *as a crown, not as an oppressive yoke over her shoulders.*

If I could change anything about the life I'm providing my daughter, it wouldn't be gifts on her birthday or a nicer house in a better street. No, if I could change just one thing about our circumstances, I'd choose to change the mother in her scenario. I'm grateful for all of my childhood comforts, but I'm most grateful for the steadfast dependability I saw in my mother, and I just cannot offer that kind of certainty to my children. They deserve a better mother than the one God or fate or providence bestowed upon them, but I am selfish enough that I've prayed not to change for them, but for the courage to walk away. Motherhood has left me feeling both helpless and worn, and I am trapped here by my fears and failures. Like the skin on my stomach after all of these pregnancies so close together, I feel as if I've been stretched far too thin to ever go back to the way I was meant to be.

It feels hopeless. I feel hopeless. But feelings, even loud feelings, lie sometimes, and I know that all too well after the past three years. Beth is one now, and history has proven that a first birthday in this family means the beginning of the end of the seemingly endless chaos in my mind and my soul. I've held on this long—by the skin of my teeth this time, perhaps, but I have managed to hold on and when the misery breaks, I'll be proud of myself for that.

Just a little while longer and I should start to feel human again. Warm emotion will gradually seep back into my soul and color will come back into my world. Silent tears will give way to genuine smiles. Sobs will give way to laughter. Fear will give way to hope. Rage will give way to calm. The urge to lash out and hurt will once again become a compulsion to love. If I can dam up the chaos...if I can hold back the storm...if I can just keep my grip on this life for a little while longer, the sun will come out from behind the clouds and life can begin again.

Happy birthday, my darling Beth.

May this year be the year life really begins for all of us.

CHAPTER TWO

Beth
1996

It's Sunday, and Sunday has always meant an open invitation for dinner at Dad's house. Once upon a time, Dad would cook a huge roast with all the trimmings, and he'd sit at the head of the table and remain the center of the conversation. Today Ruth's done the cooking, and for the first time ever, Dad isn't even here. He's been unsettled since the move last week, and the doctors have asked us not to take him out on day-leave until he's adjusted to the new arrangement. In his place at dinner tonight is a heavy, awkward grief. I suspect everyone else is trying just as hard as I am to be brave, but conversation has been through a series of violent starts and stops ever since we arrived. We just can't get the chatter to flow the way it usually does...the way it should. There's a sporadic throb in the center of my chest. My gaze is constantly drawn back to that empty chair at the head of the table.

"I'm just going to put something out there," Ruth

says suddenly, breaking a silence that stretched long enough for us to devour the meal she'd prepared. "Dad gave me and Ellis the company. The rest of you should decide what to do with the house."

Jeremy arrived back from Indonesia this morning and he's unkempt, jet-lagged and cranky. He sighs impatiently and stands to slide a bottle of merlot out of the wine rack Dad built beside the sideboard. Jeremy and Ruth are twins, and even now in their forties, they are close enough to fight almost constantly. Dad used to say they were 'just too alike', and I think there might be something in that.

"What?" Ruth prompts him, snarky and defensive.

"Stop trying to be a hero," Jeremy says impatiently. He rummages for a bottle opener, removes the cork, then starts filling glasses in silence. As he moves toward me, I set my hand over my glass, and he shrugs and continues around the table to Hunter. "Dad gave you the business because you're the only one of us who worked there. You built that company almost as much as he did over the past few decades."

"Walsh Homes is worth a lot of money, and it's not fair that I should get that *and* a cut of the house," Ruth says stiffly.

"Well, it's also not fair that we should have to watch you play the martyr now then listen to you complain about how put out you are for the next forty years," Jeremy says abruptly. I've been aware all night that there's a storm brewing among my siblings. I can see it in their stiff language…hear it in the way they are raising their voices. They're all looking for a reason to fight to distract us all from the empty space at the head of the table. I don't want to watch them quarrel, but if this is the only way to break the silence, I'll sit back and let them go for it. "Whatever we're doing with this house, we're deciding it together."

"*Whatever* we're doing with it?" Tim interjects, surprised. "Jez, there's only *one* thing to do with it. We have to sell it."

"We could keep it and rent it out," Jeremy says, frowning.

"And if we do that, how exactly are we going to pay for Dad's health care?"

There's a significant cost for Dad's care at this nursing home—it's a beautifully plush facility, but it comes with a mind-boggling fee to match, and his insurance is going to cover less than half of it. The first bills will come due early next year...maybe even sooner if Dad passes in the meantime. Dad *was* reasonably well-off, but when he retired he handed ownership of the business over to Ruth, and in the five years since, his savings seem to have evaporated. It was quite a shock when Dad signed his power of attorney over to Tim earlier this year and we realized just how little he had left. We're still not entirely sure where all of his money went. It's something Tim's "going to look into when he gets some time," but I don't really blame him for putting that task off—it's a pointless endeavor. Wherever Dad put that money, it's not coming back.

"We'll all chip in for the fees." Jeremy shrugs. "Between the four of us, I'm sure we'll find a way to come up with the cash without selling this place."

Hunter and I exchange a glance. I guess we could come up with some money if we had to, but we'd probably have to remortgage our place to do it. He's a junior partner at a law firm over in Seattle and he makes a good salary, but six years of expensive fertility treatments and now six months without my income have left us without any savings.

"I just don't think Dad would want us to do that," Tim says.

"But you really think Dad would want us to sell the house he built with his own two hands?" Jeremy snaps.

"He built hundreds of houses over his lifetime," Tim snaps back.

"Oh, come on, Jeremy," Ruth sighs. "You know this one is different. This one is *ours*."

"So you'd have us hold on to it, but then install complete strangers in it?" Tim snorts. "Makes perfect sense."

"Beth? What do you think?" Jeremy asks, and all eyes around the table turn to me. Ruth and I have arranged babysitters for our respective children—Noah is with Chiara again; Ruth's kids are with her au pair. Alicia is supposedly coming, but Tim says she's running late, and I think we all know that means she didn't want to come but didn't have the guts to admit that to him. But Ellis sits beside Ruth, and Hunter sits to my left. It's Hunter my gaze goes searching for, because I don't have the energy to buy into this debate, and I'm hoping if I deflect the attention to him, I won't have to.

"Are there legal considerations?" I ask him, my voice small.

"I haven't seen Patrick's will," Hunter says. "But generally, after he passes, the house would go to all four of you unless he's specified otherwise. And in the meantime, Tim has power of attorney, so it's up to him what happens to the house."

"I wouldn't do anything the others didn't agree to," Tim says, aghast at the suggestion. Hunter shrugs.

"I know that. I think we all know that, Tim. But the law is also clear on this—the final say is yours."

"Beth, I wasn't asking you to ask your husband for his professional legal opinion," Jeremy interjects impatiently. "I was asking you what *you* think."

"Jez?" Hunter says, and he lazily shifts his gaze from me to my brother. Jeremy raises an eyebrow at him. "You're being a dick tonight."

Jeremy opens his mouth to argue, but then closes it again abruptly.

"Okay. Maybe I am." There's a burst of quiet laughter from around the table before Jeremy sighs and admits, "I'll be honest. I just cannot stand the thought of losing our last ties to this place."

"We're not losing each other. We're not even losing Dad. It's just a house…simply an object. What's actually precious to you is the bonds the house represents, not the house itself," I say automatically.

"Well done, Jeremy. You've knocked Beth back into

therapist mode," Ruth sighs, but then she flashes me a wink. I offer her a wan smile, then divert my gaze back to my plate. If only there really *was* a therapist mode. I'd love it if I could press a button and revert back to the competent professional I used to be.

"You still haven't told us what you want to do with the house, Beth," Tim murmurs. "What *do* you think?"

I think that I'm over this dinner and over this conversation, but I have been since we arrived, and Noah isn't even here so I don't have an excuse to leave early. My feelings are muted on all of this—which is confusing, because everyone else is frothing at the mouth about what we should do next. Tim obviously wants to sell, Jeremy and Ruth obviously don't, Hunter and Ellis will keep their opinions to themselves because although they are definitely part of the family, it's really up to the four of us.

I start to think it all through—what it will look like to prepare the house for sale or lease, the packing and the cleaning and freshening up the paint and fixing the garden. It's a big job. No, it's a *huge* job, and an awful one. It's a job that no one has time for, although one of us could, theoretically, make time. And one of us is most definitely stuck in an odd rut at the moment, so...

"We'll need to get the house ready either way," I say slowly. I skip my gaze around the table, but this time avoid my husband's eyes. "We can get help in for the painting and the gardening, but sorting through Dad's things is going to be the hardest part. Maybe I should take that on, since you're all so busy."

"Wait—aren't you going back to work soon?" Jeremy asks. I *knew* that lie was going to come back to bite me.

I clear my throat and say noncommittally, "Soon. But not quite yet."

"You can't do the whole house, Beth. That's not fair." Tim frowns.

"I…" I glance quickly around my siblings, then back to my plate as I shrug. "I'm the only one of us who can make time. And I kind of want to do this. For Dad."

"You'd have to let us all help around work," Ruth says. I glance up at her, and find she's staring at me. I don't like it. She's too sharp and it feels like she's looking through me. I pick up my fork and begin to push the food around on my plate, just so I can avoid her gaze. "And of course, when you need contractors, I can arrange them."

"Good," I say, still looking down.

"Are you sure, Beth?" Tim asks, very gently. I nod firmly then force a smile before I raise my gaze to look at him.

"Noah is five months old, guys. I'm ready for a project."

Now everyone is looking at me. I feel my cheeks heating.

"It's just…you're sure you're up to this, Beth?" Jeremy says eventually. The words drip with awkwardness, and I scowl at him.

"What? Of course I am." *Oh God, please let me*

do this. I just want to feel useful again. "I had a baby, Jez. I'm not the one with the terminal diagnosis here."

"Hunter?" my sister prompts carefully, and I gape at her.

"Seriously, Ruth? Did I time warp back to the 1950s? Did you *seriously* just ask my husband to give me permission to do something?"

"Of course she didn't," Hunter sighs. "Let's talk about this later."

"No, Hunter," I say flatly. "Let's talk about it now."

"Talk about it all you want, guys, but I'm too jet-lagged to watch you two battle it out tonight, so can you do it at home?" Jeremy interjects.

"Like you can talk," Tim snorts. "You're the one who's been picking fights all night."

"Jesus *Christ*," Ruth groans, rubbing her eyes wearily. "If this is how family dinners are going to be without Dad, can we just forget about the tradition altogether?"

The reminder of that empty chair is the slap in the face we all needed, and the squabbling stops immediately.

"Sorry," I whisper, after a while. Around the table there are echoes of *me too*, except from Ellis. I'm pretty sure he's actually reading, because although he's still sitting with us, he's been silently staring at his lap for a long while now and every now and again I hear the faint rustle of pages. It wouldn't be the first time he's mentally checked out of a family function to disappear into a book, and I guess that's what Ruth gets for marrying a librarian.

"So the plan is that we clear out the house, tidy things up…then decide what to do with the property once it's all done?" Jeremy asks quietly.

"In the meantime, we can all think about whether or not we can chip in to cover Dad's health care bills," Tim suggests.

"Andrew's confirmation service is at St Louise's next weekend," Ruth says suddenly, speaking about her eldest son. "Let's have one last family lunch here after Mass."

"We can bring Dad back for that, if he's ready for a day-leave by then," Jeremy says, and that reminds me…

"Ruth, you left me off the roster this week. When do you want me to go visit Dad?"

My sister stiffens again, then offers me a thin smile.

"I thought you might like a little break before you dive right into all that."

"What? Why?" I ask blankly. It was *deliberate*? That makes no sense at all. If the doctors are right, we don't have much time left with Dad. And even if they're wrong, I've seen how fast he's declining. God only knows what his condition will be in two weeks. Besides, Dad and I are incredibly close. He's going to notice if I don't go in to see him.

"We should get going," Hunter says quietly as he rises. "We said we'd pick Noah up from Mom's by nine."

"I want to go see Dad," I say stubbornly. No one says anything, and I sigh impatiently. "Look, I'm going in with or without your approval and I know you're all busy so you may as well swap."

"Go on Tuesday in Alicia's place," Tim says eventually. I nod at him curtly, and then rise beside my husband. I glance at my sister again, and find she's staring at her wineglass.

"I'll start straightaway on the house, but I'll pack up this room last," I say with a frown. "In case he comes home for lunch with us next week, we should try to keep things nice and normal for him."

"It's settled, then," Ruth sighs, resigned. "You start the process, but promise me you'll call us for help when you need it."

"Fine."

I glance at Hunter, and I'm wholly unsurprised to see him staring into space, his face set in a grim mask.

"What are you thinking, Beth?"

We're on our way home. Hunter is driving, his face set in a stony mask as he stares ahead at the road. It's raining heavily, and now isn't the time for an argument because he needs to concentrate on driving. I keep my tone mild as I reply.

"It's just that someone has to get the house ready, that's all. The others are all so busy—"

"And so are you."

"Not really," I say. "Not compared to them." I pause, then can't help but frown as I ask, "And what was all of that about anyway? Since when does everyone treat me like I have leprosy?"

Hunter sighs heavily, then runs one hand through his hair. His hairline has just started to recede, something he's philosophical about. When we first noticed the hair loss eighteen months ago, we were in a very different place. I remember tentatively raising the issue as we were getting dressed in the bathroom one morning, and, shirtless, he'd flexed his muscles and told me not to worry, he'd still be just as irresistible once he was bald as a bowling ball. When I laughed, he chased me into the bedroom, his cheeks still covered in shaving cream, cornering me near the bed and kissing me playfully. I washed my face and reapplied my makeup but I smelled like his shaving cream all day, and between appointments with my clients, I'd pause to enjoy the scent and think about him.

"Are you feeling any better?" he asks me hesitantly.

"Better than what?" I scowl.

"Beth. You haven't been yourself for months, and whenever we ask if you're okay, you change the subject."

"We?" I repeat, eyebrows drawing down. "Who is this 'we'?"

"Me and Ruth. And the boys. Everyone can see it. Is it your dad?"

"Is *what* my dad? I just had a baby, Hunter. I'm allowed to be tired."

Hunter doesn't reply. Instead, he drives in silence for a while. Part of me wants to argue more, but I'm not sure I want to delve into this too deeply. I'm not myself, but I'm definitely not ready to explain to him where my mind is at. When we're a few blocks from home, he speaks again, so suddenly that I startle.

"I assume, since you're so keen to sort out your dad's house, you really think a project is going to help?"

"There's nothing to help," I sigh impatiently. "I'm fine. But I do want to do this for Dad and it's not a big deal. It needs to be done, and if someone doesn't take it on, the task will linger for months."

"I've been thinking that maybe you should see someone."

"See who?"

"See a psychologist, Beth," he says. I gape at him.

"Do you want to ruin my career?" I ask him incredulously.

"Do *you*?" he fires back.

"If the directors knew I was in therapy, I won't have a job to go back to."

"Come on, Beth. That's hardly—"

"That's the reality of it, Hunter!"

He pauses, and I think he's going to try to debate with me about whether or not there's a stigma around mental health professionals seeking mental health treatment. I'm getting ready to point out to him that he's a *lawyer*, and what would he know, but he draws in a sharp breath, then asks very quietly, "So if your career wasn't a factor, you would talk to someone?"

The question catches me off guard, and I stare at

him, momentarily unsure how to answer. My problem is my circumstances, not my thought processes. And maybe I'd love to talk through the tangled mess of worries I'm drowning in lately, but I just don't have the energy, and even if I did, I can't bear the thought of admitting aloud to another human being some of the stupid things that have been going through my head.

"No," I say stiffly. "You're wrong about this. I don't need therapy. I just need time."

There's a terse, awkward pause, then I relax as Hunter softens his tone and changes the subject again.

"So you're going to pack your father's house up this week? And next, I guess. It'll take a while."

"Yes, I think that's for the best."

"And are you taking Noah with you, or were you planning on asking my mom to babysit him for days on end?"

I turn to stare out the window, embarrassed that he's seen right through the reason I was so quick to volunteer for this arduous and painful job. I like it when Chiara takes Noah for a few hours. She's an amazing mother and she's incredibly comfortable with him—so much more capable than I am. I feel like he's safer with her, but there's no way I'm going to admit that to Hunter. Now it's my turn to fall silent, and I stare sullenly out the window, planning a hasty retreat into the bathroom as soon as we get home. I'm not much of a crier, but I feel pressure and heat behind my eyes, and maybe I do need to leak a few tears tonight.

When we pull into our driveway a few minutes later,

Hunter reaches across and rests his hand on my forearm. I'm not sure the expression on my face won't entirely give me away, so I don't turn to face him.

"Just think about talking to someone, babe. It seems like you really don't feel like you can talk to me," he murmurs. I open my mouth to deny this, but then I close it again. Once upon a time, I had no filter when it came to Hunter. I'd share any thought that crossed my mind, and I'm pretty sure he felt the same way. There's no denying that's changed since Noah was born. Hunter's hand contracts around my arm, gently squeezing. "If you're worried about your clinic finding out, I'll help you find somewhere you can be anonymous. Whatever you need, we'll make it happen."

"I don't need therapy," I whisper insistently. "I know exactly what a therapist would say, and I can say those things to myself for free."

We sit in silence for a moment, and then Hunter asks, "Well…what would you say to yourself, then?"

"Time," I croak automatically, as, at last, I turn to face him. "I'd tell myself to just give it more time."

Hunter nods, kisses me on the cheek and leaves the car. As I swing open my door and step out, I force a brutal moment of internal honesty for the first time in months. I don't treat adult patients anymore but I did early in my career, and I can easily picture a client sitting in my office voicing my recent struggles. I see myself as an impartial third party, listening and mentally planning my response.

My gut drops when I finally admit what I'd actually say to that client.

It sounds like you're totally overwhelmed and out of your depth. It sounds like you're struggling with your dad's situation, but that's not the biggest issue you're battling. It sounds like you're actively looking for excuses to avoid your son, and you're not coping at all when you are alone with him. You're terrified that having Noah was a mistake you can't undo. Is avoidance really the solution here, though? Let's talk about other strategies you can employ.

On the porch Hunter and his mother embrace and then I see them talking quietly. As I step out of the car, Chiara flashes me a warm smile and a wave, and I wave back, fixing my brightest smile in return. I'm certain it's convincing, despite the fact that I've just dropped a mental bombshell on myself and my gut is churning. I'm so desperate to get behind that locked bathroom door it's all I can do to stop myself from sprinting for it. Luckily, the one thing I am quite good at these days is putting on my game face.

"Sweetheart," Chiara greets me as she takes me into her embrace and kisses both of my cheeks. "Hunter was just telling me you're going to pack up Patrick's house over the next few weeks. Of course I'll watch Noah for you."

Hunter is watching me closely. Is this some kind of trap? Even if it is, the offer is too enticing to refuse. So much for changing strategies from avoidance.

"Chiara, that would be amazing. Thank you so much."

Once Chiara is gone and Hunter and I are alone in our living room, I turn my gaze to him.

"I got the impression when we were in the car that you *didn't* want me to ask your mom to watch the baby while I'm at Dad's."

"You said you need time," Hunter says, cheeks coloring. "I told you, Beth. Whatever you need, I'll make it happen."

I guess if ten years with Hunter should have taught me anything, it would be that he has my back at all times.

I just can't help but wonder if he'd still be Mr Supportive if I told him the truth: that we spent half a decade trying to become parents, and after just five months, I'm convinced it was the biggest mistake of our lives.

Grace
November 2, 1957

*I don't know what I intend to achieve with these lit-
tle notes. The first time, I actually sat down to write
a letter to Maryanne, just as I'd done so many times
before. This time I was going to do something new: I
was going to tell her the truth. I've painted such rosy
pictures of our life here over the years, but in this new
slump, I was determined to reach across the divide
with something real...something raw.*

*The problem was that when my pen hit paper, I
couldn't bear the thought of my sister knowing. Even
after all of this time and even after all of my failures,
I'm still proud enough to want her to think I made the
right choice in Patrick. I suppose that's why what came
out of my pen that day was more like a letter to myself.
I've decided it's for the best. I don't doubt that if Maryanne knew how bad things are for me, she'd blame him
and him alone—she does so love to blame men for everything. In this case, she'd feel he's proven her right,
because she tried so hard to warn me against this life.*

*I chose Patrick anyway, and that decision has
forced a distance between Maryanne and me that I've
never figured out how to close. In some ways over the
past few years, that distance has been a necessary
evil. If she knew, she'd probably try to intervene, and
I might not have much these days, but at least I have
my pride. Plus, I love that Maryanne thinks I'm a good
mother. I can't bear for her to know the truth.*

*Even so, I had the urge to write to her because al-
though there have been so many things about the past
few years that have been difficult, the isolation has
been the hardest. The irony of course is that I haven't
been truly alone in well over two years now, given I
haven't had so much as an hour without some company since the twins were born. It's not even silence I
crave. I'm starving simply to be present with someone
who doesn't want something from me. I have reached
the point where I don't fantasize about making love or
relaxing or even sleeping anymore. Now I daydream
about sitting down with someone who will listen to
me—who will understand me. And these notes have
somehow tricked my brain into thinking I'd been heard
by someone, at least for a little while, and I have been
doing so much better. Ordinarily, it takes me a few
months to rise out of the funk, but after I wrote those
notes, something immediately felt a little lighter inside.*

*Until today, that is. This relapse hit without warn-
ing, and it took me back to my very darkest months.
Ruth has a bit of a cold and kept waking up because
her nose is blocked. I got even less sleep than usual,
and maybe that's what triggered it. All I know is that
I was buttering the toast for breakfast and Jeremy
and Ruth were fighting and the noise rose all around
me like a tidal wave until it took up too much air and
suffocated me.*

*I asked the children to be quiet. I told them to be
quiet. I shouted at them to be quiet. I shouted at them
to stop. And then I screamed at them to shut up.*

That's when the thoughts came back.

I looked at the knife in my hand and I pictured myself dragging it across the smooth white skin of my wrist. I imagined the dark red blood bubbling up and the silence rushing in. I don't know how long I stood there, but when those god-awful thoughts finally cleared from my mind, I was standing beside the table in front of my four babies, who were all sitting in terrible silence, staring at their breakfasts with the kind of desperate intensity that only comes from being completely petrified.

I didn't actually hurt myself this time. I've never done something as drastic as cutting my wrists, except for that one night when I—no. I don't think about that night; it's too dreadful and too hard. Instead, these days when I feel this stretched, I have developed a coping mechanism, as awful as it may be. I sneak away to the bathroom and I scratch myself, as if breaking the surface of my skin will let all of the frustration bleed out. I always scratch beneath my clothing because I have no idea how I'd explain such a thing. It was bad enough when Patrick saw a mark on my breast and I had to lie and say that Beth had done it when I was feeding her. I was lucky that time, because it was just the smallest little thing. Other times I've scratched so hard and so long that my breasts and my belly have been speckled with blood and black-and-blue with bruises. Anything to let the frustration out. Anything to let the sadness out. Because if I bottle it up inside, it finds other ways to burst out of me...like that moment today in the kitchen.

I hurt my children today—not with the knife, but with the threat of it. My frustration and irritability and this pervasive misery drowned me in that moment and I was hopelessly out of control. Even after all these years, I don't actually know what those moments are... the moments when I can't outrun the bad thoughts. I don't see images with my eyes, more with my mind, but they swamp me anyway. Are they hallucinations? Visions? Prophecies? Whatever those thoughts are, they are vivid and real and worst of all, they are stronger than I am.

I set the knife down on the cracked white vinyl of the table and I stepped away from it. I spoke to my children in a voice that had become artificially high with panic, and I called them "my darlings" because I always call them that when I'm well, and I gently ushered them out to play. Once they were all in the yard, I locked the back door and sank to the linoleum and curled up in a little ball—my back pressed heavily against the door as if the kids could push hard enough to break the lock.

They were fine out there at first, climbing the pear tree and riding their tricycles, but the hours went on and I just kept thinking about the knife and the frustration and their scared little faces, and I couldn't convince myself to get up. Soon, Beth was crying at the door because she was hungry again. My fear and my rage had faded, but a paralyzing guilt and numbness had taken their place. I stayed on the floor, and when I didn't answer their increasingly insistent knocks and calls, Tim climbed through a window, fetched some bread from the kitchen and ferried it out to his siblings. He's such a good boy. He deserves so much better than the life I give him.

What scared me wasn't the vision or my rage or the mood I was in. It was how unexpected the resurgence of the madness was. I've walked this journey before—twice before, and the end doesn't go like this. With my first two births, as soon as I felt better, I really was better—there was no sinking in and out of funks once the babies were toddlers and the darkness had cleared. So was this just a one-off bad day, or is it a sign that I'll never truly be able to trust in my stability, not ever again? How exactly is a person supposed to live if she can never trust in her sanity?

That's why I'm sitting down with this notepad tonight. I'm hoping and praying that once these thoughts are on paper, they will break the endless echo chamber of my own mind. Left to my own devices my thoughts get louder and louder and louder, until I can't eat or sleep or do anything except think.

I need to prevent the spiral that leads to the quicksand thoughts, because once I'm submerged, I don't know how to climb out.

Don't miss Kelly Rimmer's unforgettable friends-to-lovers romance

Unexpected

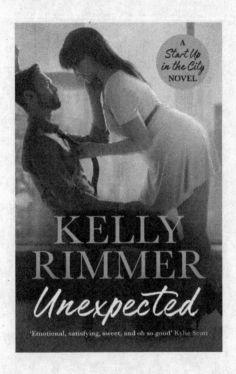

Available now!

Don't miss Kelly Rimmer's sexy, emotional second-chance romance

Unspoken

Available now!

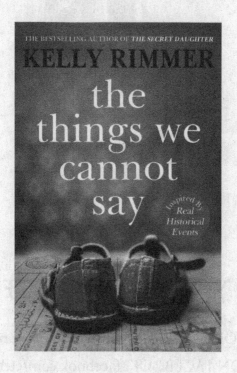

HEADLINE
ETERNAL

FIND YOUR HEART'S DESIRE...

VISIT OUR WEBSITE: www.headlineeternal.com

FIND US ON FACEBOOK: facebook.com/eternalromance

CONNECT WITH US ON TWITTER: @eternal_books

FOLLOW US ON INSTAGRAM: @headlineeternal

EMAIL US: eternalromance@headline.co.uk